Hidden Sins

KARICE BOLTON

ISBN-10:0-9899317-6-5
ISBN-13:978-0-9899317-6-2

$\mathcal{D}$EDICATION

Thank you for always being there for me, mom. I love our daily chats and appreciate all of the encouragement you've always given. And to my wonderful husband, I love you to the stars and back. I can't wait to see where life will take us next.

ACKNOWLEDGMENTS

I want to say a simple thank you to Amazon, iBooks, Barnes & Noble, and all of the other avenues available for the indie publishing world. It allows the art of storytelling to continue to flourish in unexpected ways!

PROLOGUE

Hannah

"Have you found her yet?" The male voice cut through my soul as I peered down from the hayloft. It was Miles, the father of the man I was supposed to marry. It was an arranged marriage. One that I couldn't accept, but I never would've guessed that his father was involved in this. Then again, for the first twenty years of my life, living here had seemed like an amazing gift, not a horrific nightmare that I couldn't wake up from. I steadied my breathing to ensure I wasn't heard as I watched the two men below me. I needed to stay in control. I had planned too long to fail now.

"No. It looks like she took off. Maybe two days ago. She left most of her belongings behind, but I'd say enough was missing to indicate that she's on the run. Her mother went through the house to confirm that there were items missing," the younger man said. There was something about his voice that was familiar, and I tried to focus on his features, but I couldn't place him, which was odd. The community I grew up in wasn't huge, but it was large enough that people could blend in somewhat. I guess a face could be missed here or there.

"She knows too much, Eric," Miles said, rubbing his temples.

Eric! I knew an Eric in high school, but we were told he'd left the community. Obviously not.

"Just like her sister," Eric responded. I saw a trace of a smile touch his lips as he shook his head. "But we took care of that problem, and we'll take care of this one."

What about my sister? I'd been told she left the community, ran away. My stomach turned into itself as I thought about my family. Did they know what was going on here? Was my mom actually concerned about my safety or only helping to lead them to me?

Miles took a seat and propped his elbows on the desk, glaring at Eric. "We don't actually know that you took care of Hannah's sister. Now do we?"

"I watched her fall from the cliff," Eric argued.

"No body was ever recovered."

"The authorities said that with the currents, it might never be." Eric stood his ground.

Miles shrugged as if to dismiss the argument that couldn't be won. "You're sure Hannah saw something? Two in a family calls too much attention..."

Eric paced across the floor. "We found her in the bushes close to where the other issue had been taken care of. If Hannah didn't see what unfolded, the gunshots and screams surely would've alerted her. From her vantage point, she could've seen everything. And the wild look in her eyes..."

I know more than you bastards could ever imagine.

"Enough said. Add that to the fact that she'd already gone to the authorities about Tina," Miles shook his head. "And we've got a big problem on our hands. A problem you were supposed to take care of. We're just lucky that Mark was the officer on duty when she went to the police station. We don't run our organization on luck, Eric."

My heart was pounding as I listened intently. One of the nails in the wood beam poked my ankle something fierce, but I didn't dare move.

"She couldn't have gotten far. We'll find her. My guess is she's headed to Florida, and I've got people already headed that direction," Eric said.

"What makes you think Florida?"

"I found some notes on different cities in Florida. They were tucked under her mattress."

"If this woman is smart enough to vanish without a trace, do you really think she's going to forget or leave behind a few key pieces of information? Come on. You've got to be kidding me. She's just sending you on a wild goose chase." Miles pounded his fist on the desk. "I'm taking this over. You're done. And don't tell my son any of this. You understand?"

Eric balled his fists together at the commandment. "Wouldn't dream of it."

Did that mean Brandon, my fiancé, wasn't involved? I pushed the lump down in the back of my throat as I thought about my entire life being highly orchestrated for some cause I didn't even understand.

Miles stood up, obviously agitated, and both men walked out of the office. It would take them several minutes to walk through the stables that the office was connected to, and I had no plans to come down from my perch until well into the midnight hour. I'd gotten what I came for; the last of the documents were securely tucked into my waistband. It was just an added bonus to catch Miles here, discussing my fate. At least my hunch was right. If they caught me, they'd kill me.

I shifted slightly, moving my ankle away from the nail, as my mind drifted to my sister. Four years ago she had vanished without a trace. My mother was in hysterics, but my father and brother had been completely stoic, dismissing my sister's disappearance as if the cat never came home for the night. Eventually, they had convinced both my mom and me that she had chosen to live a life outside the community. It wasn't unheard of so I was willing to blindly believe that assumption, even though my sister never gave me any reason to believe that she wanted out. In hindsight, that was my tipping point.

With every passing minute that I was stuck in the rafters, I began to doubt my plan that I'd worked on for months. I was only buying time, trying to save enough to get me out of here without looking like I was doing anymore than usual to earn money. Everything was going according to plan until three nights ago. That's when everything changed in my world. Instead of just wanting to escape, I wanted answers.

When I saw her eyes—my best friend's eyes—filled with terror, I knew I couldn't just walk away so I followed. She asked me not to, told me to stay away, but I followed her from a distance as she walked through the pasture toward the woods. I didn't know if she knew I was following until it was too late. I watched her trembling hands as she covered her face, and she sank down into the dirt, crying. She had told me that she'd been having troubles with her husband—another arranged marriage, and another reason I had no intention of following through with mine. I halfway expected to see him meet her in the woods.

Instead, two men came from nowhere, wearing masks. She didn't fight, and I didn't know what to expect. I closed my eyes quickly and took a deep breath as I readied myself to run up on them. When I heard the first shot, my eyes flashed open as her gaze landed on mine. She knew I'd followed her. Another shot echoed into the air followed by laughter from the one I could now identify as Eric.

My body trembled as the images flooded through me, and I knew if I was going to survive long enough to expose everything, I needed to create a new life. I had to forget as much as I could about this old one, until the time was right.

CHAPTER ONE

Hannah

I let out a sigh as I sat in the dusty, blue truck that had miraculously managed to make it across the country. Between the funny interior smell, the engine knocking at speeds over fifty miles-per-hour, and the tricky method for locking the driver's door, I hadn't even been sure I'd actually make it out of my hometown. I found a '99 GMC Sonoma for only eight hundred dollars, and I bought my way out of a life that wasn't my own. Or at least, I hoped I had. Only time would tell. I turned off the radio and watched a family wander into the Starbucks. My chest tightened as I thought about who I'd left behind. But it had to be done. I couldn't second-guess my decisions now. There was no turning back.

I grabbed my wallet and slid out of the truck, feeling the warm California air kiss my skin as I slowly walked across the parking lot toward the coffee shop. I wasn't used to temperatures like this in March, but I was certain I'd quickly learn to love the weather. From what I'd read, Southern California skipped over the entire winter season, which sounded perfect to me. New England winters were brutal and long— really long.

My stomach growled as I pulled the door open and smelled the aroma of coffee and pastries waft through the air. I hadn't eaten anything since the night before and desperately wanted a big cup of coffee. I'd tried not to spend much money on the long road trip in case I needed any extra cash for emergencies. Lucky for me, I'd made it to my destination without one hiccup and could splurge on a measly cup of coffee.

Yay me!

The family from outside was still in front of me, placing their order as I stood in line. The mom's latte order had so many components I lost track. It was no longer just a drink with coffee and milk. I watched her movements carefully, noticing every blonde hair was in place and her suit flawless. She seemed so in her element, and for some reason that made me feel completely out of mine. Her husband was put together just as impeccably, and I found myself running my hands along my sweatshirt to press out the wrinkles that had formed from the countless hours of driving. I was in yesterday's yoga pants, which were now technically today's, and my blonde hair desperately needed to be washed so it was piled on top of my head in a clip. I glanced around Starbucks and noticed that the family in front of me wasn't the anomaly. Everyone looked put together and ready to conquer the world. I was the odd one with tired brown eyes.

There was a brunette in the far corner who wore Hollywood shades, and her khaki capris showed off her model legs. The guy at the next table over looked like he'd just stepped out of the pages of a *Men's Fitness* magazine as he intently stared at his iPad. This had to be the best-dressed coffeehouse in America.

"Miss, I can take your order," the male barista said, as the family walked to the drink counter.

I snapped my head to see a friendly guy about my age, motioning for me to step forward to the counter.

"Oh, sorry," I said, nearly tripping to the register.

"Take your time."

"I'd like a large coffee," I said, smiling.

The guy's blond hair was shaggy and his blue eyes playful as he grabbed the white cup. "Pike Place or French Roast?" he asked.

"Pike I guess," I muttered, unzipping my wallet.

"A Venti Pike Place, and can I get your name?"

"Hannah," I said, feeling a breeze from behind as the door swung open.

A wave of shivers ran across my skin, and I started to laugh at how quickly I became acclimated to the warm weather. The barista wrote my name on the cup and called out my drink as he rang it up.

"Two-eighty," he said, as I felt someone come up behind me in line.

"Can I add a blueberry scone too?" I handed him my debit card as he nodded.

Taking my card, he quickly added the scone to the order and swiped the debit.

"So how's your day been?" the barista asked, waiting for the transaction to complete.

"Really good. Yours?" Another wave of goose bumps ran along my body, and I glanced around, unsure of the source this time. There was no breeze.

"Been great." His eyes landed on the screen, and I saw his jaw tense as he swiped the card again. "Do you by any chance have another form of payment?"

My heart sank and my body felt like it was on fire. I had no other cards, and there should be plenty of money to cover a scone and coffee.

"Can you try it again?" I barely squeaked out. "Third time's a charm."

The barista gave me a sympathetic grin and swiped the card once more.

"Sorry. Same result." The barista handed the card back as my entire body turned into a hot mess. I was absolutely mortified. It wasn't like I was trying to buy a television. I just wanted a lousy cup of coffee. And what was worse was that the money in the account needed to get me by until I could find a job in town. So where was the money?

"Umm. I'm sorry. Can you cancel my order," I whispered. All I wanted to do was run out of the coffee shop and hide in my truck. I wasn't supposed to meet my roommates for another hour, but maybe they wouldn't mind if I showed up early.

Just as the barista was about to key in the cancellation, a male voice interrupted my mini-hell of humiliation.

"I've got it covered. Technology can be such a pain." The guy from behind me took a step forward, and a surge of warmth flooded through me. His voice was gravelly, sexy, and didn't relay a bit of sympathy for my predicament. His immediate dismissal of the crisis at hand actually made me feel immensely better, like this sort of thing happened all the time. And then I felt him, his energy, wrap around me.

He was intense.

"You don't have to do that," I said, turning to see the guy take a step next to me, handing the barista his card.

My heart nearly stopped when I saw how good-looking he was. All six-foot-something of him towered next to me and I felt abuzz with delight. He was dressed like everyone else in this mystical coffee house. But on him, the black suit stretched across his shoulders in such a way that I could almost imagine what lay under his jacket. After all, I was in the land of mirages. Men like this didn't exist in my world. His wavy, dark brown hair framed his chiseled features, and his green eyes were beyond striking as he smiled at me briefly.

"Add a Venti Iced Coffee and an oatmeal cookie to the order," the man said, ignoring my statement as he placed a hand on my shoulder, sending an impossible charge through me.

His eyes connected with mine, and my entire body responded to him in a way that I'd never experienced before. I dropped my gaze and felt a warmth swell deep inside me as he continued to watch me.

"Thank you," I said.

"Anytime." His hand slipped off my shoulder.

"I'm not sure what happened. I should..."

"No need to explain. Banks screw up all the time." He smiled at me and I nodded, thankful for his ability to put me at ease.

"Well, thanks again," I said, turning to walk toward the counter where the drinks were called.

I felt his gaze on me and didn't know what to do. I felt extremely self-conscious as I thought about my day-old wardrobe and messy blond hair. I really didn't fit in here, but I better start learning how to do so.

"Scone and Venti Pike Place for Hannah," a female barista with red, spikey hair called out.

"Thank you," I said, quickly grabbing my food and drink, hoping for a quick escape.

Reaching the door, I glanced behind me and saw the guy grabbing his own drink before looking over at me. My heart stopped as his eyes locked on mine, and I knew I needed to get out of here.

"Hannah," his throaty voice stopped me in my tracks. "It was nice meeting you."

He looked so damn charming, and it was really nice of him to cover my order, but I didn't want to start calling attention to myself. Yet, I was doing that every moment I stood in the coffee house with a dopey smile on my face. I was counting on California to provide the anonymity I needed, and I was also counting on my bank account to be fuller than it was, which had me extremely concerned. I most certainly had enough funds in there to buy a cup of coffee. I couldn't do what my heart wanted me to do so I waved with the hand holding my scone bag and left the coffee house in a dash.

My truck looked like a refuge as I neared the driver's side. The fancy car next to me was parked incredibly close to my truck, and I found myself juggling the coffee and scone as I opened my door. Just as I snuck in between the door and seat, my coffee cup took a nosedive, spilling on the pavement below.

"Shoot." I tossed my scone onto the console and sat in the driver's seat, closing the door behind me. This wasn't how I'd imagined rolling into my new town. It had to get better from here, right? Opening my window, I let the warm sea air fill the car as I munched on my scone. I'd have to wait until the car next to me left so I could clean up my mess outside before taking off. Thankfully, I had some water in my car to help wash down the somewhat dry scone that kept sticking in my throat. As I looked around the parking lot and over to the beach, a deep sense of loneliness crept through me. It was a familiar feeling, but this time it was different. I had nothing to hold onto in my new surroundings. There was no one to commiserate with. There was nothing around here that provided grounding or old memories for good or bad. There were palm trees dotting the edge of the parking lot and tiny orange flowers sprinkled along the curb. It was quite different than a foot of dirty snow. I could get used to this.

I heard footsteps behind my car and glanced in the rearview. My heart sped up as I spotted the guy from inside the coffee house. It was definitely my time to exit this parking lot. I quickly put the key into the ignition and turned it, hearing nothing more than a chug and a whir. No turn of the motor. No rev of the engine.

Great!

I saw movement out my driver's window and saw the man walking along the driver's side of the car that was parked next to me. So that was his car, seemed fitting. I didn't even recognize what type of car it was. It just screamed expensive. I twisted the key in the ignition once more, and this time I was met with silence. I didn't even get so much as a grunt from the engine.

Figured!

Letting out a sigh, I thumped my forehead onto the steering wheel and began to laugh in disbelief.

"Excuse me, Hannah?" The man's bold voice

interrupted my internal comedy hour, and I lifted my head to see his concerned gaze.

"Hey," I said, pressing my lips together.

"Do you need a ride somewhere?" he asked, placing his hands on his car roof.

"No. I've got it," I said, smiling.

"Do you need me to call a tow truck?" he offered.

"Nah. I think that would go about as well as my coffee venture."

"Oh, I see." He glanced across the street toward the beach and back at me. "I saw your plates are from New Hampshire. Here on vacation?"

"Um. Kind of. No. Not really."

I didn't need to be having this conversation with him or anyone.

"Are you sure I can't help get you to where you're going? I don't feel right about buying a woman a cup of coffee and then leaving her stranded in a parking lot." His smile was dazzling and it was everything I could do not to take him up on his offer. But I couldn't afford to owe anyone anything else, let alone having him know where I was going.

He walked around the front of his car and inched his way between our two vehicles before his eyes landed on my coffee on the pavement. He was now standing directly next to me, and the breeze carried the soft scent of his cologne into the car. God, he smelled good. It was like a mixture of ocean and something else wonderful.

"Today has not been your day, has it?" A slight

smirk appeared on his lips as he reached into his suit jacket, grabbing his wallet. "Listen. Here's my card. If you need anything, give me a call. California's a huge state. One wrong turn and you're in a place you really don't want to be."

I took the card from him and he smiled.

"Thanks," I muttered, glancing at the card.

Luke Fletcher
Fletcher Security
Private Security, Risk Management, and
Counter Terrorism

"You know," he began, bending over and picking up the empty cup. "I can't, in good faith, let you leave here without a cup of coffee. I'll be right back."

"No," I called, but it was too late. He was already out of earshot on his way back into the coffee shop.

I leaned my head against the headrest and let out a garbled groan as I thought about how screwed up things were. How could things go so wonderfully well over the last several days only to end up in the worst possible scenario, without a running car and no money? I needed to get out of here before he came back. He was too much. All of it was too much. I turned the key again and this time the engine almost turned over. I counted to ten and tried again.

"Come on," I muttered.

"Trying to escape?" I heard Luke laughing as he brought me my cup of coffee.

"Uh, no. I mean," I laughed. "Maybe. That was faster than I thought."

"They remembered me and gave it to me free of charge." He smiled.

I took the cup of coffee from him and placed it in the coffee holder. I might've been sheltered for the last twenty-two years of my life, but I wasn't stupid. I wouldn't be drinking something from some strange guy, no matter how appealing he was. The more I looked at him, the closer I felt to him, which was just as dangerous.

"I've got to get going," I muttered, waving him away, but all I was met with was deep laughter.

"Are you planning on Flintstoning it out of here?" he asked, his brow arching. "I really don't mind giving you a ride."

"That's not what I meant," I said, glaring at him, but I couldn't help but laugh. "But no thanks."

"Oh, right. That was my cue. Listen, you have my business card. I don't want to make your day any worse so I'll let you do what you think you've gotta do, but if you change your mind... Call me and I'll get a cab to come for you."

I nodded and watched as he walked away from my window. He was distracting enough that the loneliness had somewhat dissipated until I realized he was leaving. Then it slowly seeped back in.

I was stranded in a parking lot twenty minutes away from where I needed to be. I had a debit card that was completely useless, and a guy who was willing to help me out. Was I determined to make my life difficult?

"Umm. Maybe, I'll save the call and say I'd love a cab ride, and once I'm on my feet, I'll be sure to—"

"You owe me nothing." He shook his head and smiled, grabbing his phone out of his pants. I watched him as he called for a cab and wondered how I'd gotten so lucky to meet such a kind soul. I had flown past embarrassment a long time ago, and I was just hoping nothing more would go wrong.

"I'll wait until the car shows up, and I'll help you haul everything from your truck into the vehicle. You don't want to leave anything in the open, even if it's tied down. What we can't fit in we'll put in the cab of your truck," he said, his eyes meeting mine.

"Thanks." I bit my lip and thought about what to say to this stranger who'd shown me more kindness in the last thirty minutes than I'd encountered in a long time. "This is really nice of you."

He shook his head, stripping off his jacket before walking over to the truck bed. I gently maneuvered between our two vehicles and stood next to him, my eyes dropping to his chest. I could literally see the ripple of the fabric from the definition of his muscles. I couldn't even imagine what that must look like underneath.

He caught my gaze and a tiny curl of his lip surfaced before I turned away, feeling the flush roll up my body.

"You like to park close to things," I teased, as I

worked on untying one of the ropes.

"It's a bad habit. I tend to get wrapped up in my own world." He loosened a knot and began on another one.

"I find that incredibly hard to believe," I said, glancing at him. His awareness and willingness to help me out of my predicament told me otherwise.

"Well, there's always exceptions to the rule, I suppose," he said, letting the first set of ropes fall to the side of the truck bed. "Especially if someone is as eye-catching as you."

I laughed and shook my head. I knew he was only being kind, considering what I looked like compared to the rest of the microcosm. My cheeks warmed as I worked my fingers against the knot, finally loosening it enough to let it fall.

Luke was on the other side of the truck bed, untying the last of the rope when I saw a black Escalade come up behind him and park.

That was odd.

"Your chariot awaits," Luke said, smiling from across the truck bed.

"That's a cab?" I asked.

"It's umm a car service I use and trust," Luke corrected, his gaze dropping away from mine. "I thought we'd have a better chance of fitting everything inside. Less hassle for you that way."

My chest constricted with the idea of leaving this kind stranger behind. His compassion was the first genuine gesture I'd experienced in a very long time. But maybe that was how it was in the real world. Maybe my new beginning would be full of Lukes.

"So it is," I said, nodding. "Thank you."

There were only five boxes and a suitcase in the truck bed, along with an old wooden chair I couldn't part with, which in hindsight, seemed pretty odd.

Luke grabbed the first box I pointed to as the driver appeared, ready to help load his SUV with my belongings. The driver was a portly, older man with dark hair, graying around the edges, and he was dressed in a black suit.

I grabbed my suitcase and pushed it into the vehicle. I went back to the cab of my truck, grabbed everything off the seat and inside the console and shoved it into a bag. It felt odd leaving the truck behind. It had become home over the last week and it was mine; one of the few things that was. The moment I figured out what happened with my bank account, I'd get my truck, but for now, I needed to get to the house and internet. I shoved my bag and purse onto the floor of the front seat.

Everything had been transferred to the SUV and relief spread through me, knowing I wouldn't have to leave anything behind in the truck. I climbed into the SUV as the driver did the same.

Luke walked over to me and stood next to the open door. "Remember, if anything else comes up, you have my number."

"Why are you being so kind?" I asked softly.

His eyes locked on mine and he smiled.

"You looked like you could use a little

kindness in your world. Welcome to California." Luke closed the door and took a step back, waving as the driver turned on the ignition and stepped on the accelerator.

"Where to, Miss?" the driver asked.

I gave him the address and his jaw tensed. "Are you sure about that address?"

"That's the one I was given. Why?" I asked.

"It's not a good part of town. That's all."

"Oh. Well, that's where I'm headed."

"Very well," the driver said, turning the vehicle onto the main road.

I looked out the window and saw Luke still following the vehicle with his gaze. I gave him a quick nod and prayed that whatever was waiting for me wouldn't be worse than what I left back home.

CHAPTER TWO

Luke

I watched as the car turned onto the main street, whisking Hannah and her few belongings away. I swear to God I could almost feel her heartbeat pounding out of her chest from here. She was running from something. That much I knew. Her beautiful smile haunted me as I let out a deep sigh, realizing I wasn't going to walk away. I felt somewhat bad about lying to her about a car service, but I didn't want her to feel awkward if she knew I had my own driver. I jogged over to her truck and peered through the window, noticing she'd left the coffee behind.

"Damn," I muttered.

This girl's luck seemed to have run out a long time ago and that made me nervous. I had three hours before I needed to be at the airport, but there was something pulling me to make sure she made it okay to wherever it was she was going. Charles, my driver, assured me that he'd call me and give me the address of where she was staying. And I was counting the minutes. But something told me I wasn't going to like his report.

In my business, I've dealt with a lot of fear and paranoia, most of it unfounded. Not with Hannah. I could almost taste the fear that was rolling off her. It was genuine fear. The kind I only see in very desperate situations, very dangerous situations. The way she constantly glanced over her shoulder or did a double take on any passerby told me her fear was legit.

I jimmied the lock and opened the truck door, hoping to find something that would give me answers in the little amount of time before I had to hop on the plane. My sister seemed to think I liked to block out all the commotion inside my head by taking on other people's problems. She also would follow it up by telling me I needed to deal with my own issues but that was no fun, now was it?

I slid my hand under the driver's seat, feeling the carpet and nothing more. I leaned over and did the same to the passenger seat, but this time my hand landed on a packet. Pulling it out quickly, I glanced at the envelope and opened it. There were several important documents, and I doubted she meant to leave them in the truck. I glanced at her car insurance, registration, and storage locker information. Definitely not something that she'd want to leave in the truck.

But I certainly couldn't show up on her doorstep with everything. She was freaked out enough without me adding to her unsettled "everyone's a stalker" mentality. I didn't need to add to her problems. I noticed a New Hampshire address on some of the documents and noted it in my phone. Maybe I could shoot by her old address this week when I was in New England. Or not. I shouldn't get myself involved, but I was never one to take my own advice.

I also spotted two different last names, Hannah Walker and Hannah Martin. Definitely a woman on the run. I shoved all the documents back into the envelope before sliding it back under the seat. I locked the door and shut it before crawling in my own car, waiting for the call from Charlie.

Hannah had gotten under my skin. There was no doubt about it. The moment I saw her standing in line, I was fascinated, but my gut turned inside out once her card was rejected. Feeling the embarrassment ooze out of her almost killed me. I wanted to swoop in and take it away. Once her eyes connected with mine, I knew she was carrying ghosts with her. Now I just needed to find out how to release them and free her from her troubles. I'd been in the security business long enough to know that if the predator didn't kill the person, the stress of thinking could—would.

My phone buzzed and I glanced down at the screen. It was Charlie. I turned the key on my Tesla and backed out of the parking spot as I answered the phone on speaker.

"What do you have, Charlie?" I asked.

"You're not gonna like it one bit."

"I was afraid of that." I pulled onto the road, turning in the opposite direction of Hannah. I needed to grab my bags from home before I headed to the airport.

"She lives on Hawthorne and Maple," Charlie explained, "and I felt horrible about leaving her there. I'd bet money on it being a halfway house or maybe even a safe house of some sort."

"What? A halfway house? Come on. You don't think she's a druggie..." My voice elevated more than I realized. That wasn't her demon.

"No, sir. I don't. To be perfectly candid, I think she's in hiding and in over her head."

I settled a bit at his admission.

"Agreed. Text over the address. Can you arrange for her truck to be towed to where she's living?"

"Absolutely."

"I'll have an envelope waiting on my kitchen counter that I'd like you to get to the tow truck driver to give her. Does that work?" I asked, pulling onto the Pacific Coast Highway.

"I'll be sure to grab it," he assured. "And, sir, one bit of advice."

"What's that Charlie?"

"You can't save everyone."

CHAPTER THREE

Hannah

The longer we drove, the more apparent the changes in the surroundings became. Rather than manicured business parks and strip malls sprinkled in every direction, homes with chain-link fences and bars on the windows appeared. We'd only driven about fifteen minutes, but apparently, it was fifteen minutes in the wrong direction. Many of the homes were small, one-story stucco buildings; the yards overgrown with grass and weeds. Every so often there'd be a home that was taken care of, but that wasn't the neighborhood standard. Concrete block walls were tagged in colorful spray paint murals. My stomach knotted as we drove deeper into the neighborhood I'd be calling home.

"According to GPS, it looks like we're about a block away," the driver said, interrupting my thoughts.

"Great. Thanks for driving me here," I replied, still staring at one rundown home after another. The car slowed and my pulse began pounding as the home came into view.

It occurred to me then that if I'd known where I was going, I might not have come. I let out a deep breath and glanced at the driver who was staring at the house. It was larger than most of the ones we'd passed on the way here. It had a half-built concrete wall and overgrown weeds in the front yard. My mind flashed back to the carefully constructed homes I'd left behind in my community, if you could call it that. Everything was in its place back home. Here it looked like everyone's dirty laundry was exposed, and maybe that's what I needed. All of the problems back in New Hampshire were hidden. Secrets filled every crevice and dirtied the soul. Here, maybe things were more transparent from the start, which might be a good thing. There was nothing worse than bearing the weight of hidden sins from another.

"You sure this is where you want me to let you off?" the driver asked.

I nodded and smiled. "Yeah. This is it."

I opened the door and grabbed my belongings off the floor as the driver climbed out of the vehicle.

"I'll start bringing your things up to the front door," the driver said.

"Thanks," I said, walking up the steps. There was a gate at the base of the stairs and it was open. "But you don't have to..."

"Orders from Mr. Fletcher," the driver said, holding up his hand to stop me from continuing.

"He's very persistent," I muttered.

"You have no idea."

When I reached the top of the steps, the front door opened, revealing a very stern woman. Her hair was long, stringy and brown, framing her harsh features and hazel eyes. She wore a pair of jeans, an orange t-shirt, and white flip-flops. Her eyes stayed on me for a beat too long and a funny feeling crept over me.

"Who's he?" she asked, looking over my shoulders.

"My driver. I—"

"You had specific instructions," the woman's voice cold and callous.

"I know. I'm sorry, but my truck broke down and..."

"Don't let it happen again," she responded, as the driver brought up a box and left it on the steps.

"You're Nancy?" I asked.

"I am."

"I really should help him," I said, setting my things down on top of the box. I marched back down the stairs. This wasn't the warm welcome I'd hoped for, and it also told me that maybe my new beginning wouldn't be full of Lukes.

When I reached the SUV, I grabbed my suitcase and hauled it out of the vehicle. The weight of it landed on the sidewalk with a thud. The driver was already carrying his third load up the stairs when I glanced back toward the front door, and Nancy was no longer there. I grabbed my chair and managed to hold it in one hand as I carried the suitcase in the other.

As I walked back up the stairs, the driver was coming down and he stopped. "Doesn't seem like a particularly friendly gal you'll be rooming with."

I pressed my lips together and gave a slight nod of agreement, but I kept walking.

Reaching the top of the stairs, I wheeled my suitcase into the entry of the home and set the chair down. The brown tile was cracked in areas, and the walls were painted a dingy, pale yellow and in need of a fresh coat of paint. Walls didn't exist like this where I came from. Every chore to keep the properties up was handled, and if it couldn't be taken care of by the occupant than it was doled out to one of the other residents.

"Miss, I carried the last box up. I'll be on my way if there isn't anything else you need," the driver said.

I turned around feeling sheepish for not having any extra cash to tip him.

"I'm sorry. I don't have..."

"Mr. Fletcher has taken care of everything." He nodded, smiling.

"Ohh... Well, thank you. No. I don't need anything else. Thanks for your help."

I heard voices behind me and watched as the driver walked down the steps. I glanced behind me and didn't see anyone, so whoever was talking must be in another room. I walked outside and began pushing the boxes into the entry when a female appeared in front of me. She looked to be around my age and far kinder than the official greeter.

"I'm Rikki." She came outside and began pushing a box inside to help me, which I was grateful for. She had blond hair, but it wasn't as light as mine and her eyes were hazel. She was dressed in frayed jean shorts and a black camisole.

"I'm Hannah."

"I know. We've been expecting you. And don't mind Nancy. She's a bit of a militant but completely harmless."

We finished getting my belongings inside when Nancy reappeared.

"Hannah, I see you've met Rikki. I'll show you around and to your room. This house has rules, and I expect everyone to abide by them...no matter what the reason. You already went against one of the first rules you were told to adhere to, which was to drive yourself here. That makes me wonder about your understanding of the situation you're in."

"I know and I apologize. It won't happen again," I replied.

Nancy gestured for us to follow her. The hall was in disarray with items stacked haphazardly on shelves, and piles of shoes and coats strewn about. The kitchen was no better. The cracked white tile on the counter was piled high with all sorts of magazines, papers, plates, and cups. It looked like someone needed to come in here and give this place a good cleaning.

"This is the kitchen that everyone shares. I keep the fridge stocked, but there's a quota per person. You can have one cup of milk, two tablespoons of butter to use how you wish, two slices of cheese, and four slices of bread per day. If you bring in your own food, make sure to mark it, to not cause confusion."

An allotment of food? What had I gotten myself into?

"You can have one tablespoon of peanut butter as well." Nancy looked at me and crossed her arms in front of her. "You understand why our rules are in place?"

I glanced at Rikki, who rolled her eyes.

"To make sure everyone gets enough..."

"To make sure we're all safe. Everyone here is running from something or someone, and if you can't stick to the rules, no matter how small, you're endangering everyone else who lives here."

I nodded. "I understand."

"I'm not sure you do," Nancy said, as she began walking out of the kitchen.

I followed her down another hall and Rikki was right behind me.

"This is the main bathroom for everyone to share. A shower schedule is posted. If you miss your time, you need to wait until the next day," Nancy said, flipping on the bathroom light. There was a clipboard with several names written down the side and times listed at the top.

"I haven't had a shower for far too long. Since

I just got here would it be okay if—"

"You don't get it. Do you?" Nancy snapped, her brow arching. "It isn't about a shower."

Apparently, I didn't get it. I was twenty-two years old and wanting to take a shower didn't seem like that big of a deal. I understood the food thing because it had to do with money and making sure everyone had enough to go around, but a shower? That just seemed like a power trip.

"If I made things easy for you and everyone here, do you think any of you would ever want to leave? This isn't a spa. It's a place for you to get your shit together and leave. So no. You need to wait until your allotted time tomorrow to take your shower. Just imagine how grateful you'll be when you finally get it." Nancy pursed her lips together and scanned the list. "We've got you on the list at eight o'clock in the morning." She flipped off the bathroom light and began walking down the hall.

"This is your bedroom." She opened the door and turned on the lights. "It's one of the smaller ones, but it's all we have available." Nancy walked into the space and I followed behind.

A twin bed was pushed into the far corner of the room, and a faded pink quilt was thrown on top of the mattress. The window above the bed had bars on it. I wasn't sure if that actually made me feel safer or not. Baby blue wallpaper with tiny white flowers was pasted on the four surrounding walls, but it, too, was in shambles as strips of the paper curled near the corners. There was a chest at the end of the bed and that was it.

On a positive note, I'd be able to stack all my boxes in the room just fine.

"Have your sheets stripped every Sunday by ten o'clock in the morning, and they'll be washed. If you don't, they won't. Okay, follow me to the great room where most everyone is watching television. I'll do a quick introduction and then you can get to unpacking. I want everything out of the entry in an hour. We need to respect the common spaces by not leaving things out."

I wondered who was responsible for littering the kitchen. Maybe the rules didn't apply to her.

As I followed Nancy back down the hall, she stopped abruptly and turned around to face me. "Just remember this. The longer you take up a bed in my house, the more you're making it impossible for me to help the next person. So the quicker you can find a job and get on your feet the better. There's a lot of people in this country who need fresh starts and new beginnings, and the longer you stay here, the less you make that possible. Got it?" Nancy's expression never changed as she stared at me, waiting for a response.

"I got it."

She nodded and started walking again. We went back through the kitchen, passed by a bathroom, and then moved into a large space where several women were watching television. The worn, brown couch looked like it was about to collapse into itself as four women were piled on it, and the recliner in the corner didn't look much better. The shade on the lamp looked like it was from several decades ago and so did the television set that sat right next to it. The room smelled of cigarette smoke and my nose began to tickle.

"Who's been sneaking cigarettes inside, again?" Nancy barked. Her eyes fell on the woman in the recliner.

"It wasn't me. I went outside. Maybe the scent just lingered," the woman said.

"That's another rule," Nancy said, looking at me. "No smoking inside the house."

I shook my head. "I don't smoke so that should be an easy one to follow."

"Girls, I want you to meet our newest resident, Hannah," Nancy said. She pointed at the woman in the chair. "That's Claire."

Claire smiled at me, tightening her ponytail before she said, "Nice to meet you. Hope you like the Housewives." She motioned at the television, and I had no idea what she was talking about.

"And that's Sherry." She pointed at a woman, who had dyed black hair and was sitting on the far end of the couch. "That's Hilary." Nancy pointed at the woman sitting next to Sherry. "Unfortunately, she's set on breaking all kinds of house records. The first disappointing one is length of stay. What are you at now?"

"Six months," Hilary said, beaming. The woman on the other side of her jabbed her with her elbow.

"What's the average stay?" I asked.

"Six weeks. And that's Reyna and next to her, Liz," Nancy continued.

"Nice to meet you all," I said, wanting to do nothing more than hide in my room and come up with a way to get out of here. I wasn't sure I'd last six days here, let alone six weeks. The sooner I found a job, the quicker I could find a different place to live. But first, I needed the internet to find out what happened with my bank account.

"Do the residents have access to internet?" I asked Nancy.

"This isn't the dark ages," Nancy scoffed as I followed her to the kitchen.

Could've fooled me.

"There's a house laptop in the kitchen or if you have your own, I can give you the wireless password."

"I've got an old netbook that I'd like to set up," I replied, glancing at my boxes.

Nancy began writing down the password on a piece of paper, and I thought about trying again with her. I'd never been one to go against the rules or try to cause trouble, and somehow, she'd managed to put me in that bucket immediately.

"Again, I'm sorry for breaking the rules you gave me. My debit card didn't work, and my truck wouldn't start right after I found out that my card was toast so I wasn't really thinking straight. A nice guy offered to help..."

"Everything has a price," Nancy said, tearing off the paper for me.

I shook my head. "I don't think so. He wouldn't let me pay him back or—"

"You, my dear, are beyond naïve," she laughed. "Just don't let it happen again."

"I won't. I just need to get online and figure out what happened with my bank account. I had plenty of money in there and I need to get my truck towed."

Nancy's eyes narrowed on me. "So your debit card was denied?"

"For a cup of coffee," I said. "So it's got me worried. I knew it wouldn't be able to cover a tow and repairs so I let someone call a car service for me."

"That's not good," Nancy said. "Did you tell anyone back home that you were leaving or had an account?"

"No. Not a soul. I'm hoping it's just a glitch."

My best friend knew, but she was killed.

"Don't count on it," Nancy replied. "If your money's gone, I can lend you the tow amount to get your truck here and if it needs to be fixed…"

"I can't do that."

"It might be your only option," Nancy said. "I'm guessing whatever you might need to borrow can be paid off in a paycheck or two, once you find a job. I'll be sure to get my money first. You can count on it."

I nodded. "I understand. I just hope that's not what it comes too."

I walked to my suitcase in the entry and rolled it into my bedroom. I heaved it onto the bed and ran back and forth between the entry and my bedroom fitting all my belongings into my tiny room. Unzipping the suitcase, my heart rate began pounding as I got closer to finding out what happened with my checking account. I turned on the netbook and typed in the wireless password. As I waited for it to connect, my mind wandered to all sorts of scenarios, but none readied me for the reality.

As my bank website flashed on the screen, I entered my username and password, and my account came up with a zero balance. I clicked on the account number detailing transactions, and my heart fell to my stomach when the transaction listed at the top of the screen showed a withdrawal and the words "account closed" scrawled on the screen. Someone closed my account today.

How was that possible? Who knew I had an account there, and how would they be allowed to close it? Someone had to have impersonated me. The nausea in my stomach increased with every passing second as I thought about who'd done this. They were obviously sending me a message. I just wished I didn't have to decipher it. I picked my suitcase up and dropped it onto the floor. Climbing onto the bed, I looked out the window, which overlooked the main street, but I couldn't help but gaze at the bars locking me inside my new personal hell. What had I gotten myself into?

Maybe I could have survived at home, played along like nothing was wrong, act like I didn't see anything, didn't know what they were talking about. I would still be surrounded by the people and places I knew; the familiarity of a life that I understood around me. Maybe that was what I should've done. I could've kept the secret, held it tightly to my chest and nothing in my life would've changed, but it was too late for that now. I had to deal with the consequences of running.

I heard a rumble of a diesel engine outside and glanced toward the street where a tow truck was pulling up to the curb, my blue truck attached behind. My heart started hammering as I thought about who called for the tow. Sliding off the bed, I ran down the hall and out the door as the tow truck driver was unhooking my truck. He wore a navy baseball cap and jeans. His thick fingers unhooked the chains as he flashed me a quick smile.

"You Hannah?" he asked.

"I am," I said, nodding.

"Great. I'll have you sign off on this," he said, grabbing a clipboard from the truck seat.

I glanced at the paperwork and noticed Luke's information in the billing section. Why was this stranger being so kind? I quickly signed my name, almost forgetting to sign my new last name. When I handed him back the clipboard, he handed me two business cards.

"This is a good mechanic I know. Trustworthy. And here's my information if it needs a tow over there," he replied. "The doors are unlocked so I'd make sure to lock it up before you head back inside."

I smiled. "Thanks."

I watched the driver climb into his truck as I headed over to mine. Opening the driver's side, there was an envelope on my seat. Ripping it open, a note and a Starbucks card fell out.

I noticed you didn't take your coffee with you, and I wasn't going to have that happen for a third time. I had to get it to you somehow. And here's a little something to make your next coffee trip a little less eventful.

Best,
Luke

I shoved the note and gift card back in the envelope and couldn't help but soften a little more toward Luke. I glanced at the Starbucks coffee cup and decided to take a leap of faith. I doubted very much he'd put something in it, and if he did, maybe I'd have a nice sleep for a change.

No. That was a horrible way to look at the world. I didn't want to become that cynical person that wandered around, doubting everyone's motives, and making snarky comments about people's true intentions. There were bad people in the world, but there were more good people to outnumber the bad.

There had to be.

Taking a sip, I spit it out onto the street. Milk and sweetness had filled my mouth instead of black coffee. I glanced at the cup and noticed it was another new drink, which explained why it was still warm. He'd managed to get me a caramel macchiato, which happened to be my favorite drink but was far too expensive for my blood. I let out a sigh and took another sip, this time enjoying the magnificent flavor as it slipped down my throat. I'd only had Starbucks maybe ten times in my life. It had been when I'd accompanied one of our groups to run errands in the next town over. I'd manage to sneak away and grab something, and it was such a victory. How odd was that? Ever since I'd hit the state line into California, it felt like my old life wasn't even real. The events too bizarre and horrifying to be anything other than imagined. But I knew that wasn't the case. It was all very real.

I took another sip and felt the delicious flavor coat my mouth. At this point in my life, I needed some sort of positive sign that things were going to be okay, and for the moment, this latte was that sign.

I looked up the stairs and saw Nancy with her arms crossed as she shook her head at me, obviously disgusted by the kind gesture that was now sitting outside of her house. I climbed the stairs and smiled, holding my latte tightly.

"Don't be fooled," Nancy said, her glowering eyes taking me in. "There are always strings attached. Don't you ever forget it."

"So you offering your home isn't out of the goodness of your heart?" I asked, walking by her. "Are there strings attached?"

Nancy remained silent, watching me walk down the hall to my room. I closed the door and decided not to unpack. I didn't plan on being here long enough to need to. With exhaustion finally crashing down on me, I grabbed a book and slid under the covers, not making it even a chapter before my eyes closed. I drifted to sleep, ready to meet my nightmares once more.

CHAPTER FOUR

Luke

I listened as the senator droned on and on about why his mistress needed a security detail. I wondered how the wife felt about that. My guess was that she or a friend did the threat sending, and it was probably completely harmless, just a good stress reliever.

These were my least favorite security tasks. From what I gathered, the senator's mistress received some death threats, and not wanting to make the matter public, the senator was now doling out top dollar to keep her safe. That was where my firm, Fletcher Security, came in. This wasn't what I had imagined when I built the company, but these were bread-and-butter cases. I had teams all over the world, protecting diplomats and other dignitaries, and my men were the best in the business. Their training and loyalty rivaled the most elite military forces in the world, but often on the domestic front, we were tapped in high-profile scandals before they became scandals.

I glanced across the lake and my thoughts drifted to Hannah. I hadn't been able to get her out of my mind; the way her eyes still managed to sparkle even though her life was quite possibly filled with more dark than light. After finding out where Hannah was now living, I had gotten some more items together before I left town and had a courier drop them off. Included in that packet was a disposable cell phone. It was an odd gift. That much I would admit, but in my line of work it was a must. I hadn't had much time before I left my house, but I was able to gather from Google maps that she was living in a house that was barely standing, run by a woman who I could say the same for. The owner of the home was Nancy Lowel, and she had a past that would make even the most seasoned PI do a double take. Between being mysteriously widowed four times, all with large insurance payouts, and several stints in prison, I had no idea how she'd managed to get into the field of helping people. I doubt she did. My hope was that Hannah would watch her back, even at her new residence. My other hope was that I didn't completely scare her off.

"Will you be able to start immediately?" the senator asked. His hair was graying slightly at the temple, and with the twinkle in his eyes, I got the distinct feeling that he actually enjoyed this little game of cat and mouse. Gwyneth the mistress sat next to him as the dutiful partner; her red hair in a loose bun and a strand of pearls around her neck. A person could almost mistake her for his wife, but the senator's wife was in Hawaii with the children and her mother.

How handy.

"Kenneth will be the man assigned to Gwyneth. I'll bring him in." I stood up and walked through the study into the foyer and motioned for Kenneth to follow me. He'd already been advised of the situation. The sooner I could get through the introductions and instructions, the sooner I could do what I really wanted, which was to drive out to the address I'd found on Hannah's papers.

"Thank you very much, Mr. Fletcher. I heard you were the best," Gwyneth gushed, and I wondered if she was looking for victim number two. Kenneth hid a smile, realizing his hands were going to be quite full with this new assignment.

"That's what we do," I replied, not amused.

The senator showed me out, and I climbed into the rental car. Popping the address into the GPS, I set course to see if I could glimpse a piece of Hannah's prior life. I had never done anything like this, but I'd never run across anyone like Hannah either.

I had spent my time disconnecting from the world, yet something about Hannah made me want to reconnect, reengage with the possibilities of...

Of anything, really.

I drove along the tree-lined drive imagining how different things would be if my parents were still alive. I certainly wouldn't be in the business of saving and destroying lives. My phone buzzed and the car answered it.

"Hey, Mr. Bigwig," my sister laughed into the phone. "Where are you at now, and since when did you start handing out my phone number to random strangers? I thought that kind of went against your protection policy," she teased. "I guess I should be grateful for the heads up you sent via text but still."

My heart pounded.

"Did she call? Is she in trouble?"

"Whoa, buddy. Calm down. No. She didn't call, but what the hell was that all about?"

"Sorry. I doubt she'll call. I just..." Uttering the words aloud would surely make me crazy so I kept them to myself. My knuckles turned white as I gripped the wheel tightly. I had to get this foolishness under control.

I couldn't save everyone.

I couldn't save my parents.

"Did you meet someone?" she laughed. "Oh, my god. You did. The poor girl. You're totally going to scare her away. You finally meet someone and you already have security stalking her. If she hasn't gone running yet, she will soon. Mark my words. Did you meet her at the club or through business or..."

"It's not like that. I met her at a Starbucks, and I just thought she could use a hand."

"Tell me more. It sounds promising."

The sad part of my sister's statement was that it probably did sound promising. I tended to only interact with clients and employees.

My sister was five years younger than me, but emotionally she seemed older than her years by far. I had raised her from the time of our parents' deaths, but in many ways, it was her maturity that made us come out okay. We always joked that she'd keep us mentally strong and protected, and I'd keep us physically strong and protected. I took my part very seriously, as did she.

"There's nothing to tell, dear sister. Listen, I got done with my client early and I'm going to go take some photographs of—"

"In the snow?" my sister teased. "So who was the client today that got you pissed?"

She knew me well. I absolutely loathed the men and women in these high profile infidelity scandals. Not everyone was cut out to be married, to be monogamous, but don't pull some poor soul along with you for that ride. If you can't handle the responsibility, don't get married.

That was what irked me. So many people tossing emotions and feelings aside as if they meant nothing, but they meant everything. That was why we were human. Life's already full of too much unexpected pain and misery. Why make someone's heart bleed with that kind of carelessness? That was why I wasn't going to be going down that path. Love was a distraction.

"Hello?" my sister queried.

"Sorry. Some senator. The usual." My sister was the only one I revealed client information to, but it was for a good cause, which was to keep her out of my personal life. If I could distract her enough with this other stuff, she rarely bugged me about finding that special someone. "His wife's in Hawaii with the kids."

"There are kids?" my sister moaned into the phone. "What a creep."

"Agreed." I turned off onto a country road where I'd be driving for the next hour. "Listen, if that girl calls, would you let me know?"

"I will. But do you plan on telling me who she is?" she asked.

"I honestly don't know."

"Okay. So I know I don't need to repeat how crazy that sounds so I'm just going to wish you safe travels and a happy picture taking afternoon. My paint should be dry anyway. Still on for dinner when you get back in town?"

"Always," I said, and she hung up the phone.

As I traveled along the narrow, two-lane road I wondered if I was only drawn to Hannah because I wanted to protect her?

CHAPTER FIVE

Hannah

I woke up with a start. The images continued to plow through my mind as I tried to steady my breathing. Hearing Tracy's screams mixed with my own cries shook me to my core. No matter how many times the images and sounds replayed through my mind, it was always like I was there, witnessing my best friend's death once again. My throat was dry and calling out for water as I calmed my breathing, promising myself that I was far away. I wiped away the dampness that had accumulated along my hairline as I shoved the quilt down. The sun was already appearing, and I quickly reached for my phone, praying I didn't miss my allotted shower time. It was a little past seven o'clock so I was safe. I'd finally get my shower. I'd slept for over twelve hours and still felt as if I didn't get a drop of sleep. Old habits die hard.

I stood up and walked toward the door, hearing a few voices drift down the hall. I opened my door and walked toward the kitchen.

Claire and Rikki were sitting at the kitchen table, both eating a piece of toast. The sight of food made my stomach rumble as I walked toward where the glasses were stored.

"Good morning, sleepyhead. You missed dinner last night. You must be starving," Rikki said.

"I'm guessing that dinner is rationed as well?" I asked.

"That it is." Claire frowned.

"I'm grateful she didn't put a ration on water," I muttered, before taking a sip.

"Don't mention it too loud. She might like that idea," Claire laughed.

I thought back to the Starbucks card and how that would provide me something beyond a couple pieces of bread before dinner. It seemed odd that everyone who was here, running from something, was willing to put up with these rules, essentially being treated as if they were twelve.

"How long have you been here, Claire?"

"Three weeks. I hope to be outta here in a week or so. I got a job last week and should be able to save enough for a deposit and first and last. I won't be living in my own place, but I found a couple places where people are renting a room, which seems like a much better deal to me than staying here."

I nodded. "And you?" I looked at Rikki.

"I've been here five weeks. But I still haven't found a job."

My heart sank at her admission.

I glanced at the kitchen clock, realizing it was getting close to my shower time. I certainly didn't want to miss it.

"Gonna go hop in the shower," I said, waving as I walked back to my room. I felt so out of place and out of my element. Was it just because I'd left the only place I'd known or was it because I was in a place I shouldn't be?

I pulled a pair of jeans and a red, long sleeved v-neck out of my suitcase. Most of my clothes were for a colder climate, but I had enough for a while until I could get more warm-weather items.

Walking into the hall, I heard the water turn off in the bathroom and waited until the door opened and Sherry walked out.

"Your turn," she hummed, a towel wrapped around her head. She was dressed in a robe and slippers and padded back down the hall toward her room.

"Thanks." I closed the door and entered the steamy palace, placing my clothes on the counter. I glanced at the sheet, wondering how long I was allowed in here. It looked to be ten minutes per person. I turned on the shower, and the water was warm instantly so I quickly undressed and stepped under the hot water. Nancy was right. The amount of appreciation that I felt toward the stinging beads that hit my skin was incredible. Feeling the water slide down my skin as I let it sprinkle through my hair was exactly what I needed. It felt like I was washing away everything from my old home and life. I was readying myself for new beginnings.

I squirted the shower gel onto a washcloth and began scrubbing my body, feeling completely revived. As the water continued to pound on me, I washed my hair and my mind drifted to Luke and his startling green eyes and the kindness that sat behind them. I let out a deep breath, knowing full well I wouldn't be seeing him again. But maybe that was what made me feel safe daydreaming about him. It wasn't reality. I opened my eyes to look for the conditioner and there wasn't any. So getting a brush through my long hair was going to be a bit of a painful process. I guess once I was on my own, I'd be ever so appreciative of the finer things in life, even if it was a ninety-nine cent bottle of the slippery stuff.

A knock at the door alerted me that my time was up. It went far quicker than I'd realized as I shut off the water and quickly dried off and put my clothes over my semi-damp body. I opened the door and apologized to the next person in line, Hilary. Holding my dirty clothes, I walked into my bedroom and threw them in the corner.

The first thing I wanted to do was find the nearest Starbucks where I could grab something to eat and start looking for a job on my netbook. I typed in the home address and saw that there was one not too far away. It looked like it was in the direction of the beach, so possibly out of this neighborhood. The tricky part was that I'd need to walk through this neighborhood to get to it. I grabbed my purse and emptied it out, leaving only my wallet inside so I could slip the small netbook into my purse. No one would be able to tell it was in there. I grabbed a brush and began working the snarls out of my hair, which took far longer than I'd imagined. But a moment of delight rushed through me when I remembered I'd grabbed a couple bottles of shampoo and conditioner from a few of the hotels on the way out here.

I looked out the window at my truck and wished it was running. I'd at least feel a little safer driving than walking, but I couldn't worry about that now. I just needed to get out of this place. As I grabbed my purse, Rikki poked her head into my room.

"Got any plans for the day?" Rikki asked.

"Yeah, was going to start looking for work," I said, forcing a smile. "I planned on walking to a Starbucks to plug in and hang out. I'm not used to this place yet, and I think the coffeehouse might make me feel a little less hopeless."

"You weren't really planning on walking, were you? I heard your truck was dead, but have you not looked around?"

I nodded. "I really was planning on walking. I don't want to spend the day here if I don't have to."

"Don't. Let me give you a ride to where you want to go. I'll give you my number, and I can pick you up when you're done. I was planning on looking at some places to rent so I'll be out and about today."

"Seriously? You wouldn't mind?" I asked.

"Not at all. Let me grab my stuff and I'll meet you out front."

My eyes landed on the envelope from Luke and I sighed as I stuck it in my purse. Taking the gift card with me would probably be a good idea if I actually planned on eating or drinking anything at Starbucks. I needed to get with it.

I walked down the hall and through the entry before hearing my name called from behind. I turned around to see Nancy holding something up.

"This is for you," she said, walking a thick envelope to me. My eyes fell to the handwriting on the outside and my insides immediately turned outward. It didn't look like Luke's. Had they found me already?

"Thanks," I said, taking it from her and stuffing it inside my purse. I didn't want to alarm anyone at the house and have a reason for Nancy to boot me out. I had no money and no other place to go.

"I don't like this one bit. Not only are you showing complete disrespect for the other house mates, you're putting everyone, including yourself, in danger."

"I'm sorry. I didn't expect this to happen. I'll tell him to stop," I replied, watching Rikki come into view.

"You're sure it's him?"

I nodded, knowing my words would betray me. But Nancy glared at me, waiting for something more. "I'll have him stop."

"Please do." Nancy turned on her heels and walked away.

"Off to the Arden Street Starbucks," Rikki announced, almost bumping into Nancy. "What was that all about?" Rikki eyed me.

"Long story."

"Being here makes me feel like I have nothing but time, so please, indulge me."

I giggled as I followed her outside toward her silver car that looked a little dinged up on the passenger side. Okay. It wasn't a little dinged it up. It had obviously been in a wreck. A bad wreck.

"It was like that when I got it. Promise," she said, noticing my apprehension. "Now tell me how you got Nancy all roiled up by day two. I think that's a record."

"I always was an overachiever," I laughed, climbing into the Chevy Spark. I began relaying everything that happened from the moment I'd rolled into the infamous parking lot at the coffee shop yesterday, all the way to landing at the house. Rikki nodded and laughed every so often as she drove us away from the ramshackle buildings that surrounded our house.

"Well, this Luke guy sounds very interesting. Are you sure you shouldn't be worried about him though, with your... with everything?"

I knew what she was asking, and we'd all signed releases that we wouldn't ask one another about our pasts, what led us to this house. Rikki was trying to ask without asking. I turned to her and smiled.

"He's harmless. Just the right guy at the wrong place and time," I assured her, trying to push away my fear about what really was in the envelope and who'd sent it.

She pulled into the parking lot of the coffee shop, and I glanced around the tidy strip mall in awe. I just didn't quite understand how things could turn so good or bad by driving less then fifteen minutes in any one direction.

"Give me your cell and I'll program my number in for you," she said, as I handed it to her.

"Thanks for the lift and I'll call you when I'm ready for a ride. But I think it will be several hours from now. Being here makes me feel far safer than being at the safe house."

She sighed and nodded. "Tell me about it." But then her eyes darkened. "You got a new cell after you left your home state, right?"

"I got it right before I left. We didn't have cell phones so they wouldn't think to look for one, if that's what you mean. Only the elders and house ma..." I had said too much.

"There's always a way to be tracked. I'd toss it and hope it's not too late." She eyed the garbage can.

"Really? You're serious?"

"Definitely."

I sighed. "I'll toss it after I text you to come pick me up." I grinned, not as worried about the predicament as she was. There would be no way for anyone from back home to track this phone. I got it the weekend before I left, under my new last name. No one saw it and I never used it, but I respected her opinion and would toss it this afternoon.

"Good call," Rikki grinned.

I closed the door and she drove off. I glanced at the coffeehouse and felt immensely better. Like I was part of a functioning society, rather than someone who was living on the fringe of it. I walked inside and smelled the familiar aromas as I stood in line. When I reached the counter, I was shocked.

"This time, I'm using a gift card," I said victoriously, pulling it out of my wallet.

The barista narrowed his eyes on me and then started laughing. "Oh, yeah. Hope you got everything settled."

"I did. Some sort of fraud alert," I lied. "So you work at this one too?"

"Yeah sometimes. Someone called in sick at this location so I volunteered. I'm trying to get as many hours as I can before school starts up again. So what can I get you?"

"I'd like a caramel macchiato and a ham breakfast sandwich." As I placed my order, I realized that I actually had no idea how much money was on the card. I could be in the same predicament all over again. I also couldn't stop thinking about what was in the envelope that was dropped off.

The cashier took the card and slid it through,

handing it back to me without hesitation. "Would you like a receipt for the balance?"

"Yeah, that would be great." I took the receipt and my eyes landed on how much remained on my gift card.

$193.76

My stomach tightened as Nancy's words ran through my head. "There's always strings attached." But that wasn't true. It couldn't be. Not all of life was about getting what you could from people, was it? I folded the receipt and shoved it in my purse, unsure of what the kindness of this stranger actually meant.

CHAPTER SIX

Luke

Driving into the small town, I got the distinct feeling that visitors weren't welcome. There was one main street that housed a pharmacy, a gift store, a Laundromat, a bowling alley, police station, and a grocery store. There was a gas station at the end of town but that was about it. As I drove through the town, the people walking along the sidewalk kept their heads down and attention turned away from me. The women were dressed in grey dresses that went to their ankles, and the men were in black pants and boxy shirts. I felt like I had landed in another century, except that cars dotted Main Street. A woman in the gift store watched me as I drove by, but once my eyes landed on hers, she pulled back into the shadows. What struck me as more bizarre than her disappearing act was her outfit.

It matched the others on the street.

The GPS instructed me to take the first right off of Main Street. I drove another ten minutes or so in the country until the GPS wanted me to turn down a private drive. No Trespassing signs were posted along a stone wall, but that had never stopped me before. If they really wanted privacy, they'd have a gate up, not just a fence. The private road turned to gravel and led deeper into the country. I glanced at the address again and wondered if this was just one large estate, but then I spotted more of the friendly people from earlier. Two women were walking in the snow. One held a shovel and the other had a baby on her hip. They stopped walking as I drove past them. It struck me as odd that they weren't in coats. It wasn't that cold out, but there was still snow on the ground. I wondered where they were coming from or where they were going.

As I slowly followed down the road, several buildings came into view. They were all similar in design, typical saltbox structures, very plain in appearance. One was painted brown, another grey, and another almost black. There were several cars parked in front of each one. I couldn't tell if these were dwellings or used for something else. I continued driving down the tiny lane and more of the same buildings came into view, but these were much smaller. There was a group of men, dressed just like the others, congregated in front of one of them. A man from the group spotted me and held his hand up as he began walking toward me.

I slowed my car as he approached and rolled down the passenger window.

"This is private property," the man's voice was gruff. He had a scruffy beard and his hazel eyes were unforgiving.

"Oh. My mistake. I thought it was part of the..."

"I ask kindly that you turn around and leave us to our meditation," he interrupted.

"Absolutely," I nodded and glanced at the other men who were approaching my car. "I apologize for intruding. I'll just turn around up ahead."

I rolled up the passenger window and stepped on the gas with no intention of turning around. The men, arms crossed, were standing in the middle of the road behind me, disdain plastered on their faces. I had no plans to turn around until I saw as much as I could. The deeper into the community I drove, more clusters of buildings came into view. There were obvious living quarters, stables, barns, and other large structures that matched the bigger ones on the edge of the property. As I drove past the houses, the doors opened and men and women stepped out of their homes, walking toward the road. They obviously weren't adverse to technology, whoever they were. Someone must have made the call that an unwelcome visitor was in town. I watched as the people lined the street, their expressions grim as I made my way to the end of the road where an old-fashioned church, complete with a steeple, sat.

I couldn't picture Hannah in this community

with her shocking light blond hair, and sexy as hell...

I stopped myself from going there. I was here to find answers, not fantasize about the impossible. I stopped my car and put it in reverse. It was time to make my exit before the group in front of me decided to confront the unwanted visitor. As I turned the car around, I was shocked at the number of people that had now congregated to either confront or intimidate me. Neither option worried me, especially as I watched their expressions. It was almost like they'd been drugged. Their eyes didn't hold the same spark that Hannah's did. There was no way she could have come from this place.

I brought my speed up and drove back down the drive and out of the makeshift community. I passed the first group of men, who were now holding batons as their eyes followed my car out of sight. How friendly. That wasn't exactly something everyone just happened to carry around.

I didn't know what this place was, but I knew enough to know that they were hiding something, and my guess was that Hannah knew exactly what that was, which was why she was in danger. Whatever the case, it had to be big to flee across the country. Now I just had to convince her that I could help. That I could be trusted. And I already knew that was going to be the hardest thing of all.

CHAPTER SEVEN

Hannah

Finding a table near the window, I opened my netbook and fished out the envelope from my purse. I quickly slid my fingers underneath the flap of the envelope, ripping it in the process. Well, at least I knew Nancy didn't open it before me. I slid the papers out and saw a map of the region with large red circles and x's marking it and a note. My heart rate raced as I tried to make sense of everything. Shaking the envelope, a cell phone plopped on the table, which scared me even more. Was it going to ring? I glanced at the handwritten note and couldn't help but laugh.

I'll be out of town for a few days. My sister's number is on the back of the map if anything comes up. I thought since I gave you my information, it was kind of unfair that I didn't have yours. I'm a problem-solver by nature and this seemed the most logical, albeit over the top. Kindly do me the favor of returning whatever feeble attempt at flirting I may toss your way via text. I don't want the minutes and texts purchased to go to waste.

Kind Regards,
Luke Fletcher

A charge ran through me as I reread his words. There was something that was beyond appealing about this man. On one hand, he had the ability to swoop in and save the day, but on the other, he belittled his entire existence with one tiny phrase. I was positive that Luke Fletcher would never give a feeble attempt at anything, which only made me dream about him more.

Somehow this man I barely knew continually managed to bring a smile to my lips when I needed it most. I couldn't keep the smile from my lips as I saw the arrows drawn on the map pointing in all directions away from the neighborhood I currently called home. I looked at the map and couldn't agree more. I needed to find a place where I could at least walk down the street without thinking I was going to get mugged or worse. There was no getting around I was in one of the scariest places to live in a twenty-mile radius. Now if only leaving were so easy. First thing was to get a job, get money, save money, and then get the heck out.

I folded the papers and slid them back into the envelope. I glanced toward the ocean and thought a walk on the beach later might be exactly what I needed. A nice reminder that there was more to my life than a crappy place to sleep at night, a truck that didn't run, and an empty bank account. There were good people in the world, and once I found them, I could expose the bad ones. The very bad ones living back home.

But in the meantime, I needed to concentrate on the fact that I happened to be living in a beautiful, warm area that had more opportunities to blend in and create a new life than anywhere else I could imagine. I grabbed the cell from Luke and turned it on. It was fully charged, and my fingers were literally tingling with the idea of texting him. It seemed kind of presumptuous. What was I going to say? I can't stop thinking about you? You're hot as hell? Run now! I sucked at flirting and blamed it fully on how we were raised, but I'd be lying if I said I didn't want to. I just had a feeling I sucked at it and never before did I have a reason to flirt with anyone. There really wasn't room for it where I came from, but wasn't I trying to leave that behind me? My other life? I needed to get brave.

I fished out Luke's business card and saved it into the phone. I took a deep breath and thought about my text to Luke. Maybe, I just wasn't a flirter. There was nothing wrong with that, right? So it began. My feeble attempt to communicate with a man who took my breath away.

Got the phone. Too much. Again. But thank you.

Taking a sip of my latte, I logged onto the internet to search for employment, but somehow my curiosity got the best of me, and I entered my hometown into the search bar, scrolling for the local newspaper. There was no mention of a woman gone missing, which was what I expected to see. Absolutely nothing. They always made us disappear, seem inconsequential, almost like we never existed. Just like my sister. Just like my best friend. They would convince my family not to take my disappearance to the authorities, and my family would agree, not wanting to go against the leaders. I scanned through the typical small town stories about the local high school theater production, the grocery store changing its hours, and the cemetery offering up new plots. A shiver ran through me as I thought about the people buried there who were far too young and held far too many secrets.

My heart started beating rapidly as I clicked away from the site. I wasn't ready to think about it, not yet. I needed to get settled before I attempted to investigate anything, if I attempted to investigate anything. Maybe all I really wanted was to start a new life and never look back. I forced a lump down as I thought about my best friend, the horror in her eyes. No. I couldn't just run. I had to get justice for her, for everyone.

My phone buzzed and I glanced down, my pulse quickening as I realized Luke already texted back.

There is no such thing as having too much kindness in the world. But besides that, I'm happy to see I didn't scare you off.

I texted back quickly.

I doubt there would be much of anything you could do to scare me off. I've got nerves of steel.

Luke replied.

I don't doubt that. Plus, you are gorgeous and I haven't been able to get you out of my mind.

My breathing hitched, and my cheeks felt like they were on fire as I read his text. And then another one came over.

See! I bet that scared you off. Knew I could do it. Seriously, though. I'd love to see you again under normal circumstances. Say, like a date?

My hands got clammy as I read the text. I had never been on a date. No. That wasn't true. I had been on many dates with the man I was told I would have to marry. Besides the fact that I tried to act like I was in another place and time whenever I spent a moment with him, I literally dreaded everything about our encounters. I wouldn't qualify those as dates, which only put more pressure on me and the fact that I was truly screwed up. I put the cell down and Googled Luke Fletcher. His security firm popped right up, along with several links about him and his company. I clicked on a Los Angeles Times article that detailed his professional involvement with several actors and actresses. My mind wandered to his personal life and whether those encounters involved any of the actresses. Not that it was any of my business. I glanced at one of the pictures and saw the driver who took me to the home yesterday. He was listed as one of Luke's employees. I picked the cell back up again and texted.

Wait a second. That guy who drove me yesterday was your employee and his name's Charlie.

He replied back.

*I told you. I'm a problem solver. You needed a
ride. I had one to offer. Problem solved. Are you
planning on avoiding my question?*

Smart ass. I put the phone back down. This wasn't what I needed to be doing right now. I let out a deep breath as I heard the scrape of a chair behind me. I scooted my chair closer to the table and knew the first thing I needed to do was find a job. Scanning the papers online, I began taking notes on different positions that sounded like a good match. Truth be told, I'd take just about anything to get out of where I was living. Secretarial, receptionist, and clerical positions were plentiful and probably the best place for me to start. Unfortunately, the hourly wage wasn't exactly what I hoped, but it was better than nothing, which was exactly what I had right now.

"Sorry," a woman muttered behind me, bumping into my chair.

"Oh, sorry. It's me," I replied, pulling my chair closer to the table. "I can be a space hog." I turned in my chair to look at the female as she attempted to plug in her laptop.

"No. You're not. I had to plug in my laptop before it totally died. They never put these outlets in a great place."

The woman's brunette hair was pulled back in a loose braid, and she was in a pair of sandals, a floral skirt, and camisole. She appeared to be a couple years older than me, at the most. Her arm looked like it was about to fall off as she continued stretching it to its limits. "Got it," she exclaimed, pulling herself back up.

"Victory," I cheered, turning back to face my screen. I heard her push the chair back in and glanced behind me.

"I haven't seen you here before," the woman said, grinning. "Not that I'm the Starbucks police or anything. I happen to live around the corner."

I laughed and turned back around. "I'm new to the area. Just looking for work, actually."

"Really? Where are you from?" she asked.

"Ohio," I lied, hoping she didn't grow up there. At this rate that would be my luck, and her father would be the Governor..

Her brows furrowed and she smiled. "Never been."

"Not many people have," I said, chuckling. "I'm Hannah."

"Liv. So anything in particular you're looking for?" she inquired.

I shrugged. "Anything really."

"You bartend?" she asked.

I shook my head.

"Waitress?"

"I haven't, but I'm a fast learner."

She narrowed her eyes as she studied me.

"What?" I asked.

"I work at a place that I think you'd love."

"Where's that?" I asked.

"Buttons," she replied. "Heard of it?"

"Uh, no. Is it a bar?"

"Of sorts. The money's great, like really great. They usually only like brunettes, but for you, I'm sure they'd make an exception. You're gorgeous.

You're a natural blonde, aren't you?" She twisted her lips as she contemplated something.

I nodded. "Wait. Is it a—"

"Strip joint?" she chuckled. "No. It's a different type of bar. You need a membership."

"For what? To drink?" I asked.

"No matter how I say it...it's going to come out weird," Liv said.

"No offense, but that doesn't sound promising," I laughed. The last thing I needed was to jump out of one group of psychos and into another underground world.

"The pay's amazing..." She smiled, watching my reaction.

"How amazing?" I asked.

"Amazing enough that I'll be leaving school without any loans and plenty in my savings come spring."

"Is it legal?" I almost whispered.

Her laughter made me feel foolish, but so did taking a sip of her serum.

"Yes. It's legal." She raised her brow. "We're in the land of Hollywood stars. And nothing makes people feel more special than thinking they have the same privileges as those who grace the covers of every magazine. This state has enough wannabes who are willing to pay to feel special. People will pay a high price for exclusivity. I'm sure it sounds ridiculous coming from where you do..." her voice trailed off.

If only she knew. The world I left behind was based on exclusivity and misuse of power in the highest form. The right to belong had a price, but it wasn't money. A shiver ran through my body.

"You okay?" she asked.

I nodded. "Sorry. Not used to the AC."

"If you're interested, how about you see for yourself? I work tonight and you can meet me beforehand." She scribbled the address on a napkin and handed it to me. "I'd rather you check the place out and see if you're into it before I introduce you to the owners."

My stomach knotted as I looked into her eyes. "How long would it take me to get enough for the deposit and rent on my own apartment?" I asked, pushing the fear aside.

She grinned and her eyes glinted with fascination. "I'd say a couple of weeks, depending on what type of place you want."

"A one bedroom, even a studio."

Liv's mouth dropped open. "Honey, you'd have enough for a place like that in a few days of work. My advice would be to save a little more and get a place right on the beach." The glint in her eye was telling. Money meant a lot to Liv, but showing it off meant even more. All I wanted was to be able to live in a safe neighborhood and maybe build a small cushion for when my truck broke down the next time.

"See that out there?" she interrupted my thoughts.

I followed her pointed finger to a white Range Rover parked outside the Starbucks.

"Yeah. What about it?"

"That's my ride."

This made no sense. Wouldn't everyone be

doing whatever it was she did? If nothing else, I wanted to see what it was this place was about, even if I didn't get a job there. I was just too nosey to let this slip by.

"Huh. I guess I'll see ya tonight then," I said, smiling, as I slid the napkin into my purse. "Thanks for telling me about it." I closed the netbook and shoved it into my purse, along with my uneaten breakfast sandwich. Glancing at the beach, I strapped my bag around my shoulder and grabbed my latte. Maybe spending some time on the beach would help me sort things out. I hadn't had a moment of peace since I'd landed in California, and within a day I'd already felt like life around here was as bizarre as where I'd left, but in a completely different way.

"See ya," she replied, giving me a quick wave before I headed out the front door.

I walked along the sidewalk to the crosswalk and pushed the button. The chirping alerted me that it was time to cross. As I made my way to the parking lot for beach access, I glanced at all the cars filling the lot. There was one shiny, new car after the next. I doubted there was anything over a few years old at the beach. And how could so many people spend a workday at the beach? I hoisted my bag higher over my shoulder and made my way to the sand. The beach was packed. Colorful towels and umbrellas dotted the sand, with children filling buckets and parents reading. There were surfers in the water at the far end, and mothers and fathers guiding their children in the shallow water. The sun was blazing and it felt like another world where problems didn't exist and every day was a new beginning. This was what I wanted.

As I trudged through the sand, I realized how difficult it was going to be in my shoes to make my way to the benches. I stopped, placing my purse on the sand, and pulled my shoes off. Feeling the sand between my toes made me feel like I was on vacation. What I imagined being on vacation felt like, anyway. I'd never been on an actual getaway. I made my way to the cluster of benches and laughed aloud as I saw the sign posted near the area.

Free Wireless Available

Seriously? At a beach? That would explain why so many people had their laptops balanced on their knees.

I took a seat on one of the empty benches and placed my purse next to me, watching the waves roll in and out. The sound of the water crashing and the children laughing in delight made me feel like everything was going to be okay, whether or not that was true. I decided to join the party and continue looking for employment on my netbook. Not that I didn't believe Liv's employment opportunity, but I didn't believe Liv's employment opportunity.

"Miss? Don't I know you from somewhere?" I heard from behind. I didn't know who the man was talking to, but the person wasn't answering.

I surfed the Craigslist employment ads,

scanning more office jobs when the man tried again. My eyes focused on the hourly wages as I continued to quickly tabulate just how long it would take me to save enough to get out of the house. It would take a very long time.

"Don't I know you?" the man's voice startled me but not as much as his eyes as he took a seat next to me.

He didn't look the least bit familiar.

"No. I'm sorry. I think you've got me confused with someone else." I said, turning back to my netbook.

"I don't think I do," his voice cold, calculating.

My heart rate pounded as I looked around this beach filled with people. Nothing could happen to me here. There were too many people around.

I turned to face the man. My gaze steadied on his dark eyes. There was no warmth behind them. His expression matched theirs. He had been sent by the leaders. How was this possible? How had they found me?

"Your car trouble seems to have been temporarily resolved. That's a shame. I'll have to do better next time," the man stated. "Pity, really, that such a nice man stepped in to help you. I imagine he'll have to be taken care of as well. No good deed goes unpunished."

My blood froze as I stared at him.

"I don't know what you're talking about," I said, moving my finger to the emergency button on my cell phone and praying I landed in the right area as I hit the screen.

"I think you do. And the less of a scene you

make, the better for everyone involved. I might even take it easy on that guy. Understand?" his voice low.

"I guess if I truly understood, I never would've left New Hampshire," I replied. "But I dare you to take me off this bench. You lay one finger on me and I'll scream bloody murder."

"You know something that can't be known. You remember something that can't be remembered," the man laughed. "Don't think for a second that we don't know that."

The sirens rang through the air as the police cars drove into the parking lot behind us. I shoved my netbook in my purse and stood up. My pulse raced as I turned to face the officers that arrived in the parking lot. They looked like tiny specks from this distance. Waving my hands frantically, I watched as the police jumped out of their cars, but it was too late. The man next to me uttered a few words before taking off, and I'd never felt so alone in the world as I did now. His last words repeated over and over again in my mind, as if I needed a reminder of the hell that had become my life.

"You can run, but you can't hide."

CHAPTER EIGHT

Luke

I sat on the couch in my hotel room and opened my laptop. Taking a swig of beer, I leaned against the cushions, trying to make sense of the popup community in the middle of nowhere. Room service had just arrived with my lukewarm cheeseburger and fries, but what I'd been really looking forward to was what I was sipping on at the moment. I looked around the living room of my suite and wondered what Hannah was doing right now. Was she safe? Was she miserable where she was now living? Unfortunately, my suspicion was that she wasn't actually free from anything. I thought about going back to the compound tonight. But what would that prove? Probably nothing and I might just be putting her in harm's way.

I hadn't had the best of luck with women, and

I was sure that tradition would be kept alive moving forward. But it was hard not to think about undressing Hannah, feeling her soft skin against mine. It wasn't like me to daydream about a woman. Yet here I was doing just that. I took another sip and shook myself out of it. Flipping on Bloomberg news, I began to search online for any type of information that might explain what I'd just seen. I wondered if they were basing their way of life on divinely inspired visions or a man who saw an opening for control and power.

My cell rang and I glanced down at the number.

Damn! It was Jessica. I forgot I'd mentioned to her that I'd be in town. We weren't exclusive, and it wasn't a long distance relationship. I really had no idea what the hell to call it, except a longstanding problem, which I'd created for myself. She was a flight attendant who I'd met on a flight from Miami to Los Angeles a few years back. She was about as interested in a relationship as I was, which just proved that there were a lot more screwed-up people in the world than anyone could imagine. Relationship runners was the official term my sister used. I let out a deep breath and answered my cell.

"Hey," I said.

"Babe, how are you this fine evening?" she teased.

My stomach cringed. That was a first. She was an attractive woman and nice. Very nice. But that was where our similarities ended, which didn't seem to bother me two months ago. Now, it was very bothersome.

"Doing well," I confirmed.

"Are you at the same hotel? Should I come over dressed in my finest?"

I couldn't help but laugh at how desperate that sounded and how desperate I must have sounded over the years trying to sling my one-liners at her. Desperate souls called for desperate measures, I supposed.

"I'm actually working on a case tonight, and I'm pretty drained." I could barely believe the words were leaving my lips.

"I could just bring by some dinner from your favorite—"

"I'm actually about to finish a deliciously dried-out burger from the hotel, but I appreciate the thought."

"I get the distinct feeling there's more to this story. How about if I come over and you can explain it to me?"

I laughed into the phone, recognizing the same loneliness I'd felt so many times myself over the years. But this thing we had between us never fixed it. It never would.

"Not this time, Jessica. I'm sorry. I'm just not... It wouldn't be right," I spoke, scrolling through the database.

"Have you found someone else?" she asked abruptly.

"No. Nothing like that." I pulled my attention away from the screen and sighed. "I think I'm done with being casual."

Jessica's laugh echoed into the room so loudly, it sounded as if she was on the couch next to me.

"Sure you are," she finally answered. "Well, I'm not... so if you're ever in town and..."

"Thank you, Jessica," I interrupted. "But I think I'll be just fine."

"All right, babe. It's been fun," she said, before hanging up.

And I suddenly felt like the cheapest date in town. As I brought the laptop to the couch, I thought back to my time with Jessica. She was fine as hell, but there was never a connection beyond the physical—in the moment—connection that could happen to anyone in the right circumstances. As horrible as this sounded, I never thought much about her before or after the encounter and neither did she. There was none of that lingering sense of need or want in between our rendezvous so why did I keep going back? Because it was safe?

I sighed, thinking how pathetic I must look if I sounded this bad. I began scanning the database again for some sign of a non-profit or something masquerading as such with her old address and was relieved when one finally came up as a match. The one at this address went by New Life, acted upon as NLC. I assumed the C stood for church? NLC was established in 1979 as a social welfare organization and has been claiming not-for-profit status ever since. I quickly put the name through one of the watch lists and it came up with nothing. I ran it through a cult database and took another sip of beer as I awaited the results. Was I dealing with a Heaven's Gate meets the Amish or what?

As I gazed at the long list, Hannah popped into my head again. The package that contained the cell should have been delivered this morning, and as if on cue, I received a text from her. She'd received the package. I tried my best to sound playful but failed miserably. Her text sounded sweet as hell and...

And then it occurred to me. What if she still had an old phone? They could track her. I opened another window and logged onto the database. Entering my credentials, I began searching for any sign of Hannah Walker or Martin. I prayed that she'd only used disposable once starting this whole move, but I couldn't be sure.

"Damn it," I muttered, seeing a cell number with her name pop up.

I transferred her number to another system and watched as the pings triangulated, giving me her approximate location.

If I could find her this easily so could they.

CHAPTER NINE

Hannah

The police cruiser pulled in front of the house behind my blue truck. The officer got out of the car and walked around to let me out. The police had managed to catch up to the guy who threatened me. They had the entire conversation recorded thanks to my phone, which I was told would give them enough evidence to request a search warrant. His name was Donald Jamison. And, at least for now, he was in custody.

"Thank you," I replied as the officer closed the door. I knew the most I'd probably get out of this ordeal was a restraining order against Donald, and we all knew how well those worked.

"If you have any questions, call or email. All my information's on the card," the officer replied. "I'll reach out to Mr. Fletcher since he's also considered a target by Donald Jamison."

"Will do and thank you." I nodded.

The officer got back in the cruiser and pulled away as I heard the front door open. Nancy pursed her lips together and shook her head.

"You have brought more attention to this house and the people in it in less than twenty-four hours than any of the other occupants ever have," her voice angry, as she glared at me.

I glanced at her, analyzing her reaction. Was it genuine? Did she really care about the people at the house or did she just care about the payment she received in the beginning? She herself said that there were always strings attached. After all, someone had to have told the people back home that I was here, and she was the only one who knew I was coming.

I pushed my way past her and walked to my room. I needed to let Luke know that he was in danger, and now more than ever I was certain I'd be taking the job tonight, if it was offered. This location was no longer safe, and I needed to get out of here as quickly as possible. Sitting on the bed, I looked around the room full of boxes and wondered if escaping this nightmare was even possible.

I heard Nancy's footsteps and looked up.

"You signed a full disclosure agreement, Hannah," Nancy said. "Would you mind telling me why the police felt the need to escort you home?"

"They found me," I replied.

Nancy's face fell and her eyes widened.

"What do you mean they *found* you, Hannah?

Who did you tell you were coming here?" Her brow arched.

"Absolutely no one. You're the only one who knew I'd be arriving. So you can imagine my skepticism as you stand here trying to act surprised that I'd been found."

Nancy took a seat on my most prized possession, the wooden chair, and looked at me. She bit her lip and her expression softened slightly. "I didn't tell anyone anything. I don't have anyone to tell, but there is no reason why you should believe that, which I understand. All the women who come here are hiding from something or someone. I've learned to never ask questions that I don't want answers to, but I'm telling you now, whoever wants to find you is dangerous, and I don't mean only dangerous to you. To all of us."

"I know that."

"Is he in custody?" she asked.

"For now," I replied, my mind drifting to Luke. I had to let him know. I had to get rid of Nancy. "But I don't know if he was the only one or if there are more."

She nodded. "When someone's running from a boyfriend or a family, the fear in their eyes is different than yours. I think it's based on some sort of acceptance or knowledge that they're one step ahead of the person they once loved. You don't have that. There's a fierceness behind your gaze."

"Your point?" I asked.

"You need to watch your back, and I want you

out in two weeks," she replied.

"Understood."

"I was once in your shoes." She pulled her sleeve up to reveal a long gash up her arm. "This should have killed me and almost did. If you're running from something and not someone, they will stop at nothing until they get what they want. They think I'm dead so I've been able to live a life, if you can call this a life. But I've accepted my fate. No husband, no family. It's a lonely way of existing, but at least I'm alive, and it's a concept you'd better get used to."

My mind flashed to Luke. She was absolutely right. The first person who I'd become acquainted with in my new town was already in danger. I couldn't let Rikki become the second, but I needed a ride tonight. Donald would be in custody for at least twenty-four hours so it should be okay. As long as he was working alone...

"If you can find out how they found you, it will help you hide better next time." She stood up and walked out of the room.

I opened my netbook and dug Luke's card out of my wallet. No matter what I put in the email I was going to sound crazy, and there was a big chance he wouldn't believe it anyway, but I had to warn him. And I had to disappear. Again. I would no longer text him, but I would hold onto the phone until I got a new one.

I created a new email account, specifically for this purpose, forgetting the password as soon as I entered it. After several failed attempts at writing, I decided to keep it short and simple.

Dear Mr. Fletcher,

Thank you for your kindness and generosity. It means more than you could ever imagine. But your kindness has put you in danger. I have received a threat, and unfortunately because of your interaction with me, you have become a target. I'm so sorry. I never meant for this to happen. I have attached the detective's information who is handling the case. He said he'd be reaching out to you, but I felt it necessary to warn you myself. And again, I apologize.

Kind Regards,

Hannah

I wanted to add a P.S. I'm not crazy, but I didn't think that would help my cause. I hit send and logged out of the email. I looked up Buttons and found the most rudimentary website ever. There was a homepage that was burgundy with the word Buttons scrawled in fancy script across the website. That was it. No information about what it was. In tiny black font at the bottom of the page there was an address. I guess the only way I'd know what Buttons was all about was to go there. I was about to text Rikki, but she popped her head in my room. She must've just gotten back from her errands.

"Hey, how'd you get here?" she asked, smiling.

"I had a bit of an issue." It was only fair I told her. "An officer brought me home. I think my location was compromised. There was a man who confronted me at the beach…"

"Oh no." Her jaw dropped open.

"He's in custody for now, but the long and short of it is that I think I found a job, but I need to go there tonight. I need to leave the house as soon as possible."

"I'll drive you," she offered. "Or better yet, you can borrow my car. Then you don't have to feel rushed during the interview or whatever it is you're doing tonight."

"You'd do that?"

"Of course." She tossed me the keys and smiled. "You've seen my car. It's not like much more could happen to it."

I couldn't help but laugh. She had a valid point.

"Thank you so much. I think this'll be a good job or at least one that pays decent."

"Where's it at?" she asked.

"Buttons?" my voice went up an octave. "Have you heard of it?"

"Of course I've heard about it. It's the place to be. How in the world did you get an in there?" she asked, perplexed.

"I ran into a girl who works there, and she found out I was looking for work…"

"Wow. Well whatever it is you have to do tonight, I'd say do it because jobs like that don't come around very often."

"She said it was like a club and she promised

it wasn't like stripping or anything..." I was hoping for confirmation.

Rikki smiled. "It's just a place where people want to be. There are all kinds of stories about what goes on there, but it's all urban legend. You'll have to tell me all about it."

"Deal. Now I wonder what I should wear," I said, feeling extremely anxious about what I'd possibly gotten myself into.

"Something stylish and revealing."

My stomach sank. I owned neither.

"I've got something that might work," she said, leaving my room.

I groaned and fell against the mattress.

Rikki came back in holding a tiny black dress that I didn't think would stretch enough in any direction to cover any one part of me. "What shoe size are you?" she asked.

"Eight."

"It's meant to be," she said, waving a pair of strappy, black heels. "I've heard there's some sort of dress code there."

"Well, I haven't been hired yet so..."

"Once you put this on, it'll be a done deal."

I laughed. "I hope so. Do you know how far away it is?"

"About an hour or hour and fifteen."

"Seriously? What time is it?" I glanced at my phone. "I better get ready. I'm supposed to meet her before her shift."

"If you need any help let me know. I can't wait to see you before you head out."

"Thanks," I said, grabbing the dress from her

before she walked away.

I quickly stripped out of my jeans and shirt and pulled the dress over my head. Somehow, it managed to cover—just barely— all the vital parts. I walked into the bathroom and did a spin, surprised by my new look. We'd always been told to dress modestly and this was anything but. I kind of liked it.

My hair was a bit unruly after a day at the beach and a ride in the police car, but there wasn't much I could do about it without a shower. And God Forbid I took a step in the tub.

I heard a whistle from the hallway, and Rikki grinned. "You clean up nice. I printed off the directions to Buttons. Do you have a curling iron or flattening—"

I shook my head.

"I'll be right back."

I began dotting on some foundation in a vain attempt to make me look like I was a solid sleeper and not running for my life. It wasn't working.

Rikki reappeared and plugged in her curling iron. "Should heat up in a minute or so."

"Thanks again for loaning me the dress."

"It's gotta get some use somehow," she said, testing the iron. "It's ready."

Without skipping a beat, she began wrapping chunks of my hair around the rod, and I looked steadily in the mirror as I drew on eyeliner heavier than normal.

"You've got this," she said, working her way around my head. "You'll be out of this dump in no time."

I smiled, hoping she was right, but also knowing I'd only stay at Buttons long enough to save enough to leave town. This city was no longer safe.

"You look breathtaking. If they don't hire you to do whatever it is they do, they don't deserve you."

I smiled at her in the mirror and chuckled. "I guess I already have one strike against me."

"What's that?" she asked, unplugging the curling iron.

"I'm a blond."

"Hairism? In this day and age? The nerve."

I started laughing and dabbed a bit of gloss on my lips.

"I shouldn't be too late. And if you need me to come back for any reason—"

She held her hand up to interrupt me. "I've got the Housewives to watch."

"What the heck are the Housewives?" I asked. "I keep hearing about it."

"A bunch of women who fight with each other over petty things, go on shopping sprees, and handle real life problems, while living in mansions. You know just living life like the rest of us." She rolled her eyes as she pointed to our surroundings.

I couldn't help but laugh. "Sounds hopeful. How do I sign up?"

"Marry a rich guy or divorce one," she teased.

"How about I just make it on my own?"

"Nah. That's not interesting. Then you can't be

called a gold-digger," she laughed, as I grabbed my purse. "Besides, we all watch it so we can feel better about ourselves."

I laughed at the irony and wondered just how low the housewives went. It sounded intriguing.

"Well, have fun with the housewives. And I owe you big for this one. I'll pay back gas money too."

Rikki pushed me out the front door, waving one last time as I walked down the steps toward the street. I glanced around the neighborhood, looking for anything suspicious, as I walked to Rikki's car and got in. So far so good. Maybe Donald was the only one out here, for now. I turned on the engine and memorized the first few instructions on how to get to Buttons. As I drove out of the neighborhood and onto the highway, I wondered what was waiting for me at Buttons. Liv said it wasn't a strip club and there was no hint of that on the website. Although, there was no hint of anything on the site. I guess it added to the mystery and intrigue.

After a wrong exit and two missed turns, I finally arrived at Buttons. The square building was stucco and brick with Tudor style windows showcasing wrought iron scrollwork. The glass had been blacked out, which only added to the mystery. The parking lot had a gate and a parking attendant stationed at it.

I rolled down my window and stuck out my head. "I'm here to meet Liv."

"She's already here." He nodded and lifted the gate.

I found an empty space right next to the building and parked. Here went nothing.

I got out of the car and tugged my dress down before walking to the entrance. Velvet ropes had been pushed along the building. It must not be open yet. I tugged on the door, but it wouldn't budge.

"May I help you?" a voice asked out of nowhere.

I took a step back and looked around, finally finding an intercom.

"I'm here to meet with Liv."

The click of the lock sounded and I pushed the door open. I took a step into the building and saw an ivory suede wraparound couch in the lobby. The lighting was beyond dim, the walls painted a deep shade of crimson, and the wood floors so dark, they were almost black. There was a hallway leading away from the area where I stood. As I debated whether or not to follow the corridor, I heard Liv's voice.

"You made it. I wasn't sure if you'd come or not." She walked out of the hallway and waved. "You look amazing. I told one of my bosses about you, but I think he'll be stunned to meet you in person."

"Thank you," I said, looking around the lobby and then back at Liv. "But I'm really not sure how being here has explained anything more to me."

"All in good time," she said. "Follow me, and I'll give you a run through about what a typical evening would be here."

Wrought iron sconces that looked like candles

flickering in the breeze lined the long hallway, creating a warm glow throughout.

"So the shifts start at five and are over by two. Generally, we have five days on and two days off. Our customers like to see familiar faces."

We stepped into a large room that looked like an ultra-modern lounge with suede booths along the walls and gigantic leather ottomans and small tables dotting the middle of the floor. There were swings hanging from the ceiling and mirrors in the corners. My heart started pounding as I looked at the open second level that looked over the main floor. Liv followed my gaze.

"That's the VIP section. It costs an extraordinary amount to sit up there. Our shifts are rotated so that at least once a week, we all get a chance to serve the VIP patrons."

My mouth went dry as my eyes landed back on the swings, dangling from the ceiling. If this wasn't a strip club, was it one step beyond?

"You might want to close your mouth," Liv said, softly touching my shoulder. I jumped a foot in the air from the contact and stepped backward. "You okay?"

"Yeah. I'm fine. I just don't understand…"

Liv grabbed my hand and pulled me across the large room, passing the bar and the good-looking bartender who stood behind it shining glasses.

"There's a male bartender?" I asked.

"There's always several male and female bartenders at any one time. For protection, really."

"What?" my voice hoarse as we walked down another hallway.

"Don't worry. None of us have ever needed protecting. It's just a smart thing to do when you have this many attractive women in one place." She winked and opened the door to the dressing room.

I was in way over my head.

CHAPTER TEN

Luke

When the email from Hannah came over, I nearly punched a hole in the wall. They'd found her and I was clear across the country. I sent an email to my administrative assistant to clear the rest of the meetings that I'd planned here. I quickly threw my things into the suitcase and scanned the hotel room for anything I might have left behind. Looked clear.

I checked out at the front desk and rolled my carryon behind me as I walked to my rental car. There were two flights out of here tonight, and I hoped I could get on one of them.

Damn it. I never should've left California.

Turning the car onto the highway, I dialed the detective's number and only reached his voicemail. I called Derek's number next. He was in charge of security personnel and could be trusted to only ask questions that were relevant.

"This is Derek."

"Hey, I've got a new client. Rather sudden. I'm stuck on the east coast, but I should be able to catch a red-eye. The perp is in custody, but I don't know how long he'll stay there or if there are others. We need some counter-surveillance set up, and I want to get a trapline on the client's old cell number."

"Got it, sir," Derek replied.

"I'll text over the client's new cell and hopefully you can trace her location. I would've but I need to get to the airport. I want a shadow detail on her."

"Anything else?" Derek questioned.

"Send me her location when you find it and if it changes."

"Affirmative. I'll get right on it."

I ended the call and drove down the exit ramp, following the signs to return the rental car. I just might make it on the next flight out of here. I pulled in behind the long line of cars and watched as the workers scanned each car back into the lot. I left the keys in the ignition and grabbed my suitcase from the backseat and set it on the pavement next to me. The guy with the scanner was two cars away, which gave me enough time to text all relevant information to Derek.

The beep of the scanner alerted me that it was my time to check the car back in.

"Bringing it back early?" the guy asked, reading his device.

"Shortened my trip," I confirmed, smiling.

The man popped his head into the car, turning on the ignition.

"Didn't bring it back with a full tank. That's going to cost $8.95 a gallon. Sure you don't want to run across the way and fill her up?" he joked.

"I'll take the hit," I assured him.

He printed off the receipt and handed it to me as I saw the airport shuttle pull up to the curb. I picked up my carryon and jogged over to the bus, barely making it in time. The bus was standing room only so I stuck to the front, gripping the pole tightly with one hand and checking my phone with the other. I texted Hannah, not expecting to receive a response and switched over to Google as the bus lurched at a stop sign, nearly tipping me sideways.

I typed in NLC and watched as the news results popped up on my screen. For an organization that had been around for so long, there were surprisingly few results that surfaced. I clicked on an image of a man, who vaguely resembled one of the men in the hostile group of greeters I'd encountered, and zoomed in on the image. It was definitely him. Miles Norman was his name. He'd been with the organization for years.

The bus came to a stop at my airline terminal, and I shoved my phone back into my pocket as I walked down the steps onto the curb. Something felt out of place. I didn't like what I was feeling, but I recognized it. The watcher was being watched. I made a quarter turn and glimpsed a man take a step behind one of the luggage carriers. Two could play this game. I stood still, my eyes narrowed at the empty space the man had occupied. I didn't have time for this, but I wanted to see who wanted to get so up close and personal. He'd budge from his post any second. They always did.

Sure enough his arm swung out and he took a step out from cover. The man's eyes turned uneasy once he realized I was waiting for him. I flashed him my best smile as I watched him squirm. His chin jutted out, giving his features a rather pronounced look, emphasizing his dark beady eyes. His thin lips stretched into an unpleasant grimace.

"May I help you with something?" I asked.

He worked his hand through his dark hair with a jerkiness.

"I was asked to escort you to the airport," the man's voice uncertain.

"Really. And who do I have the pleasure of thanking for such personal attention?"

"Client information is always confidential."

I couldn't help but laugh at this amateur.

"Well, I hope they sent their best," I said sincerely, pulling out my wallet and cell. I dug a twenty out of my wallet as I kept my finger steady on the cell camera. I took two steps forward, startling the man, and handed him the cash while my finger pressed down steadily. "Take this to cover parking and let your people know I've made it to the airport just fine. But you might not want to mention this little encounter."

The man's jaw tensed as I walked past him, seemingly unfazed and completely unaware that I just took his picture. The doors to the terminal opened, and I rushed to the airline counter and explained my wish to change my return flight to the next one. The attendant grabbed my ticket and quickly typed into the system, scanning for available flights.

"We don't have first class available," she said. "Only economy, but it's an exit row."

"That'll be great," I said as my phone rang. I glanced at the screen and saw that it was Derek. The attendant printed off the boarding pass and I thanked her swiftly as I answered my phone.

"I've located the client, Mr. Fletcher."

"Great. Where's she at?"

"She's at Buttons."

What the hell was she doing at Buttons?

CHAPTER ELEVEN

Hannah

Until recently, I had lived my life with a wide-eyed innocence. That was what initially attracted a lot of the people to the community, the innocence. In hindsight, I now saw it for what it was, ignorance. Blissful ignorance, not innocence.

And standing in a room full of women clad in lingerie made me miss that blissful ignorance. Not because of where I was, but how I got here, what drove me to create a new life, which was unfortunately discovered all too soon. I pushed the fear back down and tried to concentrate on my task at hand, getting the job.

"So, you've heard of Hooters, right?" Liv asked.

I nodded.

"Well, it's just like that, only instead of short shorts and pantyhose with runs in them, we wear lingerie."

I turned to look at Liv. "Do you serve chicken wings too?"

"Actually, we do. They aren't hot wings, though," she said, laughing. "They're teriyaki with a pineapple glaze."

I rolled my eyes just as a brunette dressed in a lacy, pink negligee bounced over to us. Her hair was braided and there was an innocence around her, which seemed quite contradictory considering everything.

"You must be Hannah," she said, forgoing the handshake and launching into a hug. "You really are gorgeous. I'm Tammi."

My stomach tightened with just how important beauty appeared to be to so many around here. Not that I was above all that or anything, I just never thought about it much until I set foot in California. It felt like I was always on display whether I was grabbing a cup of coffee or walking on the beach.

"Thanks," I said awkwardly, as she released me. "You too."

Was that what I was supposed to say? I had no idea.

"This is a fun place to work. It may seem a little weird. I know I was weirded out the first time I was approached. But it's harmless. I swear. The people are great and the money is unbelievable."

'That's what I heard," I said, nodding. I watched another girl putting on a pair of thigh-high stockings and my belly twisted. Would I really be able to do this? I didn't even change in front of people at the gym at school. I was always that girl with a towel twisted around my body as I snaked my underwear up my legs and fastened my bra over the terrycloth before unwrapping it.

"You look like your head's about to explode," Liv said, grinning. "You doing okay?"

I nodded. "Sorry. I'm just not sure I can wear one of those in front of people." I pointed at the thigh-high wearing woman with the bustier as she gave a quick wave.

"It's like wearing a bikini on the beach," Tammi offered.

"The girl grew up in Ohio. I doubt she spent much time on the beach," Liv said.

I felt marginally bad as she repeated my lie and smiled. "True. Not many beach bums in Ohio."

"At the lakes, I bet..." Tammi began.

"Nope. I was more of the stay indoors and read kind of girl."

Which was another complete lie. I loved being outdoors back home. I signed up for any chore to get me outside.

"You don't have to wear that. In fact, you don't have to wear anything revealing. A lot of the girls when they first start don't go over the top. The only requirement is bedroom attire. Most of us who work here realized that our tips magically went up on the days we wore a little less. But you could probably show up in flannel pajamas and they'd be fine with it."

That was a theory I'd be more than happy to

try out.

"I gotta get changed. All the girls here are more than willing to answer any questions you might have. And if it's something you're interested in, I'll introduce you to one of the owners. The second one isn't here, but he rarely is."

"Okay," I nodded, frozen in position. A prickle of fear went up my spine as I thought about the man who was arrested this afternoon. I didn't have the luxury to wait around and find some other job. I needed this one now so that I could get enough money to get out of here. They'd already found me, and as I'd feared, their motives weren't only to bring me back home.

Tammi motioned for me to follow her to the back of the dressing area. "This is where the members' bios are." She picked up a book and opened it, revealing photos and brief descriptions of each of the members.

"Are there any female members?" I asked.

"Actually, yes. Some of the wives are members and then there are some single females that like to just come and hang out. The guy who thought this place up was genius. He tapped right into the notion of exclusivity that so many people around here crave. It's a weird thing." She continued turning the pages and my eyes ran down the pages. There were bankers, lawyers, accountants, engineers, and executives. The list of occupations went on and on.

"And all you do is serve drinks and food to them?" I questioned.

"And conversation."

"How so?"

"A lot of the men just want to have someone to talk to."

"Why not their wives?" I glanced at Tammi who shrugged.

"Beats me. I know you're thinking this is too good to be true. But it's not. Nothing illegal goes down. And if the owners even get a hint that something might be going on that's not legal, they fire the server and terminate the membership."

I nodded, feeling only somewhat better about the situation. Besides, it didn't matter how I felt. I needed the job. I also needed an outfit to wear and had no money, so unless Starbucks started selling lingerie, I was in trouble.

"You think you might be interested?" Tammi asked, sensing my confusion.

"Definitely." I nodded.

Tammi gave a quick hop and placed the book back on the shelf. "Let's go tell Liv."

The door opened slightly and a male's voice echoed through the air.

"Everyone decent?" he asked.

The girls shouted yes in unison, and I scanned the room for Liv, who had already changed into her slinky, black slip. It was edged in lace and actually covered more than I would've thought. Maybe, I would be able to do this without feeling completely out of my element.

A guy walked into the room, wearing a black suit and silver tie. His brown hair was brushed back and his blue eyes combed the room, landing on me. "So you're the blond that Liv told me about. I'm Sean."

"One of the tough decision makers," Liv teased, and I wondered if there was a connection between the two.

My hands were immediately clammy, and my throat almost closed as his eyes worked their way along my body, and I was fully clothed.

"You are a knockout." He glanced over at Liv. "She'd be the first blond, but maybe it's time to branch out."

"She's a natural blond," Liv offered.

The man turned back to look at me, smiling. "Have the girls explained everything to you?"

"I think so," I replied, looking him in his eyes. I needed this job and wasn't going to do anything to blow it. "It sounds like a fun place to work."

He nodded, pressing his lips together as he thought about something. "Would you be willing to start tomorrow?"

My heart skipped a beat. "Absolutely."

"Perfect. Liv, will you show her to the office and have Emily give her all the paperwork to fill out."

Liv nodded, beaming.

And that was it. He walked out, leaving all the girls to finish getting ready for the night. I found a chair and sat as my mind wandered to the money I might actually get to make while working here. And if it took a membership to get in maybe it would be safer than most places to have a job. I needed safety. A shiver ran through me as I thought about running into Donald Jamison and his intentions. If he didn't want me dead, what would he do to me while I was alive?

"You ready?" Liv asked, interrupting my thoughts.

"Yep." I hopped up and followed her out of the dressing room, back down the hall to another door I hadn't noticed on the way in.

"This is the office. Emily takes care of everything business related. Paychecks, medical, 401k."

"You have medical and a 401k working here?" I was blown away.

"Pretty sweet, isn't it?" She smiled, pushing the door open.

"How much does the membership cost?" I whispered, trying to tabulate everything.

"More than I'd ever spend," she laughed. "It actually varies, depending on the client."

There was a small seating area with an office behind. The door was closed and Liv gently tapped on it.

"Come in," a woman's voice called back. Her voice sounded young and perky.

Liv opened the door and the woman sitting behind the large oak desk matched her voice perfectly. She had beautiful blue eyes that were dancing with amusement as she flashed me a big smile. "You must be Hannah."

"I am," I said. "Hannah Walker."

"I'm Emily," she said, extending her hand.

I quickly shook her hand and took a seat as Liv said her goodbyes and left Emily and me alone in the office. I glanced at her desk that was filled with knickknacks and stacks of paper. It felt like she was the glue that held the place together.

"You don't strike me as being the kind of person who'd want to work here," she stated, her brow arched.

That took me off-guard and felt like a trick question. Any answer I could give would either sound like I was putting Buttons or myself down so I just smiled and shrugged, which made her laugh.

"You don't have anything to worry about. You've got the job." She opened a drawer and pulled out a file. "So how'd you meet Liv?"

"At a Starbucks. She found out I was new to town and looking for work."

She nodded and took a packet out of the folder, sliding it over to me. "Makes sense."

Emily's eyes were kind as her gaze met mine, but I could see there was something more she wanted to say but didn't.

"So if you could fill these out tonight and drop them off before your shift tomorrow, that'd be great. The dress requirements, code of conduct, all of it is in there. Payday is every week on Friday. We do it old-fashioned around here with actual paychecks. If you aren't scheduled to work, we can mail them."

"I'll be sure to pick it up. I'm kind of in the process of finding somewhere new to live."

"Oh?" she asked.

"Really bad neighborhood and the roommates

are a bit..."

She smiled. "I know how roommates go. Enough said. Where are you looking?"

"I'm pretty open. Now that I have a job, maybe around here?"

She nodded. "I have a friend who's looking for a roommate. She hates living alone. Actually, she's the sister of one of the owners here. That's how I got the job. I bet she'd love you. So far the people who've turned up to look at the place have freaked her out," Emily replied, laughing. "That's what she gets for placing an ad on Craigslist. I can see if she's still looking."

"That would be wonderful. Thank you."

"My card is stapled to the top there so if you have any questions between now and tomorrow, feel free to give me a buzz. Actually, do you mind giving me your cell now, and I can just call you if I can get a hold of my friend?"

"Sure." I scribbled my new cell number and tamped down the little bit of hope that started to swell. After all, wherever I was going to go and whatever I was about to do was only temporary.

"Thanks again, and I'll see ya tomorrow," I said, standing up.

I found my way back through the club and waved at the bartender, who was organizing bottles. I reached the front door and swung it open. The warm air wrapped around me as I quickly glanced in all directions, ensuring there weren't any surprise visitors before I made it to Rikki's car. Climbing in, I shoved my purse on the passenger seat and looked at my cell and saw a voicemail. Pushing the speakerphone on, I listened to the detective as he solemnly updated me about the man who was temporarily behind bars. They weren't able to find enough to hold him past twenty-four hours.

My heart sank with the news, but I hadn't really thought it would turn out any different. They were always one step ahead of the authorities, which was why I didn't bother involving them anymore. I tossed my phone on the seat just as it rang.

"Hello?" I asked, as I pressed the speakerphone on.

"Hey, it's Emily. Have you left yet?" she asked.

"No. Just got in my car."

"Sweet. My friend's home and would love to meet you. I'll be right out."

And before I had a chance to respond she'd hung up.

The front door exploded open, and Emily looked around the parking lot, trying to find me. I jumped out of the car and waved. She waved back at me and glanced at the car as she walked over. I knew it looked like hell. Actually, it looked like whoever owned it was a horrible driver. Not exactly the appearance I wanted to give.

"I'm borrowing it," I offered. "My truck's on the fritz."

"So I don't have to panic at your lack of defensive driving skills?" she laughed.

"Nope. I promise."

"Well, let's take mine anyway. She's just a few blocks away, but we might as well drive."

Things were really starting to look up. I might actually be able to make it to my job if I couldn't fix my truck.

I locked the car door and followed Emily to hers, which was an adorable, white Mini Cooper.

"I can see why you wanted to drive," I said, grinning.

"Nothing personal," she laughed again, opening her door.

I climbed in as she adjusted the volume on her radio. "Sorry. I love blaring my music."

I smelled the new car scent and closed my door, buckling in tight.

"You could probably even walk to work, until you get your truck fixed." She pulled out of the parking lot and made a left toward the water when it occurred to me that I probably couldn't afford wherever it was we were heading.

"I can't believe I didn't ask this, but what's the rent?"

"You'll be fine," she said, tapping my leg. "I don't actually know what she's charging, but it's not for the money. She just hates being alone in the overly large place her brother bought her."

"Must be a nice brother," I laughed.

"He is extremely generous to his sister, but she's all he's got. And vice versa. But nice? I'm not sure I'd say that about him. He's a hard one to figure out. He owns a piece of the club and rarely sets foot in it. Whenever I've tried to say hello, he'd barely even grunt let alone smile. His sister said he hates the place so I'm not sure why he has any money invested, but he's hot as hell."

She grinned.

Emily turned down a street that brought the beach into view, and the homes peppered along the way were gorgeous and enormous. There was absolutely no way I'd be able to afford a closet, let alone an entire bedroom here. She pulled in front of a grey, three level home that sat on the corner with decks wrapped around each level.

"There's Mia," Emily said, pointing to the top deck where I spotted a woman hopping up and down waving at us. "She's adorable."

Emily opened the car door as Mia ran off the deck and out of sight. I got out and followed Emily up the stairs to the front door. There were flowers everywhere I looked. Roses in every color imaginable lined the staircase and tiny trimmed boxwood framed the steps. Hanging baskets filled with red geraniums and white petunias hung by the door.

"Mia must really have a green thumb," I said, as we reached the top stair.

"I think her gardener has the green thumb."

Of course! What was I thinking?

The front door flew open and Mia gave Emily a big hug, her eyes closing before she let go. Her green eyes landed on me and her smile grew. "You must be Hannah. Come in, guys. Let me show you around. It's far too big for me, and I really just spend my time on the decks. It's actually an embarrassment, really. But whatever. I have stopped trying to convince my brother of anything. Emily told you this place wasn't my idea, right?" she asked, closing the doors as we stepped into the foyer.

The windows surrounding the entire space let an amazing amount of light in, which made Mia's eyes even greener. She had her dark hair in two braids, and she wore a pair of slouchy jean shorts and a pink camisole that was splattered with paint.

She caught me looking at her shirt and giggled, clapping her hands. "I paint oils, or at least, I attempt to paint oils."

There was something familiar about Mia, which I knew was impossible, but her energy was infectious. It was exactly what I needed no matter how temporary my stay would be.

"You don't attempt to paint oils. You're brilliant at it," Emily said, rolling her eyes. "Not every twenty-six year old is able to open a show with every single painting selling out in the first night."

"It was a fluke," Mia assured me.

I couldn't help but smile as she ushered us through the large foyer. "That's the living room, which I rarely set foot into. Actually, I never really hang out on this floor at all so consider it yours."

"I'm not sure I'll be able to afford the rent..."

"You're working at Buttons, right?" Her brow quirked.

"Starting tomorrow."

"Believe me. You'll be able to afford it. I'm only renting you a bedroom, remember?" Her smile was kind as she glanced at Emily and then back at me.

I chuckled and shook my head. Doubtful.

"I had it on Craigslist for seven-fifty, but I like you. How about seven?" She crossed her arms in front of her. "And you don't have to pay me the first month until you get your first paycheck at Buttons."

My mouth dropped open. Seven? I had planned on getting a hole-in-the-wall somewhere for seven hundred.

"It's month-to-month so if you decide you want your own place, you can always move out."

I nodded. "This is amazing."

"So is that a yes?" Mia asked.

"It's a big yes," I laughed as Mia grabbed my hand and hauled me up the stairs.

CHAPTER TWELVE

Luke

The thought of Hannah slipping into other men's fantasies killed me, and that was precisely what Buttons offered. I'd seen the way men at Buttons devoured the waitresses with their eyes, and it was unsettling, and one of the many reasons I never showed up. I despised the fact that I had anything to do with the club, but I owed my friend, Sean, a favor and I wasn't about to let him down. He helped me when I first started the security firm and it was something I could do in return. We'd met one another in a past life, but I never expected it to bite me in the ass like this.

I stretched my legs in front of me in the airplane seat and took a sip of the red wine the flight attendant had just brought over. What in God's name was Hannah doing at Buttons? Maybe she was passing by and that's how the phone triangulated. That had to be it. There was no legitimate reason why she'd be there. She didn't even fit the profile. Sean had a thing for brunettes and a real distaste for blondes. And Hannah was definitely blonde. No doubt about it. A beautiful blonde at that. Her being a blond was the one thing I could hold onto until I could access wireless at the cruising altitude.

Damn! She was hard to shake.

I took another sip of the wine as I thought about why I was so fascinated by a woman I barely knew. The guy next to me snorted, signaling he'd already fallen asleep, which was good since I hated spectators while researching. I grabbed the newspaper out of my bag and opened it to the second page, but I had no interest in reading. My mind kept wandering to Hannah. My guys were on her so she'd be safe until I got there, but it didn't calm my fears at all. I knew too little about her and what problems were following her. There had to be a way to get her to trust me and tell me what was going on. That would be the quickest solution.

The moment the Captain announced that we had reached our cruising altitude, I opened up my laptop and began searching for information on the NLC. I also opened up another window for the facial recognition software to run my official airport greeter's face through. I scanned through my email, checking for something from Sean. Regardless of how many times I told Sean I didn't need to know nor did I care, he usually kept me apprised of all the new hires. And sure enough an email had landed in my inbox from Sean with the subject "You'll Never Guess". My stomach tensed as I became one step closer to confirming that Hannah was indeed working at Buttons. I clicked on the message, which brought up Sean's new hire confession. It had taken seven years, but he no longer felt that all blondes were the devil's spawn. Things were looking up. Too bad he was going to have to fire her.

I hit reply and began typing a message back to Sean congratulating him on his breakthrough while encouraging him to reconsider his latest hire. My blood was pumping harder as I thought about when she was going to start and how to get her out of there if she already had. I could literally taste the fury pulsing through my veins when I thought about other men looking at her. But just as I was about to hit send, it occurred to me that Buttons was safe. Membership was exclusive. I could watch her, keep her safe, and get her to trust me. I was always rational and this was the rational thing to do. So why was I so impulsive when it came to Hannah? There had to be something to it, and I was sure if I wanted to enlighten my shrink about it, she'd have a field day with it. But I was smarter than that. These feelings would be going nowhere. I would be telling no one.

I took the last swallow of wine and motioned for the flight attendant. I needed a beer. Scanning the news articles about NLC was quite informative. They had done a good job of keeping a squeaky clean image. But one thing was quite concerning. A series in one of the smaller newspapers was conveniently stopped when the journalist passed away. There was no explanation as to why the last two articles were never published. It was as if the series never existed beyond the first three articles. I took note of the journalist and kept scanning information that led nowhere rather quickly. What if the journalist had figured something out? But that wouldn't explain why the newspaper wouldn't finish up the series. I rubbed my fingers along my temple as I thought about how to infiltrate a tight-knit community like the NLC.

An email from the detective came over. He must've gotten my message. I quickly opened it up and wasn't surprised at the formality. It was a typical bland email, going over the events that had transpired and the steps that had been taken. As I read through the report listing what the man had said to Hannah, it became apparent that whoever was after her had no intentions of stopping. They wanted to find out what she knew, and after they found that out, she'd be discarded. That much was clear. From what I read, Hannah didn't tell the officers anything from her past so that had put them at a definite disadvantage. If she was unwilling to trust the police, why did I think I'd be able to gain her trust? This was going to be a lot more difficult than I'd imagined.

I closed the detective's email and began looking up the individuals who'd been affiliated with the NLC. I didn't have the luxury of time to find the pieces to the puzzle. If one person already knew where Hannah was, they all did.

CHAPTER THIRTEEN

Hannah

Somehow I'd managed to stuff the chair and the last of my boxes into Rikki's car and was on my way over to the new place. It was almost nine o'clock at night, but I was fighting the clock for a reason no one knew but me. I wanted to be situated in my new place with no ties to my old one before Donald Jamison was let out of jail. I'd decided to call in my truck to the city for impound as well. It was eight-hundred dollars down the drain, but I couldn't afford to be seen in it now, especially since he was going to be out of jail. I said my goodbyes to everyone at the house, and Rikki was sweet enough to let me use her car to go back and forth. After this trip, I was going to drive back to the house one last time and ride the bus back. As paranoid as it sounded, I didn't want anyone, including Rikki, to know where I would be living. Fortunately, or unfortunately, she understood completely.

Mia was thrilled that she wouldn't need to sleep another night alone in her too big for her house, and she promised she was a night owl and that I wouldn't be disrupting her by moving my stuff in tonight.

I got out of the car and Mia was already down the steps, ready to help with my last haul.

"Hey, girl. Welcome home," she said. "What can I help with?"

"The chair?" I asked, pointing to the backseat.

"Okay." She opened the door and slowly maneuvered it out of the tiny space, and I grabbed two boxes and slammed the trunk. That was it. I just needed to drive the car back to the house and catch the bus back.

"Follow me," she said, climbing the steps. "I emptied your new room out. It's all ready for you."

"I told you not to do that," I said, laughing and shaking my head. Once she had her mind made up, there seemed to be no changing it. My boxes that I'd dropped off from my first trip were no longer in the foyer, either.

"You hauled my things up by yourself?" I asked in disbelief.

Mia had decided the room she was initially going to give me was too small, which baffled me since it was twice the size of the one I'd just left. Her bedroom was on the top floor and mine was on the second.

"I figured if I didn't already put your stuff in

the bigger room, you'd try to argue me out of it," she said.

"True, and thank you."

I put one of my boxes on the floor and followed her up the stairs to the family room and kitchen area. It was all one big, open space that overlooked the large deck and ocean. My room was down the hall to the right.

The place was absolutely beautiful, and I was bummed that I wouldn't be able to stay longer. There were photographs of different beach scenes lining the hallway as I walked behind her to my new bedroom.

"These pictures are gorgeous," I said, stopping to take a better look.

"Thanks. My brother will be thrilled to hear you say that. Although, he'd never show it," she laughed.

He sounded like a real treat.

She made it into my room and set the chair down. "I'll go grab the other box."

"You don't have to do that," I said, as she slipped by me.

"No biggie," she said, grinning. "Hey, have you eaten? I haven't."

I started to feel like I did at the Starbucks where the complete kindness of a stranger completely threw me for a loop and then his life was in danger. I didn't want her life to be in danger. Mia was my roommate, but barely so, and she was already going above and beyond. It felt like all I did was show up and endanger whoever was unfortunate enough to be around me.

"I'm good," I said, setting my box in the bedroom.

"That's not what I asked." She gave me a knowing look with her hands on her hips. "I'll have something for us to share by the time you get back. Lock the door on your way out."

She spun around and climbed the stairs, probably headed to her bedroom. I actually hadn't gone to the third floor yet, but she said that was where her studio and bedroom were. I let out a sigh, walking down the hall and climbing back down the stairs. It felt like changes were on the way, but I wasn't sure what kind of changes those would be.

Letting myself out of the house, I locked it and walked to Rikki's car. If Mia knew that I was planning on dropping the car off and riding the bus back, she wouldn't hear of it and would follow me to the house and drive me back herself, and that wasn't what I needed. I wanted to leave the house behind me, and everyone in it, including Rikki. That was how it had to be done.

As I drove onto the highway, I thought about how crucial it was that I save as much money as I could and leave Mia's house before I put her in danger. But I doubted anyone, including Mr. Jamison, would look for me on beachfront property. And working at a private club where only members were the patrons seemed like the absolute safest job to have. At least, that was what I told myself to feel better about walking around in pajamas.

I turned off on the exit leading to the house and let out a deep sigh. I knew Nancy would be thrilled to see me go, and I didn't know many of the other house members so it would be an easy escape. As I pulled onto the street, I noticed most of the lights were on at the house. I hoped Nancy was home so I could tell her I was leaving. I'd already written a note as well, just in case. I parked the car and made my way to the entrance where Rikki was waiting for me.

"Nancy here?" I asked.

"In the kitchen," she replied.

I walked to the kitchen with Rikki behind me.

"Nancy."

Her back was turned to me as she was washing the dishes.

"You outta here?" she asked, turning to face me.

"I am." I nodded. "I called to get the truck impounded. It's of no use since they know it's mine. The tow truck usually comes in seventy-two hours or so."

Nancy nodded and pressed her lips together, wiping her hands on a towel.

"Take care and stay safe," she said, her eyes softening slightly. She was too hard for me to read. And no matter her story, I couldn't trust her. Wouldn't trust her.

"Thanks again," I said, giving a slight wave.

I glanced around the house and couldn't wait to get out of here and never return. I understood why places like these needed to exist. I only hoped I'd never see the inside of one again.

Rikki followed me outside and shut the door behind us as I glanced around. I was absolutely exhausted, feeling like I'd never be able to escape what I was trying so hard to leave behind. The darkness of the evening only led to my anxiety as I thought about all of the places people could be lurking, waiting, for me. I crawled into Rikki's car as she turned on the ignition.

Rikki let out a deep breath as we pulled away from the house. "I thought what I was running from was something fierce, but seeing what's happening to you..."

I nodded. "Believe me, we've all got our own baggage. Mine are just a little more aggressive at the moment. But I hope there's an end in sight soon."

"There will be. Don't give up."

I nodded, unsure if I actually believed her words of encouragement. Rikki pulled to a well-lit area in front of a strip mall.

"I'm going to wait until I see you get on that bus," she said. "If anything feels off. Call me."

I nodded. "Thanks for everything. I promise I'll get you..."

"Enough. It's what we do. We keep an eye out for each other while we can. There'll be a day when this will all seem like one big nightmare, not our reality."

I glanced at the clock on the radio. The bus would be coming in the next five minutes, give or take a few.

I gave Rikki a hug and got out of the car, scanning the parking lot quickly before walking over to stand at the bus stop. I watched as a car drove by and glanced over my shoulder every now and then, giving Rikki a wave. I heard the loud engine of the bus and watched it turn onto the street where I was waiting. I took a step forward as it came to a stop and the doors slammed open. I climbed up the steps and deposited the money into the machine. The driver didn't even wait until I was seated to begin driving away. I glanced at the people on the bus. A couple guys were talking to one another, sitting in the back. Another guy looked like he'd had too many and was using the window as a support system. A woman was sitting in the seat behind the one I sank into, and she looked about as disinterested as everyone else, but what did I expect at ten o'clock at night?

The air was warm from hot breaths and too many closed windows, which made it unbearable. The bus lurched at each stoplight until we finally made it onto the highway, and the sound of the engine steadied at a higher speed, bringing much needed calmness. With every bus stop we passed, the better my chances became that we wouldn't pick up anyone who might cause me trouble.

I hugged my knees and watched the neon scenery go by as our bus sped along, my mind wandering to my new home and my new job. Everything was falling into place, but I had to remind myself that it was only temporary. I couldn't let myself imagine a real life, living on the beach. It was hard enough to talk myself into the new job, but that was definitely one factor in my life that I'd like to think was temporary. Being assured by every person I spoke to that there was nothing illegal about what I was doing, didn't make me feel any better about having to show up in lingerie or pajamas. I knew there had to be more than met the eye on that one. Unfortunately, I didn't have the luxury of being picky. I was lucky that I was able to find a job and a home in a different city from the so-called safe house. A slight headache began forming at the base of my neck, and I knew it would only be a matter of time before it turned into a full-fledged migraine. I never had migraines growing up. It was only once my sister vanished that they started and never let up.

I closed my eyes and thought about my new roommate, Mia Dufort. She seemed like a genuinely sweet person, which made me even more conflicted about putting her in danger. The quicker I could leave town, the better for both of us. But in order to make things right in the world I left behind, I had to put myself first. It was self-preservation mode until everything was made right. The bus turned onto the exit and I rubbed my neck, hoping to loosen up the muscles.

When I saw the block that I needed to be let out on, I pulled the chain above my head to notify the driver. I glanced around the bus, hoping I'd be getting off by myself, and it looked like that was the case. Most people had already fallen asleep or were immersed in a book. As the bus slowed and stopped, I stood up and walked down the aisle, hopping down the stairs and feeling somewhat foolish about the amount of excitement that began pulsing through me. Even though it was late at night, being so close to the beach provided an active nightlife. There was a café on the corner with outdoor seating that was completely packed, and across the street, there was a bar that was standing room only. I waited for the crosswalk to turn green and quickly walked to the other side of the street. I was only a couple blocks away from the house and this walk was worth every step. I actually began to feel human again, like a normal person. What worried me was that if I stayed around too long, I might actually begin to forget that I wasn't normal, and I couldn't let that happen, not until I could find answers and expose everything. My jaw tensed as I walked along the waterfront, thinking about my best friend and my sister and who knows how many others who were disposed of... But for what? Money and power?

Mia's home came into view and my steps quickened. I would play things safe. I wouldn't call attention to my existence. I would slip in and out of Mia's life before anyone noticed. I wouldn't let her become part of the web.

Climbing the steps quickly, I slipped my key into the door and pushed it open. The wonderful smells of garlic and ginger surrounded me as I closed the door and skipped up the steps to the kitchen where Mia was cooking.

"Hope you're starving, new roomie," Mia said, grinning as she stirred some concoction on the stove. "I know I am. You'll find that out about me. I tend to get so wrapped up in my work that I forget to eat until midnight. But who's keeping tally, right?"

I laughed and took a seat at the breakfast bar. "It smells delicious. Is there anything I can help with?"

"Nope. Just waiting for the rice to cook." Mia turned the burner down and walked toward me. "So tomorrow's your big day. Are you nervous?" Her eyes sparkled with an intensity that was instantly warming.

"Terrified."

"I would be too." She started laughing when she realized what she'd just said. "I mean... I'm sure it'll be fine. No big deal."

The rice cooker chimed and she grabbed two plates, avoiding my gaze.

"The money just seems too good to be true," I muttered, watching her dish the rice on my plate. "But what scares me more is the lack of clothing."

"Well, if you're worried about everything being on the up and up, I can assure you that it is. My brother wouldn't be part of something shady."

My stomach unclenched slightly. "That's comforting."

"Ginger beef," Mia said, placing the plate in front of me.

"Looks and smells delicious."

Mia dished herself up and took the seat next to me. She glanced at me and smiled. "Well, I should probably fill you in on some of the important stuff about living here."

My brow arched as I watched her take her first bite.

"Like what?" I asked, praying that my showers wouldn't be regulated.

"My brother's a little paranoid about security and safety and all that so the place is alarmed up the wazoo," she said, watching my reaction, which was nothing more than complete relief. "It's like living at Fort Knox."

"Really?" I asked.

"Yeah. Every door and window has a sensor and every room has a motion detector and camera, except the bedrooms and bathrooms. I put my foot down on those. It just seemed too creepy to have cameras in there. Not that anyone is watching the footage from the cameras we have now. I'm the only one who has access, and they're only meant to be viewed if something goes wrong. I've never even looked at them, actually."

I breathed a sigh of relief. Not only was I going to be living on the beach in a new city, the home was secured.

"I love my brother dearly, but if it were up to me, I wouldn't have a system. Well, maybe some sensors on the front door or windows or something but not like this. I'll show you where the control panels are, and I'll give you the codes."

"Thanks." I nodded, not wanting to show how genuinely thrilled I was to hear about the alarm system. "The ginger beef is amazing."

"I love to cook," she continued. "And I always make enough for leftovers so if you ever come home hungry, feel free to grab what's in the fridge." Mia smiled and stretched, sliding off the seat to grab some water. "My brother's coming over on Sunday for dinner. I'd love for you to meet him. That being said, he's not really a people person."

"Oh, umm. I'm not sure what my schedule is, but—"

"No pressure. If you're free, just let me know." She smiled and took a sip of water, her eyes analyzing me. "Don't take this the wrong way…"

I started laughing. "I'll try not to."

"But I don't see you working at Buttons either."

My heart started pounding. I needed that job, but if she was able to sniff out my fear and apprehension this easily, how was I going to fake my way through it with the members or whatever they were called?

I shrugged and grinned. "Only time will tell, I guess."

"Now, do you know what you're going to wear?" she asked.

I shrugged. I'd been wracking my brain trying to figure it out. "I was thinking like an oversized button-down shirt?"

"That would be different." She nodded.

"Like different bad?" I asked, grinning.

"No. Just different. But I think a lot of guys are into that whole boyfriend shirt thing. So maybe you'll start a new trend at the club."

"Well, I guess I'll find out."

"Baby steps, huh?" Her smile knowing.

I nodded. "More like infant crawls." I took the last bite of ginger beef that was on my plate and tamped down the worry about tomorrow.

I walked to the sink and rinsed my plate off before placing it in the dishwasher. Mia was right behind me and did the same.

"Ready to tour Fort Knox?" she laughed. "I would've mentioned it when I was interviewing you, but I didn't want to scare you off."

I smiled and followed her down the stairs to the first floor where she proceeded to show me every tip and trick for securing the premises. By the time we reached the third floor, I knew the only person who would secure a house like this was someone who had a very important reason to do so.

"Did something happen to make your brother so..." my voice trailed off.

We were standing in the hallway, and she was about to show me her bedroom and her studio. She glanced behind her and then her gaze focused on me before she crossed her arms and nodded slowly.

"Yeah. There's a reason," she confirmed, but didn't say anything more.

That was when I wondered how many of us were running from something? And would there ever be something worth running to?

CHAPTER FOURTEEN

Luke

I pulled into the parking lot of Buttons and found a spot. It was twenty minutes to closing, but I had to find out if she was there. I looked in the mirror and smoothed my hair back. I had no idea what I planned on saying if she was, but I just wanted to know if she was inside, if she was safe.

That was bullshit. I wanted to see her again. I stepped out of the Tesla and closed the door before walking over to the entrance. The bouncer at the door gave me a quick nod of recognition as he opened the door for me. The club was packed with men, drinking and chatting up the servers. I glanced up and saw Liv, one of the more friendly waitresses, swinging above. This was not a place for Hannah.

"Never would've guessed you'd be here," Sean's voice called out over the pulsing beat of the music. "Making your semi-annual trek into Buttons, huh? You usually warn me." Sean punched my shoulder with his free hand as he took a swig of his beer with the other.

"Looks just like I remember," I said, my gaze scanning the crowd. "New hire on tonight?"

"Barbie? No. She's coming on tomorrow."

Hearing Sean refer to Hannah as Barbie irked me. It didn't help to see the expressions on the faces around the club as the men watched their servers. It made my anger rise again and push out all of the logical reasons why Buttons would be a good fit for Hannah, for someone in hiding.

"Do you really think it's a good idea to break the formula by adding a blond. You've got something going on here that people respond to. Why mess with success?"

"There's something special about her. Something innocent. I swear she *alone* could double the initiation fee."

"Really." I folded my arms and attempted to push down the anger, only to have it rise.

He was right. There was something very innocent about Hannah, which was why this place made absolutely no sense for her to work.

"The theme tonight?" I asked, ignoring Sean's gaze.

"What's up? You look like you're ready to pulverize anyone who gets too close to you..."

"The theme?" I asked again.

"Wonderland. But seriously, dude. What's going on? Is it Jessica?"

Oh, yeah. I was supposed to be heartbroken.

At least it was a handy excuse.

I nodded. "Called things off with her."

"No shit? I never saw that coming." Sean whistled lowly. "Are you sure about that? It's not often you find a woman who thinks like a man. She seemed like a good fit. No strings attached."

I laughed and squeezed Sean's shoulder. "There are always strings attached, especially with women. Hers just hadn't reared its ugly head yet. Needed to cut it off before it did." I pointed at Sean's beer. "How about I have one of those. We've only got a few minutes before last call, anyhow."

Sean nodded as we walked up to the bar and I got my own drink.

"Look who decided to show up." I heard Liv's voice crawl up my spine as I spun around to greet her. She must have just climbed down from the swing. She was dressed in a short, black slip and wore a bunny tail attached to the hem, I assumed to match the Wonderland theme, but she was no white rabbit. It was hard not to start laughing so I glanced over at the bartender as she slid on the stool next to me. I really didn't get this club. "What brought you in?" she asked, her eyes curious.

Liv glanced at Sean before her eyes landed back on mine.

"Thought I should show up every once in a while, especially when Sean decides to throw out his brunettes-only rule."

"I always thought it was a dumb rule in the first place," Liv said, touching Sean's chin. She'd always had a thing for Sean, but neither of them ever acted on it for obvious reasons. "She's gorgeous. I'm actually the one who brought her in."

"Was it easy to convince her?" I asked, clenching my fists as I waited for the answer.

"Not at all. I could tell she wasn't from around here since she was so oblivious. But she seemed enticed by the money. I mean, who wouldn't be. But still... I was surprised that she showed up tonight. She was really worried that this place was too good to be true," Liv snickered, and I took a sip of the beer. "But I promised her there wasn't anything compromising going on. That you guys take care of us."

I hated being lumped in with this place.

"I guess that's subjective," I muttered, watching the men slowly begin to exit the club. The waitresses still flirted with them on the way out, leaving them with that false sense of reality.

"Right, man. Cause you're above it all?" Sean's brow arched and Liv started chuckling.

"One thing I've learned since starting here is that no man is above anything. You just haven't found your kryptonite," Liv smiled at me and then at Sean, before slipping off the stool.

"Don't count on it."

"Well, the new hire will be in tomorrow. I'm training her. You should stop by."

"He never has before. I doubt he'll start now," Sean replied as Liv walked away.

"There's always a first," I muttered, pushing my unfinished beer away for the bartender to deal with. "Listen, it sounds like you've got your reasons for hiring her, but—" I stopped myself.

"Why do I think you're not telling me something?" Sean asked.

Now was not the time to get into it.

"I'm out. I'll see ya tomorrow." I shrugged and walked away.

"Two days in a row? I think this Jessica thing is bothering you more than you're letting on." Sean called after me.

When I got to my car, I saw a new text on my cell from my sister, which wasn't unlike her. She was a night owl just like me. She said her inspiration didn't even start to come until after five in the evening.

Forgot to mention. I've got a new roommate.

Why did she have such an incessant need to get a roommate? I texted back a quick reply and took off for my house.

Of course you do. Hope it works out better than the last one. And the one before that.

Since I was still supposed to be in New England, my schedule was already cleared, and I'd be able to get a lot done surrounding Hannah's case. I was itching to get more of my people on it.

Exactly! Hannah's case. That was how I needed to think about it. She was nothing more than a person who needed help, a new case, and I intended to keep it that way.

A new text came in from my sister, and I directed the car to read the text aloud. The car promptly obeyed.

She's a new hire at Buttons. I think it's a good fit. Plus, she looks like she could use a friend.

You've got to be shitting me. I turned my car onto the Pacific Coast Highway and continued driving toward my house, fighting the overwhelming urge to turn the car around and show up at my sister's house. If Hannah was in danger that meant anyone she was around would be in danger, and I wasn't going to let that happen. I'd lost too much, too early, to let it happen again. My fists gripped the steering wheel as I drove toward home, wondering how I would take care of this latest problem.

CHAPTER FIFTEEN

Hannah

After spending all day worrying about when Donald Jamison would be let out, I finally made myself concentrate on getting ready for my first day on the job. Mia had been in her studio all day, which left me plenty of time to unpack and get situated. Regardless of how long I planned on staying or not staying, I was certain Mia would figure things out pretty quickly if I left all the cardboard boxes locked, loaded, and ready to go. I glanced at the clock, knowing it was time to walk over to the club. What I was experiencing was far beyond first-day jitters, but I couldn't back out now.

I had my bag all packed and was ready to go. I locked the front door behind me and felt the warmth of the air cascade over my skin. California weather was amazing. After being locked up with air-conditioning all day, it was nice to be outside with the gentle sea breeze blowing softly. This life, imaginary as it might seem, was something I valued. It gave me hope. It told me what my life could be like someday. As long as I had hope, things would be okay.

I wandered the sidewalk, noticing the cafes and noting which boutiques would be fun to go to when I had a little cash. Once I reached Buttons, I punched in the code and opened the front door.

"Hey, Hannah," the bartender waved. It was the same guy from the day before. I decided I better make friends since he seemed to know my name, yet I knew nothing about him.

"Hey," I said, placing my bag on the cherrywood bar. He gave me a quick handshake and smiled.

"I'm Kevin," he replied. "If you ever need anything, I'm your guy."

I started laughing.

"That sounded cheesy, didn't it?" His deep grin showed off the sharpness of his features. He was good-looking with his dark hair and deep-set brown eyes, but meeting Kevin reminded me of my reaction to Luke, and my non-reaction to Kevin, which was similar to the reaction I had toward my fiancé. But at least I wouldn't have to worry about Luke anymore since I'd left the last place he knew where to find me.

"It could've been worse," I assured him. "So how long have you been working here?"

"Two years. There are three other male

bartenders, but I'm the best looking."

I laughed harder and his gaze steadied on mine. "Another bad one, huh?"

I shrugged. "They could be fabulous lines for all I know. I've been out of the dating world for far too long to know."

"Really?" He looked puzzled as he flipped a bar towel over his shoulder. "You've got a boyfriend?"

I shook my head. "No. I was engaged."

At least that sounded halfway normal.

"Oh," he nodded. "Did you...he..."

"I broke it off." I smiled.

Kevin leaned over the bar and smiled. "Listen, if you have any questions don't hesitate to ask me or anyone behind the bar. We hear and see everything from our vantage point." He tapped the beer tap and pulled back and smiled.

"Thanks. I'll remember that. Now I guess I better go and get ready for my first shift," I said.

"Is that my girl?" Liv hollered from the other side of the room. "Get your butt down here before the doors open."

My stomach immediately went into a free fall as I waved and hurried over to Liv. This was it. I'd finally get to see what everything was about inside these walls. I glanced up at the swing and wanted to kick myself.

Why did I look up?

"So you got your outfit for tonight?" she asked, pulling me down the hallway.

"I do." I didn't want to tell her what it was for fear of it being vetoed.

"Well, make it snappy and we'll get through this. The first night is always the hardest." She swung open the door and led me to a corner vanity and small closet. "This will be where you can get ready. Although it looks like you're all already to go, except for your clothes."

"Yeah, I did my makeup at home."

Liv smiled and nodded. "Awesome. So you'll be working my tables tonight, and I'll be right there with you every step of the way."

I placed my bag on the chair and looked at Liv, hoping she'd get the hint. She didn't. I opened my bag and turned my back to Liv as I pulled my dress over my head. I was in one of the few matching lingerie sets that I owned, which even though it was matching was more toward cotton comfy than lacy racy. I said a silent prayer that Liv wouldn't notice and slipped the button-down over my head. I quickly buttoned up the shirt and turned around to see Liv, her mouth gaping.

"This is brilliant. Why didn't I ever think of this? The men are going to love it." She reached over and unbuttoned a couple of the buttons up top where I had just securely fastened them and smiled. "There. All better." Then her eyes dropped to the bra that was edging out from under the white cotton. Her mouth went into a disapproving pout, followed by a huff. "At least it's black."

"Exactly," I agreed.

Liv took a step back to give me a once over, and my fingers immediately pulled down at the hem of the shirt, trying to stretch it to my mid-thigh area.

"That's a no-no," Liv said. "No fidgeting."

"Sorry. Things are just breezy."

Liv laughed and glanced at the clock on the wall. "We've got fifteen minutes before the members can start to arrive. Tonight might be a little slow, which will be good for you."

I reached into my bag and grabbed the water I'd brought along, taking a swallow. "Thank you so much for telling me about this opportunity, by the way."

"Hopefully you'll still be thanking me after your first shift."

I was startled by her honesty but couldn't help crack a smile as I began to feel a little less anxious.

"Believe me. We all go through the first week jitters. I remember I was always on-guard, thinking that something awful was going to happen or that something more was expected of me that I wouldn't be comfortable with. But that never happened and to this day, I've never felt bad about my time working here. Think of it as Hooters for wannabe millionaires."

I nodded and put my water back in the bag before following her out. The music had just turned on, and I was shocked at how quickly the club had changed. It felt far more intimate but strange.

"Tonight's theme is the *Phantom of the Opera*."

"There are themes?" I looked around trying to see how the Phantom fit in with what the room had transformed into. The curtains surrounding certain booths had been changed out to black velvet, and there were large floral arrangements placed around the club, but the theme was lost on me.

She nodded. "It keeps things fresh. See over there?" She pointed to the corner. "It's subtle."

I saw nothing that referenced anything to do with the Phantom. Instead, I was looking at a huge ice sculpture that was meant to look like something, but I had no idea what. It spilt onto a glass table where shot glasses and rose petals were scattered.

"I don't get it," I said, turning back to Liv. "How is this the Phantom at all?"

Liv laughed and motioned for me to follow her over to the table. As I got closer to the sculpture, I recognized a man's face covered with a mask carved into the ice.

"Oh, okay," I said, nodding. "That's kind of stretching it."

"We all have to wear a mask." She smiled.

"Seriously? The whole night?" I asked.

Liv twisted her lips, scanning across the room. "Yup."

Knowing that I'd be able to hide under a partial mask made me start to feel less exposed and more at ease. I could do this. At least tonight I could do this. All I could do was take it one day at a time.

"So follow my lead. We take drink orders, food orders, and we stop to listen, to chat with the members. You need to learn to read their moods, their expressions," Liv replied. "Our job is part server and part listener. One thing I've learned is that men don't necessarily want to discuss things that are bothering them. Meaning they don't want to hear our take on the matter. They just want to vent and take a swig of whisky."

I nodded, worrying that there was still something more behind this job than she was letting on, but I guess only time would tell. I also liked to think that men were more complex than Liv's assessment. As I glanced around the club, I focused on the fact that only members would be in here tonight. This was one of the safest jobs for a person in my predicament, and I needed to quit worrying needlessly. I could handle this.

Kevin, the bartender, gave us a slight nod, which seemed to tell Liv something. She walked us over to the back hallway where one of the girls, who I hadn't met yet, was handing out the white masks.

"It's showtime." She squeezed my hand. "Here's to a night of splendid tips and easy customers."

I smiled, unable to resist her jolly attitude. I turned back around and watched as a hostess led two men to one of the seating areas in the center of the club. One of the men sat on the couch, while the other sat on the ottoman. They were deep in discussion, and one stood back up to take off his suit jacket before sitting back down. The hostess took it from him and walked back to the front.

"Do we need to go over there?" I asked.

"That's not our section. Tonight, we're

covering the exterior booths."

I nodded and she secured the mask over her face and I did the same.

"Too bad this doesn't cover up my whole face," I teased.

"That's the spirit," Liv said, rolling her eyes. "Looks like our first table is being seated. Have any questions?"

I shook my head. "Not yet."

I followed Liv's lead and walked over to the large booth that now housed four men. Two of them looked to be in their early fifties and the other two maybe thirty? Guessing age was never my thing.

"Who do we have here, Liv?" One of the younger guys asked. He was dressed in a polo and chinos, and his blonde hair was slicked back. I smiled at him as his eyes fell along my body, and I instantly knew this wasn't going to be easy.

"This is Hannah. It's her first night, so behave," Liv responded. The guys ate it up.

"Don't we always?" the man asked, smiling. "Nice to meet you, Hannah. I'm Greg."

"Nice to meet you," I responded, commanding myself not to fidget.

"Your usuals?" Liv asked.

They all nodded, but Greg spoke up. "Make Jim's a double."

They all laughed and we walked toward the bar. "Not so bad, was it?" Liv asked.

"I don't want to jinx it," I whispered.

"Okay, so Greg drinks a gin and tonic. Jim drinks a White Russian, and the other two have

Merlot. The gentleman with the white hair is Todd and the one sitting next to him is Barry. Got it?"

I nodded as I tried to commit their names and faces to memory as Liv waited for the bartender to make the drinks. There was a steady stream of customers and the music was nothing like I expected. I assumed it changed based on the theme of the night, but tonight was a nice mix of classical. Hearing the piano made my fingers restless as I thought about not being able to play my violin, having nowhere to play and no instrument.

"Drinks are ready," Liv said, interrupting my thoughts.

I grabbed the tray and noticed a long-stemmed red rose placed in between the drinks.

"What's this for?" I asked.

"Every night we pick a favorite at the table." Liv caught my expression and her lips pressed into a thin line.

This was so gimmicky. It was hard for me to fathom that anyone fell for this. I followed Liv to our table and began serving the drinks, trying very hard to remember which name was paired with which drink.

"I think the new girl should pick her favorite," Greg replied, grinning. I felt his eyes cascade down my body and was grateful I was buttoned up in my oversized shirt. I had no idea how'd I'd be able to do this in lingerie.

My stomach clenched and I smiled as Liv took the tray from me. I wrapped my fingers around the stem and held it out toward Greg, waiting for him to grab it.

He didn't. Instead, he slid over in the booth and tapped the seat. I glanced at Liv, horrified, and she nodded, her gaze tightening on me. A wave of nausea swept through my body, but I fought it down and took a seat next to Greg. He smiled and sat back in the booth, finally grabbing the rose.

"I've always preferred blondes," Greg said.

Preferred blondes where? In what context? I didn't think there was anything like that going on here. My body began to warm up as fear pulsed through me. What were Greg's expectations?

"So tell me about yourself," Greg asked.

Sensing my unease, Liv slid into the booth across the table. The men moved down slightly to let her in.

"She's from Ohio," Liv answered for me.

"Is that so?" Greg chortled. "A small world. My sister lives in Dayton."

Of course she did.

I smiled and nodded. "I lived up north in Akron."

Greg nodded. "Well, I think you're going to be a lovely addition around here." He took a sip of his drink and handed me the rose. "You take this and keep it to remember me by. At least until next time."

I smiled and took the rose back from him. Liv stood up from the table and walked over to me, grabbing my hand. "We need to put that in water then. Is there anything we can get for you before we do that?"

All the men shook their heads. "Only drinks for now," Jim replied.

Liv's grip was tightly wrapped around my fingers as she nearly dragged me off the floor and down the hallway.

"You have got to loosen up," Liv commanded. "I know first nights are always uneasy, but you looked like you were about to pop."

"I'm sorry. I'm not used to that type of—" I stopped myself. Whatever was about to tumble out of my mouth wouldn't make sense. Not to someone who didn't understand where I actually came from.

"Type of what?" she asked, pushing open the dressing room door.

"Interaction."

"Well, you better get used to it and quickly." She grabbed a vase, filled it with water, and shoved the rose in it. I took the vase from her and placed it near my bag.

"I will. I promise I'll step it up."

And I did. The rest of the night as the booths filled up and men were introduced, I turned myself into a commodity. I smiled. I laughed. I teased. I touched their hands. And by the time I left for the evening, I wanted nothing more than to take a nice long bath to rinse everything away. I only needed to do this for a few weeks at the most. It wasn't that big of a deal. But it was.

"Nice work," Liv said, as she followed me outside.

"Thanks. I told you I'd get the hang of it," I

said, grinning.

"You walking home?" she asked.

I nodded.

"Have a nice rest of your night. You did awesome," Liv said, waving as she walked off toward her car.

I waved and walked over to the sidewalk. Even though it was late at night, the streets were surprisingly full. I glanced around looking for anyone or anything suspicious, but I didn't see anything out of the ordinary. Just couples making their way back home and the typical groups of men and women winding down from a night full of drinking. As I made my way down the street to my temporary home, I decided to walk right on by the house and visit the beach. I'd been dying to visit it since I moved in, and now seemed like as good a time as any.

The crashing of the waves beckoned me over as I walked along the sandy beach. It was a beautiful, warm night, which made it difficult to believe we were in the month of March. Such was the life in California. Even though the sidewalks had been full of people, the beach was empty. Exactly how I wanted it. I set my bag down and kicked off my flip-flops. I felt the sand run between my toes. If I could only find peace in the middle of the night so be it. At least it hadn't been completely taken from me.

I looked back toward the house and saw the lights from the top floor blazing and a shadow dancing along the wall. Mia must have been painting or dancing. Maybe one led to the other.

There was something comforting about Mia, about my new home, no matter how temporary. I turned back toward the ocean and sat down on the sand, closing my eyes and listening to the waves crash gently against the beach, imagining that this was what my life could always be.

The sound of an engine running interrupted my dreams, and I turned around quickly to look behind me. Had someone found me? My heart began racing when I saw a car idling in front of Mia's house, my house. The headlights were blazing, which made it difficult for me to see what was going on or who was in the vehicle. I moved slowly, hoping whoever was there wouldn't see me. When the driver's door swung open, a large figure jumped out of the car with the engine still running. I heard him on the phone, talking about "finding the girl" and my chest tightened in horror. They'd found me.

Again.

I blocked the light from the headlights with my hand, hoping to glimpse a bit of the person, but he took off running toward the front door. My heart raced with fear, but instead of running away, I ran toward the door, toward the man. I couldn't let anything happen to Mia. This was my problem. Not Mia's.

CHAPTER SIXTEEN

Luke

Damn it! I had decided against going into Buttons on Hannah's first day. I didn't want to give her any reason to run, and my hunch told me she already had plenty of them. So instead, I turned into the guy hanging out in the parking lot to keep an eye on her. Something about this scenario had to change. This wasn't how I operated, but I didn't want to scare her. I might only have one shot to prove to her that I could be trusted, and I didn't want to blow it. So, here I sat in the parking lot in the middle of the night to make sure she was all right. How was that not creepy, again? I changed the satellite radio away from rock to classical. I needed something calming.

It was a few minutes past closing, and I expected to see her walk out any second. I knew she didn't have her truck any longer and planned on walking home, which did nothing to calm my fears about how this girl operated. She was on the run, yet she was still too trusting when it came to strangers. I think she actually thought if someone tried to attack her in public, a stranger would step in. Unfortunately, that wasn't how it worked in our world.

The door opened and the bouncer smiled as two women walked out. My heart quickened when I spotted Hannah. She was laughing, carrying a bag and holding a rose. My stomach knotted with the thought of how she got that rose. Some man had already claimed her, and she didn't even know it. Liv forced a smile as she appeared to be giving Hannah some sort of advice. Whatever it was, it made Hannah cringe slightly, but I doubt Liv even caught it. I wish I knew what Liv had told her.

Liv walked to her car as Hannah walked out of the parking lot. I waited for Liv to get in her SUV and pull out of the lot. I didn't want to attract attention and Hannah wouldn't be getting very far with the traffic signals around here. They were slower than molasses. I watched as Liv drove by, talking on the phone. I wondered who she was talking to in the middle of the night. Last I knew of she had no significant other, which was why Sean was her target of the moment, and I doubted he'd be willing to go down that path. It was too cliché. Club owner dating one of the waitresses, but who knew; he was apparently a changing man.

I pulled out of the parking stall as Liv turned down the street. Several cars were lined up at the stoplight as I inched my way out on the road. Scanning the sidewalks for Hannah, my heart began to race. I didn't see her. There were more crowds on the street than I expected, but then again, all the bars and restaurants were closing so everyone was being pushed out. She had to be here. I gripped the steering wheel, cursing the red stoplight until it turned green. I continued skimming the sidewalks, my eyes landing on any blondes that I could see. And in California, they were all over.

Where the hell did she go in less than five minutes? I turned down the street that led directly to my sister's house, my eyes still watching for any sign of Hannah. She had to be here somewhere. Maybe I'd passed by her. I pulled over and grabbed my cell. If I texted Mia, she'd know immediately that Hannah was the woman from Starbucks. I tapped the shifter with my thumb as I debated whether or not to text Mia. Maybe Hannah hadn't walked home, maybe she had jogged home, which would make her there already. I looked in my rearview mirror, canvasing the group of bar patrons, still not seeing any sign of Hannah.

I let out a sigh and typed a text to my sister. It was bound to come out anyway.

Hannah back to the house yet?

Minutes ticked by and no response. She must

be in the middle of one of her works, which meant the music was up and she was in her zone. There was no getting through to Mia unless she happened to glance at her phone.

It had been fifteen minutes since Hannah had left the club. Even if she walked extremely slow she'd be back at the house by now. I shook my head, knowing what I was about to do.

I put the car in drive and pulled back onto the road. If something happened to Hannah because I didn't just lay it on the line with her, I would never forgive myself. If they got to her…

My foot pressed harder on the gas as I thought about the information I had found out earlier this evening. It was time to come clean with my sister. My car flew by parked car after parked car until the beach finally came into view. I was only a block away. There was still no sign of Hannah and the anger inside of me was beginning to boil over. I didn't follow protocol, and I let my personal feelings for her overshadow her safety.

I pulled in front of my sister's house and jumped out of the car. The lights were on upstairs so my sister was working. I reached for my keys to open the door when I realized I'd left the car running. My hand grabbed the door handle and pushed it open. Mia didn't even lock it.

Wonderful. I was glad to see the security system had a chance.

"Mia," I hollered, climbing the stairs two at a time. "Mia."

The music was louder with each step I scaled.

There was no way she'd hear me until I was right in front of her. Another thing we'd need to discuss. It wasn't like our family was in the clear either. There was a reason she had an alarm system.

Her studio door was slightly ajar, and I pushed it open the rest of the way.

Nothing would have prepared me for what I saw in front of me. I had to look away.

CHAPTER SEVENTEEN

Hannah

That man was on a mission, whoever he was. My heart pounded as I climbed the porch steps two at a time, and I jumped into the entry. He didn't even bother to close the door. I'd left everything on the beach and was completely empty-handed. I didn't know what I thought I was going to do, but whatever it was, I couldn't be without some sort of hard instrument. My fingers curled around a small iron sculpture tucked in one of the wall alcoves. It would have to do. I scrambled up the stairs, my blood on fire with each step toward Mia's floor. Car still running, door wide open. Whoever was in here was being careless, guided by his heart, not his head. Was it an old boyfriend of Mia's? Was that why her place was so secure? Who did she have after her and why didn't I pay more attention?

Out of breath, I reached the top of the stairs, greeted by thumping bass from Mia's studio. As I turned down the hall, I saw a man slowly backing out of her studio. His movements were unnatural, nervous—possibly angry. There was no sign of Mia. Then I heard it over the music, a woman's voice moaning.

I quickly considered my options. Wait until he turned around and saw me and then lunge? Or hit him now and apologize later, if needed.

Second option!

I jumped toward the man, grabbing the back of his suit jacket, which threw him off balance only slightly. He stumbled backward as I swung the piece of metal toward the back of his head. Missing his skull completely, I plunged it into his neck. But it was too late. Before I even realized what had happened, he had me slammed against the floor. My eyes clenched shut with pain, as he pinned both of my arms above my head, his knee digging into my waist.

But then as quickly as he'd apprehended me, he let me go.

"Oh my god, Hannah," the voice spoke, the voice that the heavens were built upon.

My eyes flashed open.

"Luke? What—"

He hopped off of me and knelt next to me. "Are you okay?" he interrupted. "I had no idea it was you."

"Why would you?" I asked, rubbing the base of my head. My heart rate immediately began to calm as I looked into his eyes.

He shook his head. "I'm so sorry." He ignored my question. His fingers gently ran along my shoulder, sending the fear straight out of my body as an amazing pulse of electricity replaced it. "Let me get you some ice or help you to—"

"What about Mia? Is she okay? I heard..." The bump to the head was starting to pound.

His expression fell and he answered before I could finish. "She's just fine. A little occupied at the moment."

Was Luke her ex-boyfriend?

"Oh," I said, realizing what he meant. "You didn't—"

"I did. And I wished I hadn't."

I let out a stifled laugh, which brought a trace of a smile to his lips. "Well, you might want to go take care of your car. If someone hasn't stolen it yet, they will shortly."

"That would fit my luck tonight," he laughed, helping me up. "You sure you're okay to leave alone for a minute?"

"A minute? Yeah. I think I can handle that. I'll live. Can you maybe grab my stuff on the beach?" I smiled.

"Sure." He turned around and my eyes cascaded down his body. It was hard not to admire it. Squeezing my shoulder muscles to get the kinks out, I decided to follow him down the stairs as I thought about what just happened.

I went into the kitchen and grabbed a plastic baggie and filled it with ice. I'd do the same for Luke, but I wasn't going to lie to myself. Whatever injury I had attempted to inflict on him, didn't happen. But what in the world was he doing here? Mia's last name was Dufort.

I smacked the baggie of ice to the back of my skull and took a seat at the breakfast bar as Luke walked into the kitchen.

"Car still there?" I asked, adjusting the ice.

"Amazingly, yes." He smiled, and I couldn't help but want to say something funny to keep that smile there. But I couldn't think of anything even slightly humorous. He placed my bag from the beach on the floor.

"So you know Mia how?" I asked, watching as he made himself at home, grabbing a glass.

He bit his lip and glanced at me as he filled up his glass with water.

Yup, ex-boyfriend.

Instead, he placed the water in front of me on the granite counter. "Drink up. It'll help."

"Nice evasion tactic," I said, before taking a sip.

He filled up a glass for himself and leaned against the counter. How hard of a question was this?

"Since I got your email," he replied, his eyes focusing on me. "I've been in contact with the detective."

I felt a slight turn in my universe as his gaze stayed on me. No. The room wasn't spinning. Okay, maybe it was a little bit. This bump to the head must be bad. As his gaze continued to stay fixed on me, I knew it had nothing to do with the injury.

"Yeah?" I asked, shifting on the stool.

He nodded. "I know you're running from something. I can help."

I shook my head. "You can't help. And you're still not answering my question."

"I'm Mia's brother."

My stomach did a somersault at this revelation. He wasn't an ex-boyfriend.

"Oh noooeees, and you saw?" I laughed.

He smiled and shook his head. "No. Thank God. I would've jumped out the window, ended it right then. I saw a little evidence and someone I never expected to see in the room with her. That was too much for me."

"Things get juicy in the outside world," I muttered, smiling to myself.

"Excuse me?" Luke asked.

"Nothing. So do you mind telling me how out of all the people in the world, I managed to move in with your sister?"

"I was wondering the same thing," Luke replied.

I studied his features, thinking about how it possibly was that no matter how I tried to separate myself from him, he reappeared time and again. "I'm sorry about attacking you. Although, it wasn't much of one, apparently." I massaged my shoulders.

His smile deepened. "So, you thought Mia was in danger? And came at me?"

I nodded. "I figured with the security system and all, maybe some crazy ex was after her or something."

"And you'd put your life on the line for hers?"

His brow arched.

Debating what to say and what not to say, I heard the music from above turn off and looked at my empty glass. Whatever it was, I needed to hurry and get it out. After all, he was familiar with part of the story. I'd already managed to make him a target just by having him buy me a cup of coffee.

"Initially, I was worried it was the same person who was or is after me," I offered. "And the thought of an innocent person getting hurt because of me." I shuddered. "But then I realized whoever came in here was guided by their heart. The people after me have no heart." I steadied my gaze on Luke. He didn't flinch at my words. "So I knew I needed to help her." I couldn't help but laugh. "But apparently not."

"Huh." He ran his thumb along the slight stubble on his jawline. His green eyes were piercing as he watched me, debating what to say.

"So why don't you give me your spiel? I'd love to hear why you came barging into her home in such a frenzy. Leaving your car running and the front door open?" I eyed him, watching his jaw tense. "Seems a little extreme for an innocent brotherly worry if there was no sign she was in danger."

He let out a sigh and dragged his fingers through his hair. His gaze fell away from mine as his mouth formed into a small 'o' before he began to speak. It was hard not to admire the curvature of his mouth, and it was even more difficult to understand where these feelings kept coming from. I'd never before had thoughts like these, not until him.

"I'm waiting." I smiled. He brought his eyes to mine, and I felt that charge run between us.

"I was worried about," he stopped himself and glanced at his sister and the man behind her in the hallway.

It was Sean.

Ooh. This didn't look good.

"What the hell, man?" Luke said, his fist balling.

Sean smirked and his eyes fell to me. "Hi there, Hannah."

I looked from Sean to Luke and then to Mia, feeling like everything in my life had become highly orchestrated, which made me absolutely sick. As I looked at everyone standing around me, I wanted to run. Had Luke somehow planted Liv to get me to work at Buttons and then this renting a room thing magically fell into place? Anger began pulsing through me as the thought continued to expand. I had been controlled and manipulated long enough by a system I didn't believe in. I didn't need to have that happen again. I had no idea what was going on, but I no longer wanted to be in the dark. I needed explanations.

"So you had Liv follow me?" I stated more than questioned, completely unable to hide my anger.

"What?" Luke asked bewildered.

I couldn't read if it was genuine or not.

"You were the missing partner. The partner

who never shows up to the club? It figures." I shook my head, feeling completely betrayed.

"It's not like that," Luke said. "I know what it seems like."

"This just seems a little too handy. I mean it would follow along with just about everything else you've done. The coffee, the coffee again and again, the cab that wasn't a cab, along with the truck showing up at my old place?" Just repeating it aloud made me livid. "You probably just had Liv show up to—," I stopped myself. "And how did you even know I was at that Starbucks? It wasn't even in my neighborhood."

Luke shook his head, the expression on his face bordering between horror and hurt. "Hannah, I promise that I never ever sent Liv to follow you. I can guarantee you that I would never have wanted you working at Buttons."

"Enough with bashing Buttons," Sean interjected, running a hand along Mia's shoulders as she watched what was unfolding between her brother and me.

"You know I hate that place," Luke replied, flipping Sean an icy stare. "I'll deal with you in a second."

"Why would you hate something that you own?" I asked, crossing my arms.

"He owed me a favor," Sean replied before Luke could say anything. "I helped get his security firm up and running when he couldn't afford to hire employees. I worked for free. Once it got going, he helped me get my dream going and he's made me feel like shit about it ever since."

"Unlikely story. What guy wouldn't want to be surrounded by beautiful women?" I asked, turning my attention to Luke.

"It's not about that. I don't like what it stands for. I wouldn't want anyone I care about working there. Or dating someone who thinks it's okay to run a place like that." He stared at Mia.

"But I didn't think anything was shady about the place," I stated sarcastically.

"Listen, honey..." Sean began.

"Don't call her honey," Luke cut him off. "That right there is why I wouldn't want anyone I care about working there. There is nothing shady about the place. At least that I'm aware of, or I'd pull my percentage. But the place objectifies women and that's not something I condone."

"Right because you're so above it," Sean shot back, rolling his eyes. "I wonder if Jessica would agree about your virtuous ways."

Wait. Who was Jessica? My stomach twisted into knots.

"There's no reason to bring her into this," Luke replied.

"Well, if you're going to talk about objectifying women..." Sean replied. "I don't know of many who like to be strung along."

"She wasn't strung along," Luke said through clenched teeth. "We were both adults choosing—"

"Exactly," Sean almost shouted. "Adults choosing to participate. Just like Buttons. I don't force the waitresses to flirt. I don't force them to work for me. I don't force them to do anything. They are choosing to be servers at Buttons, just as the members are choosing to pay for the promise of nothing."

"It's not a promise of nothing," Luke replied. He glanced at me.

"So you didn't send Liv to recruit me?" I asked.

"God no."

"Listen, it's been fun. But I'm out." Sean gave Mia a quick kiss and I thought Luke was about to pounce on him. Instead Sean showed himself out, and Mia came over to me and took a seat.

"So I'm completely confused. As far as I knew, you worked at Buttons and Emily knew I was looking for a roommate and voila. And now you've got ice on your head. But how the hell does my brother play into this and what on earth are you doing here this late at night?" She asked bemused, turning her attention to Luke.

"Yes, please do tell what brought you here?" I smiled, hoping to finally get some answers.

CHAPTER EIGHTEEN

Luke

With all my careful planning and nonstop worrying about how to proceed with Hannah, this was how it all came to fruition. Hannah sitting with an icepack on her neck, my sister wondering why the hell I broke into her home in the middle of the night and, finally, finding out my sister was seeing my best friend.

Priceless.

I watched Mia and Hannah as they sat next to each other, seemingly unfazed by tonight's events, patiently waiting for my answers. Answers I had full intentions of giving them but not this way. I had planned on taking them both aside and explaining events differently to each, catering to their reactions. Now that wasn't going to happen. It was going to be one story that would anger one and enlighten the other, or baffle one while making the other run for the hills. Either way it had to be done.

"Let's say I put on a pot of coffee," I replied, turning toward the machine.

"Grounds are in the top cupboard," Mia said, turning to smile at Hannah. "So what the hell happened at Buttons to make you need an icepack? You didn't get on the swing, did you?"

Leave it to Mia.

Hannah's laugh floated through the air, and I immediately wanted to shove this sordid mess aside, give her a reason to keep laughing, keep glowing. As I poured the water into the coffeemaker, I watched her cheeks redden at my sister's question. There was such an air of innocence to Hannah that I loved, but at the same time seeing where she came from, why she had that innocence, saddened me beyond belief.

"No, I had a tumble with your brother," Hannah said, her eyes flicking to mine.

"A tumble with my brother?"

"Yeah. Your new roommate tried to attack your poor, unsuspecting brother," I laughed, closing the top of the coffee maker.

"I doubt that," Mia said. "You're never unsuspecting, and you certainly aren't poor."

"No. It's true. I attacked him," Hannah said, flashing me a smile.

Damn. She was gorgeous. She didn't have a clue what that smile did to me. It was the unraveling of me, why we were in this situation in the first place.

"Well, I don't blame you. If he was sneaking

around here, I would've too," Mia said, smiling.

"See? The landlord says I'm off the hook." Hannah moved the icepack.

"So the icepack?" Mia prompted.

"Should I start at the beginning of the debacle?" Hannah looked at me.

"Might as well." I threw my hands in the air in surrender.

"I was on the beach, unwinding and wondering if I'd really be able to last at Buttons. Want to tell me your story?"

I grabbed three mugs and began filling them with coffee. "Your story first. Then mine."

"I'm gonna hold you to that," Hannah laughed, as I placed the mug of pseudo adrenaline in front of her.

"Anyway, I was on the beach and a car pulled up in front of the house and a crazy guy jumped out without even turning off the car. The next thing I know, he was running into the house and I got worried. I thought someone was after..." Hannah paused. "Well, at first I thought they were after me and then I got terrified that they were after you. Either way, I went in ready to mess someone up. I couldn't just stand around and do nothing."

"You put yourself in danger for me?" my sister asked.

"Well, I certainly wouldn't just sit there and watch. Anyway, by the time I got to the top floor I saw some guy backing out of your studio. He was acting suspicious. What topped it off was I heard a..."

Mia grinned. "Gotcha. Bad to worse."

"Tell me about it," Hannah muttered. "That's when I tried my superhero moves and failed miserably. Your brother had me on the ground and pinned beneath him within a second."

Mia eyed her brother and took a sip of coffee. "You were in the studio?" her voice was almost hoarse.

"I guess it's my turn," I replied. Coffee didn't seem like enough. "Have any Bailey's?"

"I've got some Kahlua in the fridge," my sister offered. "Must be a good story."

I opened the fridge and found the bottle. I quickly poured some into my mug and then poured a little more for good measure.

"First, I'm asking that both of you give me a chance. I was coming from a good place." I took a drink and motioned toward the family room. "Mind if we go in there?"

They both nodded and slid off the stools. My sister had decorated the family room in very neutral colors and even though I'd begged her not to, she had several of my photographs displayed along the far wall. I grabbed the fireplace remote and flipped it on. I needed all the help I could get. Hannah took a seat in the overstuffed chair, and she tucked her legs underneath her. Her blond hair was slightly messy and beyond sexy. This was the problem. I was too attracted to her, unable to deal with her the way I would a typical client. Shit. She didn't even know she was a client. That was another problem.

I took a seat on the couch next to my sister. "I'm not going to start with tonight's events. Doing that would only make things sound worse than they are."

"Sounds like a great introduction," Mia said. Her brow curved as she looked at me with disapproving eyes, slowly cluing into who I'd been so worked up over these last several days. It had all been about Hannah. "Especially since you think the story will lead to how or why you were in my studio in the middle of the night when I was with Sean."

I ignored her.

"I ran into Hannah at a Starbucks. She had a bit of trouble with her purchase. I stepped in to help and since then my world hasn't been the same."

My sister's jaw dropped open, and I wanted to beg her to please tone it down a tad or it wasn't going to be an easy confession. Instead, I forged ahead.

"Something told me there was more to Hannah's story than she was willing to let on. Between plates from out of state, and the way she constantly looked over her shoulder, I had a bad feeling. I had my driver take her home. Got her address, looked some things up."

"What do you mean you looked some things up?" Hannah asked, her voice trembling slightly.

This wasn't going well, and I'd only gotten a couple sentences out. I needed a new approach.

"I was curious about why a girl would travel clear across the country to move into a home that left so much to be desired, so I investigated. You intrigued me, Hannah." I shrugged. "I'm not going to apologize for being interested in you."

My sister's gaze caught mine, as she gave me a warning look.

"I didn't expect to find out what I did, which in all honesty wasn't much. When I heard someone had attempted to hurt you, all bets were off. I was back in New England on a business trip when everything happened, when I received your email." I watched Hannah stiffen as my words tumbled out. "I went to your old address. I saw where you came from."

Hannah shook her head, her hands moving slowly to her mouth. "You've put yourself in danger. You don't understand these people."

"I was worried about you. My job is protecting people. I wanted to protect you. I wanted to help."

"I'm completely lost," Mia replied, glancing at Hannah. "I thought you were from Ohio."

Hannah shook her head slowly.

"She's a member of the NLC."

"I was a member," Hannah corrected.

"What's the NLC?" Mia questioned.

"It's registered as a non-profit in New Hampshire. They've done a pretty decent job of keeping out of the news. The address I went to was a compound of sorts," I continued. "But in all honesty, I'm hoping that Hannah will learn to trust me enough to tell me what it was I was actually seeing. What it is she's running from."

I looked over at Hannah. Her eyes were

vacant. She'd gone to a place far away. She was going to leave. I could tell. I only had one shot at this, and I was already screwing it up.

"The short of it is, I figured out Hannah was your new roommate, and I learned she was working at Buttons. I couldn't believe it, and I'd fully intended to talk Sean out of letting her work there. But then I thought about her situation and as much as I hated it, at least this job would keep her out of any public spaces, for the most part."

"And why don't you let Hannah know how you pieced this all together," Mia said, pressing her lips together.

I looked at Hannah who was watching me, her eyes still void of any emotion.

"I used my resources."

"Which means?" Mia pressed.

"I put a security detail on Hannah and had some of my guys investigate..."

"I've heard enough," Hannah said slowly, standing up. She didn't look angry, more hurt than anything. Maybe hopeless. Whatever the expression was, it killed me inside. "I've caused enough turmoil in your lives. I'll be out by the next payday. I don't want to cause any trouble for either of you. Luke, thanks for trying. But it's bigger than that."

It was like she'd stabbed me in the chest. I watched her walk out of the room, and it took Mia grabbing my hand to not follow after her.

CHAPTER NINETEEN

Hannah

I'd been manipulated, controlled, and watched long enough in my life. The thought that I'd fled one situation only to somehow land in another one had me worried, had me questioning what it was about me that attracted this type of situation, or person, to my life.

I quietly closed the door to my bedroom and fell onto the bed, feeling the squish of the comforter surround me. I looked around the bedroom, which was one of the few places I had that felt safe, not watched. It was such a peaceful room. Everything was white. The walls, curtains, throw rug, furniture, comforter, even the paintings on the wall were pure white. It felt a little angelic. The only bit of color was next to the window. A crystal vase filled with blood red seashells.

I liked it. I liked this place. I liked Mia. I liked Luke. I really didn't want to leave.

But I was tired.

Tired of the life I knew I was about to lead, one where I would always be looking over my shoulder, always on the run. Until I could prove what the NLC was doing.

It felt like all I did was trade one struggle for another. I thought leaving the NLC would be the hard part, not trying to make it in the normal world. Certainly, I knew I might have some difficulty getting on my feet, possibly staying on my feet, but I didn't count on anyone finding me, at least not so quickly. I also hadn't counted on some stranger feeling the need to start checking up on me, following me. But it was Luke. Actually that made it even harder. I liked Luke. A lot. His kindness, concern...Nancy's words ran through my mind, "Always strings attached". It was such a cynical way of looking at the world. I didn't want to become that person, but I was starting to understand that worldview.

Making my way to the bathroom, I let out a sigh. I still wanted to wash away the creepy glances I'd endured during my shift tonight. As I turned on the water and squeezed soap into the tub, I thought about Luke. What all did he find out? What did he know? Was it more than even I knew?

Stripping off my clothes, I dipped a toe into the water, testing the temperature. It was perfect. I slid into the warm water and dunked my head. The feeling of warmth touched my scalp, and seeped through my skin, penetrating clear to my bones. I hadn't realized how cold I was. It was a familiar chill. The chill of fear. But what was I afraid of this time?

Pushing myself back up through the water, I opened my eyes and groaned. What was I going to do? I'd get money and go. Go where? Where no one believed me? Where no one cared? I thought about the documents I had managed to get my hands on. Those were everything I had to go on. On my way into California, I rented a storage locker and placed them in it for safekeeping. Maybe it was time to get them out. I just didn't know.

I heard a faint knock on the bedroom door and Mia's voice.

I analyzed my bubble coverage, which was plentiful and called out that I was in the bath, but covered if she wanted to enter.

The bedroom door opened, and I heard faint footsteps through the bedroom.

"I'll just stand out here," she said. "I don't want to make you uncomfortable."

Too late for that.

"Listen, I don't expect you to believe me or find any reason to hear me out, but my brother's a good guy. His business is protecting people. Sometimes the lines become a little blurred. He should have told you. I don't argue with that, but I just want you to know his intentions are good. He meant well. I've had to come to terms with his secretive ways myself, set boundaries with him. But he's my brother, and I've learned to deal with it. I'll understand if you don't want to. Okay, I'll let you have some peace and quiet. Anyway, have a good night." I'd already heard her beginning to move away from the door.

"Mia?"

"Yeah?"

"Thank you."

I heard her walk out of the bedroom and shut the door. It was the middle of the night, and yet I was wide awake with my mind running wild with questions.

What if this was my one opportunity to find someone who could help? What if I run away from the wrong person? The alarm beeped, signaling the house was secured. That probably meant Luke left. My stomach fell and I cursed myself for caring. There were bigger things to be concerned with. Even though I was more confused than before my presoak, I felt better— less anxious, which was puzzling. I dried off quickly and put some sweatpants and a tee on. I glanced out the window and didn't see Luke's car below. Why did I care?

Wandering out into the hallway, I heard soft music coming from upstairs. Mia must be working again. I didn't want to interrupt, but for once in my life, I wanted to talk to someone. I climbed the stairs to the third floor and decided I'd peek my head into her studio. If she'd already started, I'd go to bed and not worry about it. The door was open and the room was lit up from every direction. I spotted her in the corner in a pair of paint-covered overalls and a hat. She was holding a brush, standing in front of a large canvas that equaled her height.

What I saw both horrified and intrigued me. I saw myself in the painting. Splashes of red dotted the perimeter of the face, but the face I was looking at was mine, and the eyes... The eyes were vacant, haunted.

I knew I'd told myself I'd turn around if she were busy, but I couldn't. I was anchored to the floor, anchored to her process, anchored to her unveiling. I needed to watch her work. I needed to see the layers as they were peeled back, my layers.

Mia's head bobbed up and down slightly, as her brush touched the canvas, bringing swirls of crimson alive next to my hair. Another brush, a different stroke added a streak of black along the base. But the eyes, she wasn't touching the eyes. I didn't even know how long I'd stood there. Nothing shook me from my position. I was mesmerized until I heard her mutter that she had finished. Even with that admission, I still couldn't move. I needed answers. I wanted to know how she saw that in me. I felt so exposed. Not violated, just unmasked by an almost stranger.

There were so many evils in this world, many of which I carried close to my heart, and it was as if her painting caught them all, exposed them all to the world in a violent blaze of color. A shiver ran through me as I watched her clean her brushes. Every so often she'd glance at the piece, and I wondered what she was thinking, what drove her to paint it, to paint me. I didn't have enough courage to ask, not yet. Not to mention I already felt as if I were prying, watching a personal dance between artist and work.

"Hey," Mia's voice was kind. "You okay?"

I looked away from the painting, my eyes focusing on Mia. "How do you know? How did you capture it?"

"I'm sorry?" Mia asked, not following my line of questioning. She wiped her hands on a towel and walked over to me. "You can come in." She bit her lip and held out her hand, which I took. She led me through the studio. There were various sized canvases stacked along different tables, along with tubes of paint, pencil sketches, and other works in different stages of completion.

"It's just..." I began. "I don't know how you captured everything...everything I feel, think."

Mia squeezed my hand before letting it go as we stood in front of the painting. "I apologize for not getting your permission to paint you. I just had to get it on canvas before the inspiration left, literally." Mia stopped herself. "I shouldn't have."

"Please don't apologize. I'm in complete awe. I don't understand how you saw this, all this." I gestured to the emotion rolling off the canvas.

Mia smiled. "It's not as difficult as you might think to read you, Hannah. You wear your emotions for everyone to see, or in some cases, lack of emotion."

"Oh," I whispered.

Mia turned to face me. "Do you know what

bothered my brother more than walking in on Sean and me?"

"What?" I asked, shaking my head.

"Seeing this painting. It wasn't finished when he saw it, but it was the portrait that tore him up. Sean just happens to be the poor guy he'll take it out on. And believe me, he'll take it out on him."

I laughed. "I don't doubt that. He was pretty upset about Sean. I don't think it was the painting."

Mia shook her head. "Nope. That's how I operate. I don't do relationships and sometimes certain things need to be taken care of. I'm sure you can relate. My brother and I don't go there in conversation, but he's well aware of my late-night tendencies for a booty call. So whatever he led you to believe, my dear, is not the case. It was the painting that caught him off-guard. It's you that catches him off-guard."

My mouth was dry with her confession. It was such personal information to share with someone she barely knew. Not to mention, I never would've guessed it. She seemed like the relationship-type girl.

"Sorry. I hope that wasn't too much information," Mia replied, grinning. "I'm pretty open about it, but I'm getting the feeling you're not..."

I shook my head. "I actually..." I stopped speaking and looked back at the painting. "I can't really relate. I've never felt the need for anything to be taken care of, so to speak."

I can't believe I just told an almost stranger

about my bedroom leanings, or lack thereof.

"Oh. I had no idea. I didn't even think..." She reached out and touched my arm. "Sorry. I shouldn't assume everyone is as emotionally bankrupt as I am."

I let out a laugh. "That's impossible."

"What's impossible?"

"You being emotionally bankrupt. I mean look at your work. You capture the very essence of being human, having emotion. You couldn't do that if you were bankrupt."

Mia sighed, "Touché."

Besides, I was the one emotionally bankrupt.

"The eyes. Is that really how you see them, see mine?" I asked, glancing back at the painting.

"At times." She nodded, crossing her arms. "I know there's a lot of pain you're carrying around. I recognize it because I was there once, where you are. I'm sure there are different causes for each of us, but I see it. So did my brother. I'm sure that's what messed him up at Starbucks when he ran into you. He's very perceptive, to a fault. He's got an amazing heart, and he always wants to fix things, fix people."

"Some situations can't be fixed. Some people can't be fixed," I said, pressing my lips together.

"True. And that's something I've been trying to tell him for a long time." She bent down and turned off the music. "Has he told you anything about why he started the business?"

"The security firm?" I asked.

"Yeah."

I shook my head.

"Well, that's his story to share, but I can share my story with you. Maybe that will stop you from running away from us. At least so soon."

Her words were like a blade to the soul. She knew I wanted to run. I really was transparent.

I shook my head and followed her out of the studio, back down to the kitchen.

"I don't know about you, but I need some white tea, or I'll never get to sleep tonight," she said, her voice cheerful.

"Sounds great," I said, sliding onto the stool. "It probably didn't help that I had coffee."

She put a kettle of water on the stove and grabbed loose tea from the pantry, sprinkling it into the infusers.

"My brother filled me in briefly about you. Or at least what he thinks he's learned about you. Sometimes data retrieval and triangulation isn't all it's cracked up to be. Humans are complex beings." She shrugged her shoulders. "I won't pretend to know that I understand your views on anything, your reasons for wanting to hide. But I can tell you that I understand feeling like you can't trust anyone." She poured the boiling water into the mugs and placed one in front of me. I looked at the colorful pieces floating around, imagining what she was going to tell me. Nothing came to mind.

"There's a method to my brother's madness. We all have our ways of dealing with fear. It takes some of us longer than others to come to terms with it," Mia said, sitting next to me.

"Agreed," I said, taking the infuser out of the

mug.

"Our parents were murdered," Mia replied bluntly, her gaze landing on mine. "By our aunt and uncle. More specifically, my dad's brother and sister-in-law were the murderers. Truth be told, we don't even know who all was involved, how many family members. Hence, Fort Knox and my brother's obsession with security."

A lump formed in the back of my throat as grief entered me from every direction. My mind flashed to my sister and my best friend; the loss I'd been doing so well at pushing out, but even with keeping it in the proper compartment, it was daring to expose itself.

"I'm so sorry," I said, my voice hoarse as I attempted to hold back the tears.

"It's okay. It was many years ago. We've had years to work through it. Although, I say work through it rather loosely since apparently my brother and I can't form personal meaningful relationships, for the most part." She smiled, trying to infuse humor, but I felt the pain—understood the pain—she was talking about.

"Grief is a difficult thing to understand," I said.

"I'm not sure it's meant to be understood," she replied. "But it certainly does mold us, doesn't it?"

I nodded, thinking about my mom. I left her, but I couldn't trust her. I couldn't trust anyone. But that didn't make the pain any less. It wasn't like I could just cut them off from my memory. It wasn't like I didn't have good memories to go along with the bad ones.

"I never would've guessed my aunt and uncle could be so evil. Blood relatives willing to kill their own brother and his wife?" Mia shook her head. "It made me think about being human in much different terms. Therapist after therapist and nothing felt better. I felt no better. It was as if language betrayed me. I could find no words, so I began painting, and I've never stopped." Mia let out a sigh before taking a sip of tea.

"And grief for the living. That's almost worse isn't it?" she asked, looking at me.

That was it! That was what she captured in the painting; my grief for the living—the ghosts of my past that wouldn't let go, wouldn't stop following me no matter how far I ran. I thought of my mom and the life I'd left behind. It didn't matter what reason drove me to leave, I still missed them, or the idea of who I wanted them to be.

"Yeah. Grief for the living can be worse," I confessed, taking a sip of my tea and praying that there was a way to leave it all far behind.

CHAPTER TWENTY

Luke

I was at the office, going through paperwork for one of our jobs that had just ended, trying to distract myself from the encounter with Hannah several nights earlier. Work was usually all-absorbing, and that was what I counted on, especially this morning. But I was just exhausted, mentally fatigued. And instead of letting go of Hannah like I should have, I placed a guy on her. Something told me she was about to flee, and the least I could do was make sure that wherever she ran to, she'd arrive safely. What was the old saying? If you love something? I laughed at myself. Loved? Lack of sleep certainly wasn't a stabilizing force in my life.

I turned my attention back to the case I was marking as closed. It had brought us a lot of money, and it had a happy ending. I should be elated. A man we'd been tailing had finally been arrested before anything devastating happened. In my mind, one of the little flaws of our criminal justice system was waiting for the worst-case scenario to occur before any actual law enforcement happened. That was the benefit of hiring private security firms, but how many people could actually afford to do so? Very few.

Stalkers generally got slapped on their hands as if they were just being naughty, and it wasn't until someone was hurt that the law was really enforced. When had a piece of paper ever defended someone who really needed protection? When had it deterred someone who wanted to cause harm to someone else? It was a travesty. The general public only heard of the high-profile celebrity cases, but the truth was that with social media and other ways of creating connections, average citizens were the bulk of reported cases. Unfortunately, because they didn't have the celebrity presence behind them, their cases didn't always end so favorably. And that was exactly what I didn't want to have happen to Hannah. It wasn't a case of stalking so much as attempted kidnapping. Or at least that was my assumption based on the evidence at hand. She knew something that someone wanted kept quiet and people were trying to make that happen. What I needed was to find out more information, but I kept hitting quite a few dead ends. If she would only open up, I'd have a shot.

My laptop beeped, and I saw a status update had just come in from Kenneth about the senator and his mistress. Apparently the wife didn't take very kindly to having the mistress guarded by our team. She was planning on going to the tabloids and didn't care who all went down with her. In my book, she was definitely the one who'd sent the letters to the mistress. The senator still wanted Kenneth working on the case, so we would comply. It was definitely going to make the national news. The senator was going to need a good PR firm too.

My phone rang and I saw Sean's number coming in on the hardline. Did I really want to talk to him?

Not really.

Was I really mad at him about my sister?

Doubtful.

They were both consenting adults. It was just bad timing.

I ignored the call and thought back to the portrait my sister was painting, the one that stopped me in my tracks when I went into her studio. It wasn't completed, but I knew it was Hannah. I had no idea what possessed my sister to paint it, but she was always an amazing visionary when it came to capturing life's moments on canvas. I just wasn't sure how Hannah would feel if she discovered it. Another thing I shouldn't be giving the time of day to, I supposed. I needed to quit thinking of Hannah in terms of personal association. She'd made things quite clear by not returning any of my texts over the last several days. It also didn't help my ego to find out that she hadn't mentioned me once, not once, to Mia. My sister tried to let me down easily, but it didn't work. If I'd heard that about any other woman, I seriously doubted I'd care. But with Hannah, the news was crushing. Crushing enough to make me want a cigarette, and I'd never picked up the habit.

My assistant, Kimberly, stuck her head in the office and smiled. "You look like hell."

"Thanks," I laughed, glancing in her direction. She was an attractive woman with long dark hair and a slim physique. Kimberly was working her way through law school. She worked harder than anyone I knew, and because of that I afforded her the flexibility in her work schedule for classes and studying. I didn't care if she got her work done at noon or midnight; I knew I could count on her to do it, and that was what I valued more than regular hours.

"I've got something rather interesting," she said, bringing an overstuffed folder into view.

I straightened in my seat. "Really?"

"Yeah. I couldn't go to sleep after class last night so I started typing different combinations into RAID…"

I leaned forward and motioned for her to continue. This sounded like a possible break in the case.

"Well, in between making popcorn and watching…"

I raised my brow and folded my arms. She was an amazing sleuth, but she had a tendency to give every single detail on the path to discovery.

"Sorry. Habit. Anyway, I tried hundreds of

word combinations using NLC and nothing until I typed in the word ambush. I mean why that popped into my head, I have no idea. Actually, no. I do know why that popped in my head. I was watching the Discovery Channel and these naked people were worried that they were going to be ambushed by monkeys or some wild creature in the jungle."

I couldn't help but laugh. This was just how Kimberly worked.

"But what that word brought up was an event that occurred over four years ago involving the NLC. And you know your hunch about NLC and the C meaning church?"

I nodded.

"It's not a church. It stands for community. At least according to the Justice Department's papers," she said, sitting down and dropping the folder on the desk with a thud.

"That makes sense with everything I saw. Although, they did have a church at the end of the road," I replied. "Must be for good measure."

"So you went there?" Her brow quirked. "When was this? Never mind. I don't want to know. Actually, I think I know. It was when you had me clear the schedule. Okay, so back to the ambush. This is where it gets interesting. From what I could gather, some members of a very large drug cartel ambushed three NLC leaders. All three died and the cartel members went poof."

"That doesn't make me feel any better about the situation at hand."

"There wasn't anything else that came up. But despite the FBI's assertion, I doubt the cartel just happened to pull the trigger on unsuspecting people. There just might be a connection between at least those three members and the cartel."

Kimberly nodded and continued, "I kept digging and while the top members of the NLC look clean, I was able to trace, rather faintly, an active line between some distant relatives and their propensity to only vacation in Columbia and Mexico. These relatives do not associate with the NLC whatsoever. They don't even live near the compound. I'm sure we can come up with some ideas as to why those are the hot destinations though." She smiled. "But it looks like lodging is always covered because the NLC owns homes in both countries. So these family members may not be members, but they certainly get to enjoy the benefits."

"Interesting." I sat back in the chair and thought about Hannah. She's going to need far more protection than I even imagined. If drug money was involved, the stakes were enormous. And if Hannah had the power to take them down, they would ensure they'd take her down first. "It makes me wonder what happened to the cartel and why they didn't pursue anything else with the NLC, especially with the south of the border family connections."

I knew all too well how it worked with the feds. They were willing to turn the other way on certain events if they had an undercover operation ongoing.

"I know it's not my place, but I find it odd that we are spending so much time, and pardon me for saying, resources on something that isn't on the books," Kimberly said.

"Would you want this on the books? With the information you just found out? I think at this point, it's safer for us all to keep it off the records. And to be candid, I think you've done more than enough. I'll take it over from here."

Kimberly nodded and walked out of my office, pausing at the door. "I can see it in your eyes, Luke. Whoever this girl is, she must be really special." Her eyes connected with mine and she continued. "She's really lucky to have you on her side."

CHAPTER TWENTY-ONE

Hannah

Even though I'd been planning to make a run for it, there was something inside of me slowly shifting. I wasn't able to put my finger on the specific reason, but things were starting to sort themselves out. I don't mean in the sense that rainbows were shooting through the sky and butterflies were following me everywhere I went, but that I was able to get through what I needed to get through without losing my mind. That was key.

I'd worked a total of seven shifts at Buttons without even a hiccup. Not one. I'd managed to memorize most of the men's names, their favorite drinks, and what they enjoyed talking about. I'd even become somewhat fond of a few of the members. I said *a few*.

Some were single men who didn't want to go

to that next step, meaning strip clubs, but still enjoyed a woman's company in a more intimate setting. And then there were what I called the marrieds, which were guys who didn't seem to really understand the concept of idolizing the women they already had at home. However, the more I got to know those men, I actually found myself feeling sorry for them and wanting them to see the light. I thought a gentle reminder here or there about how good they had it wasn't the worst thing I could do. I wanted them to recognize that the life they were missing out on was their own, not the fantastical one that Buttons somehow managed to create. And it was a fantasy! We were a fantasy.

So far, I'd managed to commiserate with men that their corporate job was the worst job in the world and that nobody understood; I'd listened to the couples as they convinced one another it was okay to admire other women, as the wives shot me dirty stares, and I'd also gotten my butt on the swing during *The Great Gatsby* evening. It wasn't so bad and it got me out of having to talk to the clients.

Now, I'm not naïve enough to say that all was peachy in the world of Buttons. And maybe some of the scenarios I created in my head were just to deal with the underlying sleaze factor, but hey! That was an improvement from when I started, namely with the incessant need to take an immediate bath every time I left the place.

It also wasn't like I wasn't paranoid and worried that the NLC would find me. In fact, I knew they would. I just was hoping it would be far into the future and on my own terms. That was what I found insanely amusing about myself, actually; my innate ability to use time to my advantage and adjust, bounce back, and cope with adversity without missing a beat. That, after all, was how I survived living in the NLC commune. How I ignored being told who I was going to love, who I was going to marry. How I learned to forget about what happened to my sister until the time was right.

But was I still looking over my shoulder at every turn? Yes! However, now I did it without thinking, and I didn't let it bog down the rest of my existence. I had finally gotten into a rhythm, knowing full well what I needed to accomplish in order to get me to the next stage, and Buttons was what would get me there. I needed money—plain and simple.

And time, which was turning into my lovely friend, would distort the harshness and reality of the situation, because the longer the time went by where I wasn't bothered by the NLC, the less of a worry that became. Granted, if a letter arrived on my new doorstep or I received a double take from a stranger, the worry level would be off the charts once again. But for now, I felt in control. I knew what I needed and I knew how to get it.

And as long as I didn't let my mind think about Mia's brother, the equation was an uncomplicated one. We hadn't mentioned him since the night he confessed to having me followed and him going to my old address, and I'd planned on keeping it that way. Because in truth, he was too captivating, too enticing. The moment my mind drifted to him, I wanted something more tangible. His chiseled features and piercing green eyes were almost impossible to shake. And if I was being completely honest, his body was out of this world. Or at least how I'd imagined it.

"Hey, girl. Nice work tonight," Liv said, smiling. "Today's payday."

She tossed an envelope in front of me. I really had no idea what to expect since so much was dependent on tips. And it wasn't just the tables I worked. Everyone's tips went into a large pool and then were divided equally between the servers in order to ensure we all tried our best.

"You gonna wait until you're home to check it out?" Liv teased. "The privacy of your own place?" Liv snorted as she opened hers and glanced at the printout. Her expression fell. That didn't seem good.

"What?"

"Let's just say, bringing in some fresh blood must have rejuvenated these guys," she replied.

"How so?"

"Biggest. Check. Ever." Her lips broke into a grin.

"Well, now you've done it." I tore through the envelope and scanned for the amount. "No way."

"Yes way. Aren't you glad you got over whatever it was you had to get over?" She grinned.

I smiled, stuffing the envelope in my bag. "Definitely could get used to this."

I still hadn't advanced to skimpy negligees, but maybe I didn't need to. I glanced down at my cotton pajama bottoms with pink hearts and my white camisole. I grabbed a sweatshirt and slipped it over my head and traded my pajama bottoms for some jean shorts. Time to get out of here.

"You know, somehow you've got the innocent card really figured out. I'd almost believe it if it weren't for something sitting right behind your expression," Liv said, her brow arched.

"What's that supposed to mean?" I asked, bewildered.

She shrugged her shoulders. "Ready to walk out?"

I nodded and looped my bag over my shoulder as we made our way through the dressing room. A cheer erupted from the corner.

"Hannah, we owe you," one of the girls shouted. "I think I'm gonna try rocking some flannel boxers and a t-shirt."

Another woman nodded and started laughing. "Ditto. Who knew?"

I shook my head and waved, as I followed Liv through the bar.

"Sean better be careful or we'll all start showing up in yoga pants and stained sweatshirts," Liv replied, holding the door open.

"Whatever works, right?" I winked at her and turned toward the street, nearly running into Luke.

"Well, have a goodnight," Liv said, as she made her way to the parking lot. But I didn't even respond. I was too caught up with the man standing in front of me.

Luke was no more than six inches from me, dressed in a pair of jeans and a tight fitting black t-shirt. I didn't know a man could look so good in something so basic. I glimpsed the edge of a tattoo sticking out on his left arm and I wanted to rub my fingers over it. What had gotten into me? There was something really hot about it, about him, and I never imagined my body would respond this way. It certainly wasn't something I was used to.

"You haven't returned my texts," Luke's deep voice was soothing as it wrapped around me, his tone pleading for me to look at him.

He reached out, and his hands firmly gripped my upper arms, anchoring me in place. His touch sent a corkscrew of emotion down my spine. His touch was what I'd been craving, dreaming about, but it was exactly what I needed to avoid.

"Yeah. Sorry. I've been busy. Trying to pick up as many shifts as possible." I stared straight in front of me, my gaze focused on his chest, not his eyes. I had to stay away from those suckers. They would be the end of me.

"Which tells me you have no plan to stick around," he murmured more to himself than to me.

"It's not safe. You of all people should know that," I replied, looking into his striking, green eyes. His gaze immediately locked on mine, as if begging for something he knew he would never be able to have.

The longer he stared, the more my body responded, sending waves of warmth through my veins. Feelings that I'd never experienced were pulsing through me at a ridiculous rate and rather than trying to escape, I stayed in his grasp.

"I won't apologize for wanting to keep you safe," Luke said. "But I do apologize for how I went about it. Do you forgive me?"

His straightforwardness nearly knocked me over. There was no beating around the bush, no back and forth, and all I could do in return was offer the same level of directness.

"I do, but I won't forget. I felt violated."

His expression hardened and he pulled his hands away. "Understood."

"You could have just asked what you wanted to find out," I replied, already missing his touch.

"Would you have told me the truth?" he asked, his brow arching.

I felt my cheeks warm. "Probably not."

"What a quandary," he mused.

"I guess it could be for some," I admitted.

"It's late. Why don't you let me drive you to Mia's? At least give me the satisfaction of doing something useful for you that's out in the open."

I nodded, unable to hide my smile. "That's a start."

He gently touched the base of my spine and guided me toward his car. He gave a slight wave at the parking attendant before opening the passenger door for me.

"Chivalry isn't dead?" I teased.

"Would you want it to be?" he asked, as I slid into the seat.

I laughed, shaking my head. His gaze fell to my legs as his eyes moved along my bare skin, which did nothing but excite me.

Luke closed the door and slowly walked around the front of the car. I watched his careful movements as his eyes scanned the lot. He was a man always on alert, which I appreciated. He opened the driver's door and sank into the seat, turning on the engine before he even buckled in. He popped the car into drive and drove off the lot.

Being in such a confined space with Luke was difficult. Really difficult. The light scent of his cologne, soap, or something just Luke filled the air. If he weren't sitting right next to me, I'd probably take a deep, exaggerated breath in to absorb everything about him.

"I don't want you to run away again," Luke said, taking me off guard. "I can protect you much easier if you're here."

"Who said I needed to be protected?" I asked, glancing at him. "I can take care of myself."

"I don't doubt that for a minute, but why chance it? Wouldn't it be nice to have a little peace of mind, knowing that you weren't by yourself in this world?"

I looked out the window as we whipped by the clubs and restaurants, which were shutting down for the night, the lights extinguishing one by one as I thought about his words.

"It's not an alternative that I've given much thought to, honestly," I responded, as he pulled in front of Mia's.

"I'm not asking for an answer this second, but I want you to think about it." He turned off the car. "And I want you to think of something else."

"What's that?" I asked, shifting in my seat.

"Go out with me. One date. Before you leave." His voice was low, pleading.

I let out a sigh.

"Well, that's a first," he joked.

I smiled and turned to look at him, which was a big mistake.

"I'll tell you what," I began. "If you can find a place that is built upon dreams and is filled with nothing but happiness and another existence, then yes, I'll go on a date with you."

Luke smiled and laughed, giving me a sideways glance. "Then I've got just the place."

CHAPTER TWENTY-TWO

Luke

I was standing in line to grab a quick lunch when I got the information over email I'd been waiting for. Donald Jamison was no longer in California. Flight records showed that he'd left L.A. two days after he'd been released, but that didn't lessen my worry about Hannah. My guess was that the NLC wasn't pleased with Donald's ineptness and traded him out for someone new. But who knew if that someone else was already here. These were all things that I wanted to discuss with Hannah, but I knew we weren't there yet.

She had softened slightly toward me. I noticed it in small ways. The way her hand grazed mine and stayed there a second longer than it needed to. The way she looked at me, smiled at me, the fear diminishing. There was no denying the connection we felt, but I could see that she was fighting it every time we were together, which only drove me more insane for her. It was the little things about her that had me completely at her mercy; how her gaze would dip slightly when I smiled at her or when her cheeks would redden when my gaze stayed on her for a beat too long. Those were the moments I couldn't stop thinking about. The moments I wanted more of.

My fear was that the more I dug into her past without her permission, and the longer it went, the less she'd be able to forgive me, both on a personal level and a professional one. But there was something making me take it slow on both accounts, which was my fear of losing her before I had the chance to have her, feel her, against me.

"Sir? Sir? What can I get for you?"

I looked up to see about ten feet between the cashier and me. All of the other customers had already placed their orders and paid while I stood here like an idiot daydreaming. This was definitely not something I was used to. No woman had ever taken up every single thought I had.

I made it to the counter and ordered a burrito, everything on it, for me and two crispy tacos for my sister. We were meeting for lunch so I could fill her in on everything I'd learned about Hannah, and to gauge her ease about being in the same house with someone who's being targeted. I already knew where Mia would stand on the issue, but I thought it was only right to give her an easy out. I could find another place for Hannah.

I walked over to where the orders were called when I saw my sister walk into the restaurant. She gave me a quick wave and pointed at a corner table near the window. I nodded and grabbed our tray of food.

Mia looked refreshed. It was a familiar expression, one that usually appeared after she'd finished a piece. I placed the tray on our table and smiled.

"Hey, big brother," she said, hopping up and giving me a quick hug.

"How are you doing?" I asked, sliding into my seat.

"Better than you I'd say. You look like shit." She grinned right before taking a bite of a taco.

"Appreciate it. Wish I could say the same of you, but you look great."

"I finished a piece. I'm sure you know which one I'm talking about. And I started another. Hannah's agreed to let me paint a series. At first, she wanted nothing to do with it. Not a model, blah, blah. But once I explained to her how easy it would be, she finally agreed. Actually, I think it was the modeling fee that helped persuade her."

"Ah." I nodded. "Another way to stockpile money for when she's ready to hit the road."

Mia nodded sympathetically. "Yeah. Probably so."

"Do you think she's a flight risk?" I asked.

My sister burst into laughter.

"Sorry. Lack of sleep."

"Glad you apologized because I didn't want to have to beat your ass. You and I both know she's

201

not just a client, a flight risk. And you better figure out which way you want to go with her because it's one or the other with her. She can't be treated like your past girlfriends."

"I haven't had girlfriends. You know I don't do girlfriends."

"Exactly. That's my point. She's too—" my sister stopped.

"She's too what?" I prompted.

"Nothing. I don't want to say. It's not my place."

"Oh, no. You can't stop and start like that. She's too what?" I asked, digging my fork into the burrito.

My sister looked at me, her brows furrowed. "Inexperienced."

And the water continued to be muddied.

"You okay over there?" she laughed.

I nodded and took a bite of the burrito. "Listen, I've found out some more information about the group she used to be involved with. There's some evidence that ties the NLC and at least one drug cartel together. I think she found out something about it and they know that she knows. At least that's my guess."

"Shit. Are you gonna get the feds involved?" Mia asked.

I shook my head. "Not yet. I need her cooperation. And there are too many loose ends that I need to follow."

"Poor thing. No wonder she's scared shitless."

"I think she'd probably clobber you if she heard you say that." I smiled.

"You've got it bad. I've never seen you like this."

Ignoring her, I continued, "You okay with her staying at your place? I mean if you actually used the security system I set up for you, everything should be just fine. But getting you to do that is an entirely different story."

"She needs somewhere to be," Mia said, her expression softening. "And I can't let the subject of my paintings run off. I'll see about dragging it out. The one thing I've learned about her is that she never wants to let anyone down. Remember that."

I smiled. "Thanks. I've gotta head to San Antonio tonight. New client."

"A real client?" she teased.

"Yes. It's a paying client. Thanks for the concern. But not nearly as interesting of a case as Hannah's."

Swallowing another bite of the burrito, I began telling my sister everything that I'd uncovered about Hannah and the NLC's mysterious connection to the drug world.

CHAPTER TWENTY-THREE

Hannah

Several days had gone by and I'd heard nothing from Luke. Apparently, finding a place to meet my specifications was just as hard as I'd predicted, which was what I wanted, right? Pick a place that didn't exist so I didn't go out with him. But the truth was I was hugely disappointed. I had two days off from Buttons, today and tomorrow, and both were taken up with modeling for Mia. I stayed in my bed and stretched out my legs, feeling the cool crispness of the sheets against my skin. There were plenty of days where I just wanted to hide from everything and stay in bed. Today was one of those days. It had been extremely uneventful since moving into Mia's home and that had me worried. The NLC wouldn't let me off this easily, not with everything I knew.

Yeah. This was definitely a day I wanted to stay in bed. I let out a sigh and shifted onto my side, grabbing my cell. My heart sped up when I saw there was finally a text on it. There were only two people who would text me. One was upstairs and the other was Luke. I quickly opened the message.

Sorry for the delay. I was out of town and your request took a bit of time. I've got the perfect place all lined up. I'll pick you up tomorrow at eleven.

My heart pumped with excitement as I reread his message. I wondered where he was taking me, but then my mind raced with worry. Where was this going? It couldn't go anywhere. But I wanted it to so badly. And then I thought about Mia. I had promised her I'd sit there for her all day tomorrow.

I promised your sister that I'd help her with something tomorrow. I can't back out. I'm so sorry. Is there another day?

I actually felt relieved sending that message. This wasn't what I needed to do. What I needed to do was continue stockpiling my money in preparation to leave.

Nice try. Mia's fine with it. I'll see you at eleven.

My heart fluttered, and I texted back.

Looking forward to it.

He texted back.

Sure you are.

I tossed my phone on the bed and let out a laugh. This would be good. We'd go out. He'd see how boring I was, and then he'd no longer feel the need to interfere. Easy as that. I threw off the covers and walked into the bathroom to brush my teeth. I heard Mia in the kitchen, grinding coffee beans. There was something so easy about living here. I didn't feel out of place. I felt safe, and I felt like I fit in without any judgment.

I'd felt nothing but judged back at home. I always felt out of place, slightly out of step with everyone else. And no matter what I did, I never felt comfortable in my own skin, and that was a horrible feeling. I assumed it was because I didn't really know who I was, but the longer I was away, I realized I knew exactly who I was. But the problem was that I knew there was no place for me in the only world I'd known. Scary thought.

I tossed my toothbrush on the counter and decided on a cup of coffee before a shower. Then I could find out what Mia wanted me to wear for our little session. I had to admit there was a tiny part of me that was excited about being painted. This would be considered so taboo back at home. Art was considered a frivolous commodity. But when I looked at Mia's paintings, I knew her works were an expression of being, of existing, in a world that made no sense. Her paintings provided a feeling of empowerment, and that certainly wouldn't be what anyone in the NLC would want its members to feel.

"Good morning," Mia said, pouring a cup of coffee. "Want some oatmeal?"

"Sounds great. Thank you." I grabbed a mug and poured myself a cup of coffee as Mia scooped the grains into the bowl and added water.

"Today's going to be amazing. I can feel it."

"You're going to have to tell me what to do every step of the way. I've never done anything remotely like this. We didn't even have school pictures," I almost snorted.

"That's not a completely bad thing," she joked.

"True." I took a sip of coffee. "So what's my wardrobe?"

"I wanted to start with the most difficult one so you'd see even the most complicated session is no big deal." She smiled.

"So says the woman on the other end of the brush."

"Seriously. You'll see. There's a boutique down the street I thought we could hit up. I called down already and asked them to pull some dresses that fit the feel I'm going for."

I took a deep breath in. "Okay. I'll follow your lead."

The microwave beeped and Mia took the bowl of oatmeal out and placed it in front of me.

"Eat up. It's going to be grueling," she teased. "I'll go hop in the shower."

I grinned and nodded as she wandered down the hall. This was going to be fun and getting paid on my off day didn't hurt either. I quickly downed my oatmeal and went to get ready. It wasn't until I hopped out of the shower and got dressed that I saw another text had come over my phone. I wondered what else Luke had to say. Maybe he was cancelling. I picked up my phone and clicked on the message, nearly dropping my phone the moment I saw the words.

You can run but you can't hide

I didn't recognize the area code, but I didn't need to. They'd found me. Again. There was no playing pretend in my life. What few moments of relief I had were few and far between. My hands trembled as I put the phone on the nightstand. I didn't understand how they got the number. Did that mean they knew where I was staying? Or were they trying to flush me out, hoping I'd make a mistake so they could find my location.

"You ready?" Mia asked, knocking gently on my door.

Heat began rolling up my neck, settling in my cheeks. I wanted to tell her.

But I didn't.

"I'm ready," I said, opening the door, trying to sound as bright and cheery as possible.

"Well, you seem extremely happy."

Damn! I went too far. I wasn't a very good actress. My mind flashed to the plans I had with her brother and was thrilled I at least had an excuse. "I'm looking forward to today and tomorrow."

Mia grinned. "Enough said."

I followed her down the stairs and she stopped in front of the door but didn't open it. She grabbed a bag of supplies. "I need to confess something."

"What's that?" I asked.

"It's not going to be just you and me today."

My heart fluttered at the thought of Luke joining us.

"Who else will be there?"

She twisted her lips and glanced out the window.

"My brother's intentions are good. Please don't get the wrong idea. He's worried about you, about me being with you."

"Okay..."

"So, he's got one of his guys on us. He promised it would only be for a few weeks. He figured he'd let me tell you so that you wouldn't get mad at him and cancel your date tomorrow."

I laughed.

This was another example about my theory on people's coping abilities. We could pretend that things weren't as bad as they were and let time essentially dampen the fear. Yesterday I would have been upset because I'd convinced myself things had gotten better. I let time play its cruel trick on me, letting me think I was in control. Today, reality hit me like hammer to the toe. There was no escaping my reality, and I was grateful to have an extra pair of eyes watching over Mia and me.

"I'm glad it was you who delivered the message," I replied, smiling.

She opened the door and waved for the stranger who was standing on the sidewalk to come over to us.

"This is Mitch," Mia said. "He's been with my brother's firm forever. Since the beginning, right?"

Mitch nodded, keeping his stern expression in place. I was surprised Mia wasn't able to crack it.

"Nice to meet you," I said, as I walked outside.

"Pleasure is mine." He took a step back and I was impressed with his size. He had to be at least a foot taller than me, and I wasn't particularly short at five-foot-seven. He was dressed in a dark suit and wore aviator shades.

"Won't he stick out like a sore thumb everywhere we go? He looks like secret service on steroids," I asked Mia.

"My brother wanted the message to be loud and clear to whoever's going to try to say hi to you next."

I nodded and followed her down the stairs with Mitch close behind.

"We'll see which dress feels the best, and then we'll walk over to this amazing botanical garden that's about two blocks away. It's a hidden gem in this town. The white camellias are gorgeous right now, and I think if we can find something like a vivid red to put you in, it will be spectacular."

Mia stopped in front of a storefront that

looked like a cross between bohemian and vintage. I'd never been able to splurge on anything other than the basics, but I'd always dreamed of being able to dress in a way that made a statement.

"I'll be stationed here if you need anything," Mitch replied, his expression unchanged. He stood next to the entrance, and I couldn't help but chuckle once I turned around. He definitely wouldn't be the store's idea of a welcoming committee.

"Hey, girl," a woman from behind the counter crooned.

"Morning, Melanie," Mia sang, giving her a quick kiss on each cheek. "This is my friend, roommate, and latest victim, Hannah."

"She's lovely. I can see why you'd want to paint her," Melanie said, walking over to greet me. Her lips began to make their way to my cheek and I froze in place, but Mia's laughter somehow put me at ease, and I reciprocated the air kiss before turning to teasingly glare at Mia.

"Melanie works in sculpture," Mia said.

"But to pay the bills I work in this lovely establishment," Melanie informed me. "But enough about the struggling artist. I have several lovely gowns for you. I've got mermaid and empire pulled out. They're hanging in the back dressing room," Melanie said, pointing toward the hall. "I'll let you two be."

"Thanks, Melanie," Mia replied, grabbing my hand. "This should be easy enough."

When we got to the dressing room I was

beyond dazzled with the selection. It seemed like there was every shade of red imaginable in our small dressing room, and I wanted them all.

"I think this might be the one," Mia said, handling a flowing, red dress with a neckline that was a deep v. "Beautiful. Look at this detail."

I held it up and she took a step back. "Yep. Gotta try it on," she said, smiling.

Mia began taking it off the hanger as I slipped my shirt over my head. She helped bring the dress over my shoulders as I felt the fabric fall around me. Working my shorts off, I flung them in the corner and glanced down, shocked by the amount of skin that was showing.

"Perfection," Mia whispered.

I looked in the mirror in awe as I imagined another life, another way of existing where I would slip this on for an evening.

"You like?" Mia asked.

"It's perfect."

"Well, that was the easiest wardrobe selection in my career. You might as well keep it on and we'll just keep your clothes here for after. Melanie lets me borrow the merchandise. Although, I think if my brother saw you in that dress he'd buy it for you."

My chest tightened when she mentioned her brother, but all I did was laugh.

"We found it," Mia told Melanie as I followed her back into the shop. "Mind if I keep these here?"

"That is the one, isn't it?" Melanie said, nodding in response to Mia's question.

"Exquisite."

"Thank you," I muttered, a little unnerved by the amount of attention. "I just realized I'm going to have to walk to the garden in this."

"Don't give it another thought. It's L.A. No one will think twice. They'll probably think you're famous and it's their fault for not knowing who you are."

I laughed as we walked outside to greet Mitch, who looked like he hadn't moved a muscle, and all three of us began walking down the sidewalk. Regardless of what Mia had said, I was sure we were quite a sight.

"Okay. Here we are," she replied, standing in front of a gated entrance. "They're closed to the public today so we've got the place to ourselves." She pressed a button on the gate and a woman's voice greeted us.

"It's Mia."

"Thought it might be," the lady replied, as the lock clicked.

The gardens were absolutely gorgeous. It was amazing to think that this many things could be blooming at this time of year. It definitely wasn't like this back at home.

Home. I needed to quit saying that. I took a deep breath and smelled the fresh scent of foliage and flowers as I followed the path through the gardens alongside the Victorian home.

"I think we'll head to the back," Mia explained.

"Sounds good to me," I laughed.

The front was beautifully manicured, but the

backyard was more natural. There was a wildness about the landscape, and the flowering shrubs and meandering paths only added to the mystery that surrounded the space.

"I was thinking we'd start over there," she said, pointing to the far corner. She set her bag down and began grabbing equipment out of it. "If we can tuck you in there, make it look like you're coming out of the woods..."

"That would be amazing," I finished

"Let's get your shoes off. Do you mind?" she asked.

I flung off my flip-flops and laughed, realizing I'd never even given my shoes a thought. They really wouldn't have worked. "Good call."

Working with Mia turned into such fun as she pulled me in one direction and then tugged me in the other. Many of the shots had me wrapped within the greenery, and I couldn't even imagine what the images might look like. After hours that felt like minutes, Mia surprised me with her announcement.

"One last shot and I think we've got enough for this session."

"I'll give it my all," I promised. "And I'll be the first to admit that I'm happy you talked me into it."

"I knew it. Okay, flip your head over and work your fingers through your hair," Mia instructed.

I started laughing as I followed her directions and worked my fingers through the blond strands. There was something about the sea air that made my hair tangle more easily.

This was the last shot of the afternoon, and I was a cross between exhausted and disappointed. I'd had far more fun than I thought I ever would, and it took my cares completely away. Plus, it was added money. During all of these shots with Mia, it somehow made me reflect on what I needed to do. I knew tomorrow I would tell Luke everything, including about the text I got today. It was time to stop running and start facing my reality. But I didn't quite want the fantasy to end.

As I flipped my head back over again, my breath caught as I saw Luke standing next to his sister, taking me in, his eyes devouring me with such desire my legs almost gave out.

My gaze darted from his, but it was too late. He'd cast his spell on me.

"Beautiful. Absolutely beautiful," he murmured, as Mia gave me the last few instructions, but I barely heard her. His words shook me to my core. I worked on autopilot as I fought down the emotions running through me as Luke looked on. The way he looked at me held such promise for something more, but I refused to get my hopes up.

"We did it," Mia announced, hopping on her toes. "I can't wait to begin painting. I only use the photographs to capture certain aspects. I'm no photographer. In fact, I suck so horribly that no one but me will get to see these."

"That's completely unfair," I groaned. "I had counted on getting to see them all afternoon."

"You'll get to see my paintings as long as you

stick around. I promise, but you should let my brother capture you with the lens. I bet it would be breathtaking."

I glanced at Luke and his gaze hardened before he looked away. He obviously didn't like being put on the spot by his sister.

"Will you be needing anything else with Hannah?" Luke asked his sister.

Mia looked amused as she watched her brother. She shook her head and flashed a smile in my direction. "I do need to return the dress to the boutique."

Luke shook his head. "No. I don't want her to change. It'll work well for where I want to take her tonight. Tell Melanie I'll cover it."

My heart fluttered as his gaze fell to mine, and I wondered how on earth I'd be able to resist him.

CHAPTER TWENTY-FOUR

Luke

"Anything out of the ordinary?" I asked Mitch.

He took a sip of coffee and shook his head. "Nothing, sir. They're around the corner. While Hannah was taking a break, Mia told me this would be the last group of shots."

"Is that so?" I glanced behind the house and saw my sister. "I'll take over from here, Mitch. You can go home now."

"Thank you, Mr. Fletcher. Call me if you need anything."

"Will do."

Mitch walked away as I slowly made my way over to where my sister was kneeling down, adjusting her camera. She glanced at me and beamed as she pointed toward a pergola. My gaze followed her finger and my heart nearly stopped. Hannah had her head flipped over, her blond hair flowing as her fingertips gently teased the strands. Her body was wrapped in a crimson dress that hugged every curve, leaving very little to the imagination.

She flipped her head back up, her gaze catching mine.

"Beautiful. Absolutely beautiful." I hadn't meant to say it aloud, but she literally took my breath away.

My sister began taking more shots, and I watched how Hannah's gaze teased the camera. With every movement of her hips, swing of her arms, all I could think of was holding her tight. It took everything I had not to rush over to where she stood and press my mouth against hers. It was unfair of me to assume that she'd even want that.

I had our plans all set for tomorrow, but the idea of spending tonight with her was all I could think about. There had to be a way to convince her to have dinner with me. Not even hearing what my sister and Hannah were talking about I interrupted, "Will you be needing anything else with Hannah?"

"I do need to return the dress to the boutique." Mia grinned at me, completely amused.

"No. I don't want her to change. It'll work well for where I want to take her tonight. Tell Melanie I'll cover it."

Hannah's eyes fell to the ground, and I wondered if I was too forward, too presumptuous. I hadn't even asked her.

"Whatever your plans are, I hope dinner is somehow included," Hannah replied, her eyes meeting mine as she took a step forward.

Mia quickly gathered her things and gave me a quick hug and whispered next to my ear. "Be careful," before turning to wave goodbye to Hannah.

"Thanks for such a great start," Mia said. "I'll see ya back at the house."

Hannah nodded but her gaze quickly connected with mine as Mia walked away. Hannah looked like she wanted to tell me something, like there was something bothering her. I hoped it wasn't about tomorrow. God, how I hoped that wasn't it.

"You are absolutely radiant in front of the lens," I said. What I wouldn't give to get her in front of my camera, but there was no way she would agree. I already knew that.

"Thank you. It turned out to be really fun. I can't wait to see what your sister does..." Hannah's voice trailed off as she slid into her flip-flops. She was only a foot away, and the breeze carried a light floral scent that smelled as wonderful as I'd imagined. Hannah smiled and glanced at the house behind me. "Such a great location."

"It is. You should see it in the summer. There really is nowhere else like it." I slid my hand along her waist. As innocent as the gesture might be, I was unable to help myself from touching her. Her body tensed, but she didn't pull away. Instead, she gathered the long skirt of her dress in her hand and looked up at me, her big brown eyes curious. My gaze fell to her lips, but her words interrupted my plan.

"Is this your way of getting out of tomorrow?" she teased.

I grinned and shook my head, taking a step back. I needed to get a hold of myself, but it was pure agony being so close to her and not being able to do what I wanted to do.

"Far from it," I answered, leading her to my car that was parked out front. I opened the passenger door and watched her climb in, my eyes glimpsing her naked legs.

Closing the door, I grabbed my phone and quickly made a call to ensure a table would be ready for us.

I felt her gaze on me as I slid onto the seat.

"All set for dinner. I hope you like seafood."

"I love it," she said, her smile fading.

"Everything okay?" I asked, putting the car in gear.

She sighed and glanced out the window. "Actually, no."

Her answer took me by surprise. "You want to tell me about it?"

I glimpsed a slight tremble of her hand, and without thinking, I linked my free hand with hers.

"Not yet."

We drove along the coast, mostly silent as Hannah looked out the window. I felt her body tense more and more, and I worried I shouldn't have made her come to dinner.

I turned the car into the parking lot of the restaurant and parked. It was set on a cliff and on a normal night, the view would be the focus of dinner. Not tonight.

Hannah's eyes were filled with dread and it tore me up inside to see such pain set so deep within her. I wanted so badly to take away all of her hurt, but I knew that was impossible. Giving up sorrow was never that easy. Instead, I traced my fingers along her arm. Her breath caught and she shifted slightly in the seat.

"Ready to go in?" I asked.

"I am." She gave me a quick look over her shoulder as she climbed out of the car. "And I'm starved," she added.

I stepped out of the car and watched as she stood by the edge of the cliff, watching the waves crash into the boulders. There was a long stretch of beach that was framed by these awesome cliffs. I had hoped to take her for a walk later, but now I wasn't so sure. I walked up behind Hannah and slid my fingers along her shoulder. Feeling her body tremble slightly, she turned to face me. Her eyes glistened as she dotted away the tears with her fingertips.

"Sorry. Something caught me off guard..." she stopped and turned to face me. "Have you ever wanted a do over?"

"Many times," I said, wiping away the stray tears that stained her cheeks. I knew not to press. I needed to trust that she would tell me, that she would trust me eventually.

She bit her lip and glanced over my shoulder

toward the restaurant.

"Ready?" I asked.

She nodded as I slipped my hand into hers. As we walked in silence toward the restaurant, I thought about my parents, the loss I felt every day for them, the grief that never subsided and the anger toward whoever wanted them gone. It was that same loss I sensed in Hannah. Someone she loved was ripped away from her. There was more to Hannah's story than what I'd been able to dig up, and I wasn't sure which ghosts were worse for her.

I opened the door and she walked through it, letting go of my hand.

"Mr. Fletcher, it's nice to see you again." The hostess flashed me a warm smile, but it slipped slightly as she glimpsed Hannah. She grabbed two menus and motioned for us to follow. The restaurant was perched on the cliff overlooking the ocean, and the architecture took full advantage of that feature with windows facing every direction. A koi pond was centered in the middle of the restaurant, which the hostess led us around, and I caught Hannah slowing to take a peek. The waitress set the menus down and pulled out the chair for Hannah. I took a seat and thanked the hostess before she left.

"Gorgeous views," Hannah said, scanning the sunset. "Sometimes I imagine making a life for myself in California and then I wake up."

"Maybe I can help you make that a reality," I replied, holding her gaze.

The sommelier appeared and Hannah looked

relieved to have the interruption.

"Would you care for wine this evening?"

I looked at Hannah and raised a brow. She glanced at me and blushed. "Whatever is fine."

"We'll take a bottle of the Merlot, Harlow's Vineyard," I responded.

"Very nice selection." The sommelier smiled and walked away.

"Why are you so interested in helping me?" Hannah asked, bringing her gaze to meet mine.

"I like you."

"You don't know me," Hannah replied, taking a sip of water. My gaze strayed down her collarbone, and I forced myself to look away. But her skin was intoxicating. She was intoxicating.

"I know you enough to know I'd like to get to know you more," I replied, returning my gaze to hers. "So let's start from the beginning."

CHAPTER TWENTY-FIVE

Hannah

I took a sip of the wine and glanced at Luke. The sound of other diners echoed through the space, giving us a sense of privacy.

"Do you not like it?" Luke's deep voice washed over me.

"No. Yes. It's good, nice flavor," I replied, feeling the connection deepen between us.

Luke smirked and sat back in the chair. The intensity that his gaze held made my body react, just a look from Luke made my body sizzle.

"What's your favorite drink? Would you like a cocktail instead?" he asked.

"No. This is wonderful." I took another sip to prove my point.

Luke leaned forward, his gaze steadying on mine. "What do you feel comfortable telling me?"

My body began feeling warm, and I glanced at

my almost empty glass of wine. Luke still had most of his in the glass.

The server came to our table and Luke ordered our meals.

"I can keep you safe," Luke began. "But there will come a point when you will get tired of running, tired of always looking over your shoulder."

"How can you be so sure that you can keep me safe?" I asked.

"It's what I do," he replied. "But if you open up to me, it would make my job a hell of a lot easier."

My stomach knotted. Had I been confusing his intentions? Maybe I was just a pity case to satisfy his do-gooding tendencies.

"Is this all part of the job? Something you do with every client?"

"Which part?" he asked.

"Dinner."

I caught a glimpse of mischief in his green eyes as he debated what to say, and before I had a chance to say no to more wine, the sommelier refilled my glass.

"I may meet with potential clients over dinner, if it suits their schedule," he replied, a bit of a smile tracing his lips.

The sting of his words surprised me, but I wasn't sure what I'd expected.

"I don't really think that's what you're asking, though," he continued, his eyes amused.

I saw desire in his eyes. The same desire I felt. My stomach knotted as his eyes darkened with the knowledge of what he did to me.

"You seem like you have it all together," I said at last. "And I can't fathom why you'd want to spend time with someone who, well, doesn't."

Luke smiled and reached over to my hand and held it across the table. "I'll let you in on a little secret."

"What's that?" I asked, leaning forward.

"I don't have my shit together. Not at all."

I laughed as he squeezed my hand gently before letting go.

"You could've fooled me," I replied, glancing around the restaurant.

"I'm good at what I do. No doubt about it. Professionally, things came together for me. But personally? Not a chance." He took a sip of wine and studied me. His gaze darkened. "There's something about you that I think can change that for me, if you stop running."

I was frozen in place by his gaze and the feelings shooting through me. I shook my head.

"I'm afraid of what they'll do to me," I whispered.

Luke pressed his lips together and let out a sigh. "I know. But Hannah, what are you going to do when you get tired of running? They'll still be out there, unless you deal with it, deal with them."

"I know you're right. But I've barely had time to come to terms with anything and..."

The waiter placed our meals down and asked if we'd like anything else. We both shook our heads, and I glanced back at Luke, his eyes still on me.

"And I know there is no winning with these people," I finished.

"How much has my sister told you about our background?" he asked, taking me off guard.

"She told me that your parents had been murdered by family."

He nodded. "That's partially true."

"What do you mean?"

"The people who ordered their deaths are still out there. We don't know who they are or why they targeted my family."

"I thought your aunt and uncle?" I stopped myself.

"They carried out the act, the actual murders," he replied, his gaze darkening. "But according to them, someone else made them do it."

"How can you make someone commit murder?"

"Exactly my thought, but if I were to believe what my aunt and uncle said, they were doing it to save themselves, their own family. They botched the job, actually, but they never told the authorities who ordered them to do it. They were too fearful for their children's lives to say anything more so they were sentenced to prison and that's where they've stayed."

"How so?" I asked, my mouth feeling extremely parched.

"We were supposed to be in the house when it caught fire. For some reason, my mom wanted me to take Mia to get a Blizzard, just out of the blue at ten o'clock at night. I didn't want to, but she wouldn't let up so I finally did. We came back to a house in flames."

"I'm so sorry," I whispered. "How'd your aunt and uncle get caught?"

"A series of mistakes led the authorities straight to my aunt and uncle."

"That's why you're so protective of Mia..."

"I'd be far more protective if she'd let me, but she's tired of running. She wanted to live normally. Who wouldn't? My job has allowed me to channel all of my energy into protecting people. I couldn't save my parents, but I can save others. I can help you."

"There are so many people involved," I said, taking a bite of halibut. It was delicious even though I no longer felt like eating. "It seems impossible to put together all the pieces."

"Why do you think you need to?" Luke asked.

"It won't make sense unless I can prove what I think is going on."

"That's usually the job for the authorities," he offered.

"It worked well for you," I said, without realizing it. "Sorry. That came out wrong. I didn't—"

"No need to apologize. I know exactly what you mean. But what makes you so certain you can get the proof you need?"

"I have most of it already."

"And that's why they want you alive?"

I nodded. "But I can tell you there are just as many minutes in the day when I fantasize about leaving it all behind, not trying to bring any justice about, just wanting to hide and start over."

"You don't have to go through this alone."

I didn't answer. I wanted to believe him, but everyone I'd ever trusted turned out to be a monster in disguise.

"Let me try another way..." Luke glanced out the window before returning his steely gaze to mine. "Running into you at the Starbucks was meant to happen. Just like taking my sister out for a Blizzard was fate stepping in. Let fate step in, Hannah. Don't go at this alone." The muscle in his jaw tensed as he waited for my reaction.

My heart was pounding but not as much as my head. The feeling of wanting to flee was still at the surface of every thought, but as I looked into Luke's eyes I knew I belonged exactly where I was tonight. I wanted to believe there was a way out of this mess, and he made me feel like there was.

"Remember how you promised to go on a date with me if I could find a place that was built upon dreams and filled with nothing but happiness?"

I nodded, smiling. "I didn't actually think you'd come up with a place."

"Ouch," he laughed. "How about starting now, we just enjoy our date tonight? Put everything else aside until another day?"

"So tonight is a date?" I grinned.

"I thought that was rather obvious."

"You've seen where I've come from. I wouldn't assume anything is that obvious," I giggled, finishing off my second glass of wine.

"Speaking of that, how do you like living with my sister?" Luke asked.

"It's amazing. She's amazing."

"She is."

"So how'd that whole thing with Sean go over?" I enjoyed what the wine had done to me. It loosened me up. Anything that popped into my mind had no problem making its way out.

He smiled, taking another bite of his meal. "She's an adult. It shouldn't bother me."

"But it did," I finished for him.

"Yeah. It wasn't a highlight for me. But truthfully, they're both looking for the same thing."

"Which is?" I prompted.

"Nothing with meaning."

"Wow. That's sad. I can't imagine," I muttered.

His eyes flicked to mine. "Relationships aren't for everyone."

"Are they for you?" I asked.

Giddiness floated through me right before it was quickly squashed with the look in his eyes. I felt like I sputtered and stalled all in one fluid motion, and he hadn't even uttered a word.

"They haven't been my thing in the past, but I think I'm starting to see the light... How about you?"

And we're off.

"I've never had a serious relationship, in the normal sense."

"How about the abnormal sense?" His brow arched.

"I was engaged."

His expression fell and confusion filled his eyes.

"But I have a feeling the expectations are different in my old community. There were certain limitations and expectations. It was arranged."

This made him smile, his gaze intensified.

"Limitations?"

"I think you can imagine what I'm saying," I said, enjoying the power I seemed to suddenly have over this man. My candidness rendered him speechless and I loved every second of it.

"In other news, I'm thinking about getting a new car. Well, a new old car," I replied, beaming.

"Tell me it's not going to have as much character as your truck."

I laughed and nodded. "Actually, I'd say more. It's another truck, but this one's a '77 Ford Ranger."

"Where do you find these beasts?"

"Craigslist," I replied. "Have you heard of it?"

"I suppose there's no talking you out of it."

"Not a chance. My other one got me all the way across the country and would still be chugging along if it hadn't been for the tampering. I just don't see the point in spending lots of money on something that just moves me from one place to another."

The waiter came and removed our plates, asking if we'd like any dessert. I shook my head and the server left to get the check. My heart fell knowing that meant the evening was winding down. I didn't want it to be over. Things were just starting to feel normal, no matter how make-believe.

"Thank you for having dinner with me," Luke replied, as he exchanged his credit card for the bill.

"Did I have a choice?" I teased.

"Probably not."

"I really enjoyed it, choice or not." I smiled. "And I think that wine has gotten the best of me."

"Is that so?" He signed the receipt and let out a sigh as he glanced outside.

"I feel very relaxed," I confessed.

"Then my work here is done." He stood up and walked over to my chair, his gaze fastening on mine. Taking my hand in his, he led me through the restaurant, but instead of walking through the lobby, he took me to a side door and pushed it open.

"I'm not quite ready to say goodnight," he said smiling, and a wave of excitement came rushing through me.

I walked out with him onto the large wooden deck, toward a steep, wooden staircase that led down the rocky cliff, spilling onto the sandy beach.

"Do you mind?" he asked.

"Not at all." I looked up at him. "I didn't want the night to end, not yet anyway."

His smile lit something inside of me that I didn't even understand, a way of being, of existing. He made me think of the future and the after all of this, and that wasn't something I'd ever allowed myself to do. I always stayed in the now to avoid disappointment.

"I can just imagine capturing you on the beach, a storm off in the distance..." his words trailed away as he helped me down to the sandy beach. My stomach tightened as his words settled over me and I imagined the same.

"I'm sure you're referring to your photography." I smiled, his eyes brightening as he led me toward the waves.

"What else would I have been referring to?" He feigned innocence.

I went to speak, but I couldn't. It felt as if he was peeling layer after layer from my soul, and I wanted that. For once, I wanted to be exposed.

"I want to help you, Hannah. I can help you... If you would just trust me, trust my sister." He grabbed my wrist, pulling me into him.

My palms rested flat on his chest as I watched the waves crash in the distance and slowly roll onto the beach. The smell of the sea surrounded us, and I wanted this to be my home. It felt right. But it wasn't safe.

My mind wandered to the girls back at Nancy's house. Many of them had been running a lot longer than me. I remembered their tired eyes, but their absolute resolve to conquer their particular plight. I wondered how Rikki was doing, if she'd managed to leave Nancy's yet. I scanned the water and the seabirds attempting to catch dinner and thought about the fairness of life.

I barely rolled into California and managed to fall into a job that got me out of Nancy's almost instantly. I landed in a house that was beyond my wildest dreams, and now I stood next to a man who was not only exquisite but had a heart of gold. He was willing to stand by my side and help me face whatever was in front of me, if I'd let him. Life wasn't fair, and I felt so undeserving of it all because I was still running. I hadn't made the problem go away. I didn't stop the men from doing what they were going to do or what they did.

"You doing okay?" Luke asked, his voice gentle. "You look like you're a thousand miles away."

"A few thousand for sure," I confessed.

"You want to talk about it?" he asked, his hands slipping into his pockets.

"Life's not fair," I said, turning toward him.

He shook his head. "Nope. It's definitely not fair."

I let out a sigh and took another step toward him. The way he looked at me made me want him even more. We were less than a foot from each other, and the energy running between us was profound. The way his green eyes darkened told me he was feeling it too.

"I just feel so undeserving," I whispered, thinking back to everyone who I'd left behind and how little I'd done to help.

"Wait. You're thinking about how unfair life is to everyone else?" Luke's voice deepened. "I thought you were referring to how unfair life had been to you."

"I've had it lucky. I mean look where I am," I

said, motioning to the beach around me. "The people back at home. Sorry. I have to quit referring to it as home. But anyway, they can't even imagine life another way. They don't know what the NLC is actually capable of, that they are all pawns. And the girls I left behind back at Nancy's had been scrounging everything they had to get out of there for weeks, months even, and then somehow I just ran into the right people."

"And you're running from some very dangerous ones," he replied.

"I know, but..."

"You *are* deserving. In fact, you deserve so much more," Luke whispered, his hands circling my waist. "You deserve to be able to imagine life another way."

I looked into his eyes as his words etched through the many layers of guilt and confusion that had become my comfort. My gaze fell to his mouth as he spoke and my mind ran wild with possibilities.

"You aren't responsible for what's happened to the people back at home or out here. You're doing the best you can and that's all you can ask of yourself," he murmured.

I placed my hand on his shoulder as I leaned my body against his. "How do you know the right thing to say?" I asked, almost breathless.

"Years of therapy." He smiled, pressing his forehead against mine, looking down at me.

The rawness of the emotions that swirled through my body was nothing compared to the feelings of desire I had for this man. The heat from his body rolled through mine, and I wanted nothing more than to be kissed. He ran his fingers along my spine as I felt my pulse quicken, his firmness pressing against me.

"The diners might be able to see us," I whispered.

"Then let's give them a show."

"I'll do my best." I smiled, his lips only inches from mine.

I fisted my hand in his hair, as he brought his mouth to mine. Closing my eyes, I felt the softness of his lips caress mine, sending a shot of desire through me. It was even more spectacular than I had imagined. His kisses tugged at the wall around my heart, threatening to make it crumble bit by bit. The rhythm of his kisses quickened as my lips parted, and I silently begged for more. His hands shifted lower to my hips, pulling me closer to him as his kisses deepened, needy, as my worries melted away. The hunger for more awoke something inside of me.

The fire coursing through my veins intensified with every flick and circular motion of his tongue, but right when I thought I couldn't take anymore, he stopped. His lips left mine, and I trembled with the loss of connection to this man, my breathing ragged as I opened my eyes. His eyes searched mine before his lips crashed down to mine once more. My fingers tangled in his hair as a shockwave of emotion travelled through me, the craving for him only deepened with every passing second. My hand skated across his chest, the firmness of his muscles apparent underneath the fabric. But it wasn't enough. As if sensing my longing, he traced his mouth along my jaw down the side of my neck, sending every nerve into overdrive. My mind tried to understand how something so simple could feel so good. It was like nothing I'd felt before.

The gentle touch of his fingers softly trailing along my arms, his breath dancing off my skin, teased desires I didn't even know I had until now. I dreamed of his lips moving along other parts of my body, and my head fell back as a quiver ran through me. His mouth moved along my collarbone, making me feel like I was his to be claimed, and I wanted to be claimed. I wiggled against him, my body craving more as the desire between us grew to an extreme.

"You're so beautiful," he whispered. Even though every touch and caress was heated, his eyes held nothing but tenderness and that made me want even more.

I traced my fingers along his neck, guiding him to kiss me once more, but as I slowly lowered my head, I caught a glimpse of someone in the distance, watching.

My breath caught and Luke backed away, his gaze followed mine. The man disappeared just as quickly as he came. But I sensed it. We both did. The man was looking for me and he'd found me. The fantasy over before it even began.

CHAPTER TWENTY-SIX

Luke

I'd never been as aroused as I was with Hannah and that was just a kiss. Damn! I can't even imagine more. But this right here was the problem. I kept letting my personal feelings for her disrupt what I intended to do, which was to protect her.

"We need to get out of here," I replied, the feelings from moments before gone in seconds.

"It could just be a coincidence," Hannah muttered.

"Are you willing to stake your life on it?" I asked, grabbing her hand.

"No." She hesitated. "There's something I didn't tell you."

"I think there are a lot of somethings." I pulled her through the sand, her legs barely keeping up. "But let's wait until we get to the car."

We climbed the stairs, and once we reached the top, I glanced around the lot, looking for anyone suspicious. I saw nothing. But I felt something. Reaching the car, I helped her into the passenger seat and closed the door. I hurried around the back of the car and slid into the driver's seat.

"They texted me," Hannah said, as I reversed the car out of the lot.

My pulse quickened. Why didn't she tell me?

"What did it say?" I asked, gripping the wheel.

"You can run but you can't hide," her voice went hoarse on the last word. She grabbed her cell out of her bag.

That was what Donald told her on the beach. I remember seeing that in the police documents. My fingers tightened around the wheel. I spoke to my hands-free set, commanding it to dial Mitch's number.

"Toss your phone out the window," I directed. They'd somehow found out her cell number and pinged her location.

She rolled down the glass and flung the cell out of the opening.

Mitch picked up immediately. "Mr. Fletcher."

"I know I dismissed you, but I need your services tonight. I'd like you to keep an eye on my sister. I'll call and let her know to expect you. There's been some developments. I'll send over details when I have them."

"Absolutely, sir. I'll get right on it. I'm only a few blocks away from her house, grabbing some dinner."

"Wonderful. I'll let my sister know." I ended the call.

"I'm so sorry," Hannah whispered.

Her pain echoed in every syllable.

"You have nothing to be sorry for," I replied, squeezing her hand. "Nothing."

"I'll text Mia," she offered. "Using your cell."

I nodded. "Thanks. Did you give your cell number to anyone?" I asked.

"You, Mia, the detective. Those are the only people I've given it to. Oh, and it's on the paperwork at Buttons."

"You didn't give it to anyone from that house you first stayed at?" I asked.

"No. I've broken all ties with everyone. I didn't even let Rikki know where I moved to, and I borrowed her car. No one besides the people I told you have my number."

I shook my head. That made no sense. They got it somehow, texted her, and even managed to ping her location. I was sure of it.

"The organization is well connected. I tried going to the authorities, but the NLC has contacts, ways of making problems disappear, making people disappear. I don't want to be one of them."

"Did you know Donald Jamison?" Luke asked. "Did he live on the compound?"

I shook my head. "No. And it's not the first time I've run into someone who's involved but not living on the compound."

I spotted a car behind us getting a little too close for comfort as we drove along the Pacific

Coast Highway. I increased my speed slightly and so did the other vehicle.

"Who else?" I asked.

"Some guy I knew in school named Eric magically appeared out of the blue. We'd been told he'd ran away from the compound, but I saw him the night I left, talking to the leader." Her voice caught. "My fiancé's father."

Jesus!

"It's okay. You can tell me," I pressed, keeping my eyes on the rearview mirror.

"Eric killed my best friend. And my sister," her voice trembled.

"I'm so sorry. That's what made you run?" I asked, trying to place the events.

Hannah shook her head. "I'd been planning it for years, but the final few months made it clear I had to do it soon. I kept pushing it off. I guess no matter how awful a place is, the overwhelming fear of the unknown outweighs common sense sometimes."

"The unknown can be frightening, but it can also offer a new beginning," I offered.

The vehicle behind began flashing its lights, which made it difficult to see now that the sun had set, especially on this windy road. I didn't want to alarm Hannah, but she needed to know our visitor had followed.

"I knew what the NLC was into was bad, but I didn't understand what depths they'd go to keep their sins hidden. I saw Tracy get murdered right in front of my eyes. My best friend's screams haunt me every night," Hannah whispered. "I thought my sister ran away, abandoned me, but Eric pushed her off a cliff. Or at least that's what I overheard."

I let out a sigh and watched as the vehicle fell behind.

"We've got a situation. I think our friend from the beach is saying hi. He just dropped back, but I don't think it'll be for long."

"What?" Panic echoed through her words. "Are you serious?" Hannah flipped down the visor and looked in the mirror. "I don't see a car."

"It's there. He's been riding my bumper, flashed his lights, and then disappeared. I'm calling it in."

As much as I didn't want to, I lowered our speed to maneuver the upcoming hairpin turn.

"Place a call to Mitch..." I spoke to the hands-free set.

Two headlights from behind sped up, only this time they weren't slowing down. Before I could finish the phone command, it was too late. Hannah's hand slid to my knee as the first tap from behind spun our vehicle as I tried desperately to keep the car on the road.

CHAPTER TWENTY-SEVEN

Hannah

"Sir. Sir," Mitch's voice echoed through the car. The sound of screeching tires and branches scratching the metal competed with Luke's calm voice.

I watched as Luke turned the wheel, correcting the spin, just as the other car lost control. Luke gunned the accelerator to avoid the vehicle that was now barreling toward us onto the narrow, gravel shoulder.

I didn't have time to panic or let fear settle over me as our car hit the even pavement while the other vehicle went sailing by. I turned in my seat and watched the driver's door swing open as the car flew over the railing. But it was too late for whoever was inside.

Luke finished giving Mitch our location and was already on the phone with the police. He parked our car, and I opened the door and got out of the car.

"Hannah," Luke called.

I walked over to the shoulder of the road, unsure of what I expected to see. Sirens in the distance placed a sense of urgency, but I was numb. I knew I should be feeling something, but I didn't. Every single emotion I'd started to feel had been placed back in the vault of my soul. It could've been us. We could've been the vehicle down below. I took one more step and looked over the edge. The wreckage came into view as my legs began to give way. Once more, I'd almost tasted death.

Luke's arms wrapped around my waist as I stared at the wreck below. There was no fire, flames, or smoke jetting from the mangled pieces of metal. But there was the incessant beeping of the horn. My body trembled as I thought about how close we were to being on the rocks below.

"You're okay," Luke whispered, pressing his lips to my hair.

I shook my head, trembling. "We could've died."

"But we didn't," Luke whispered, holding me closely.

The first police car arrived on the scene, the ambulance still on the way.

"Over here," Luke called out, his embrace only tightening.

Another police vehicle arrived on the scene as an officer jogged over to us.

"I doubt the person survived," Luke muttered,

as the officer looked down at cliffs below.

The other officer began cordoning off the area as the ambulance appeared on the scene.

"Can you tell us what happened?" the officer asked, his expression concerned.

"He was trying to drive us off the road," Luke began. "And he failed."

I saw the expression harden on the officer as he took in Luke's blasé attitude.

"You're certain that was his intent?" the officer questioned.

"Absolutely. You can tell by the tire marks that we were almost down there joining him."

"Was it a road rage incident? Did you incite him?" the officer asked.

I felt Luke's heart rate speed up at the questioning so I took a step away.

"Not at all," Luke replied, his lips pressing together.

"This just seems unlikely," the officer replied.

"Not in my profession," Luke replied, his brow arched.

The officer was getting more agitated.

"And exactly what would that be?" the officer asked, not amused.

"Is Captain Rodriguez on his way out here?" Luke asked, ignoring the officer's question.

"Why won't you answer my question?" the officer asked.

"After being the victim in a case that turned deadly, I don't enjoy being treated as if I'm the criminal. You're focusing on the wrong end of things, I can assure you."

I would never in a million years dream of talking to a policeman like this and it, quite frankly, scared the crap out of me. I watched the medics swiftly move the gurney to the edge of the cliff, knowing full well they'd only be lifting a dead body back up. The thought inched a prickle down my spine.

Luke turned his attention away from the officer and dialed a number. Bringing the phone to his ear, he waited.

"Captain," Luke's voice almost jovial, followed by a slight pause. "Yes. It's been too long. I seem to have encountered..." Luke glanced at the officer's tag. "Officer Anderson at the scene of an accident that I was involved in."

Silence while the Captain spoke and the officer's anger rose.

"Yes. I'm fine, but the other driver didn't fair so well. He was after a client I had with me. Attempted to drive us off the PCH. Unfortunately, he lost."

More silence.

"That would be much appreciated. I'd like to get my client to safety."

Officer Anderson was incensed as Luke handed him the phone. The discussion was quick and the officer ended the call, handing the phone back to Luke. "Mr. Fletcher, my apologies. If we need anything more, we'll be in touch."

"Thank you, Officer," Luke replied, as he wrapped his arm around my shoulders and led me back to our vehicle.

I slid into the seat and glanced back at the

officer who no longer seemed enraged. Rather, he looked on as if he'd just met someone he admired. I turned my attention to Luke as he climbed into the car, shutting the door behind him.

"What was that all about?" I asked. "That's not how it works for normal people."

Luke smiled. "There's a lot we need to learn about each other. You're not going to my sister's tonight."

He turned the car in the opposite direction from where we'd been headed and my stomach tightened.

"Then where are we going?" I asked.

"My house. It's not far from here."

I looked out the window into the darkness. "Thank you."

"Don't thank me until it's over," Luke replied.

"What if it never ends?" I asked.

"It will. You just have to learn to trust me." He touched something on his dash and Mitch's voice appeared in the car.

"Everything okay?" Mitch asked.

"Been better. Listen, I'd like you to bring my sister to the house. Things have gotten a little more interesting."

"She's going to fight it," Mitch replied.

"I know, but it's for the best. Let her know Hannah will be there and she might soften up a bit."

"Will do."

And the call ended.

"So do you really think hiding us is going to

solve the problem?"

"Not at all. But I think three minds are better than one."

I nodded and reached for the radio, but he flipped it on from the steering wheel first.

"Something soothing?" I asked.

He found a classical station that was playing a cavatina and my body immediately relaxed, even though my mind could not.

"This okay?" he asked, his voice husky.

"It's lovely. It makes me wish I had my violin."

His eyes caught mine and his jaw tensed. "You play?"

"It was one of the few hobbies we could take up. I've played since I was four, maybe? But I stopped when my sister left. I mean when I thought she left. We used to play together."

"I'd love to hear you sometime." He turned the car off the Pacific Coast Highway onto Malibu Canyon Road.

"I've never really played in front of people, except my sister," I confessed.

"There's a first for everything," he said softly.

"Are we almost there?" I asked, changing the subject.

"About ten minutes away," Luke replied.

I still felt completely exposed. How did they keep finding me? Sure, I'd thrown the cell phone out the window, but if they knew I was with Luke at the time of the accident, it wouldn't take much for them to find out where he lived, or maybe they already knew. I wasn't sure going back to his house was actually all that safe considering everything.

Luke rubbed his hand along my knee, and instead of moving away, I wanted more. His ability to turn off the desire to run was unnerving, and the comfort his touch brought was alarming. I worried it would make me do things I wouldn't normally do. Stay when I wouldn't normally stay.

I didn't like how I didn't have an escape plan. I always had an escape plan, even when I was at the NLC. I just never used it until it was almost too late. If only I'd left when I thought my sister had. I never would've found out the truth. I could've just lived my life, thinking my sister was still out there somewhere, while I blended into society never to be heard from again. I never would've learned the things I learned. My life wouldn't be in danger. They never would've come after me. There wouldn't have been any need. But I would be a coward.

Luke turned onto a narrow road that edged along a cliff overlooking the ocean, and that's when I realized it wasn't a road. It was his driveway. A closed security gate was up ahead and the car slowed as he punched in a code on a control panel. The iron gates slowly rolled open and we proceeded up the drive.

"My guess is that Mitch and Mia will be here within an hour or so."

As he drove up his driveway, my eyes focused ahead on the large estate. Even in the pitch dark, I saw that the home situated on the tip of the cliff was gigantic. Solar lighting lit up the driveway and dotted the front yard, allowing just enough light to see the Mediterranean features of the home. The large garage door opened, and we drove into a garage that housed several cars in many different directions. But rather than park, we drove down a ramp where more cars were parked. This wasn't a normal garage. For starters, it was two stories.

"Do you moonlight as a mechanic?" I asked. "Or maybe Batman?"

Luke laughed as he slid into one of the vacant spots and turned off the car. "You've found me out."

"I knew there was something slightly off about you," I teased. There was nothing off about this man.

He opened his door and climbed out of the car and I followed his lead. He met me around the side of the car and pointed toward a door. "There's an elevator over there we can take to the house or we could just walk up the ramp."

"Let's walk. That'll give you time to explain why one man needs so many cars." Without realizing it, I slipped my hand into his as we walked up the ramp.

"There are two reasons. First, I love cars. Second, it behooves someone in my profession to have different options. They are not all my personal collection. Depending on the job, employees will use vehicles that fit their cover," Luke said, as we reached the top of the ramp. The garage door had lowered behind us and I looked around the large space.

"Likely story."

"I'm sticking to it." He grinned.

My mind flashed back to the man who'd been chasing us. "Do you think he's dead?" I asked, already knowing the answer.

"Yes," Luke answered, leading me through the garage toward a door. "You'll be safe here."

"How can you be sure? If they know I've been with you here and there, they'll surely know to look for your home. They'll find your home."

Luke's eyes brightened. "I really do need to tell you more about what I do and the resources that are available to me and my firm," he said, unlocking the door with a simple press of his thumb.

"Seriously?" I asked, looking at the thumbprint pad.

"Yes, seriously, and I will program your print into the system tonight."

"I know I owe you an explanation—"

"A very long explanation," Luke interrupted.

"But I almost wonder if yours will be longer," I said, as he pushed the door open.

The room in front of us was vacant, empty of anything and everything. It was small with a door on the opposite wall. There was no furniture. The walls were a stark white and the floors a pure white marble to match. My pulse quickened as I looked around the bare space.

"Haven't decided what to do with this room?" I asked.

"No. It has a purpose," he replied, not offering any more explanation as we made our way across the floor to the next door. It, too, had a fingerprint ID pad that he quickly pressed his thumb onto.

He opened the door, and a tiny surge of relief entered my system when no more mystery rooms were unveiled. I was now standing in a beautiful kitchen with walnut cabinetry and ivory granite. A Viking six-burner stove was in the island and double ovens were in the wall to the left.

"You cook?" I asked.

"It's the best way to be able to eat." He smiled. "Would you like something to drink?"

I shook my head, unable to believe that an hour ago I was feeling pretty good from the amount of wine I'd consumed, and now that was all a distant memory. Instead, I was left with a pit in my stomach and the inability to focus on much of anything.

I took a few steps into the kitchen and saw a great room a few steps below. Windows covered the far wall, but sheer drapes framed the windows. A large, ivory sectional was centered in the room. It was quite beautiful. My guess was in the daylight I'd be looking at the ocean in the distance.

I turned and paused. "Before I start guessing incorrectly, would you mind telling me what that empty room off the garage is for?"

His eyes filled with mischief and his smile broadened. "Why don't you tell me what you think it's for? We could use some levity for the evening."

"I have an active imagination and I'd just embarrass myself. Thank you very much. Please just do me the courtesy."

"If you don't at least throw out one of your ideas, I'm not going to tell you." He folded his arms in front of him.

"Fine. I'll just wait until Mia gets here, and I'll ask her."

"What makes you think she knows?" His brow arched. He was calling my bluff.

"It looks like it can be cleaned easily. Almost like you could just spray it out."

"And why would I need to do that?" He was entirely too amused.

"Maybe it's where you bring captives..."

"Captives?" he repeated.

"Like for deeper questioning," my voice lowered. "Interrogations."

Luke broke into laughter and I wanted to nail him. "I told you I had an active imagination."

"You weren't kidding," he continued to laugh. "I'm not CIA. I don't waterboard people. I wouldn't bring anyone back here that I didn't implicitly trust anyway."

"Sooo I'm part of the inner circle?" I asked, smiling faintly.

"Indeed."

"Well, I gave you one of the many ideas that came to me. Now spill the beans."

"I use the room for photography. The ceiling opens up and lets light in."

Oh. My. God.

"Uh-huh. Yeah. That was my second guess," I

said. "I was just putting you on notice."

"Is that so?" he asked, taking a step toward me.

"I wanted you to know that I understood all this spy stuff."

"I'm not a spy," he corrected. "I just own a private security firm."

I looked around the house and smiled. "A very successful security firm that makes policemen apologize. I also have a feeling you know more about me than you're letting on."

"I don't know enough," Luke replied, seriousness dismissing my playful intent.

"Same could be said about you," I whispered.

"I don't deny it, but I'll try to do better. Starting with giving you a tour of my home."

"I guess that's a start," I said.

"It'll have to do until Mia gets here."

"Well, show away." I smiled and his gaze fell to my lips. A complete swarm of butterflies crashed inside my belly the way his gaze lingered on my mouth. I found myself moistening my lips as his gaze intensified.

"I give you way too little credit," Luke muttered, his eyes connecting with mine.

"How so?"

"I think you know exactly what you do to me."

"I have no idea what you're talking about." I hid my smile at his admission.

"Oh, I think you do." He grinned. "But two can play that game."

Luke's fingers grazed the small of my back as he pushed me gently forward, guiding me to see the rest of his house. I felt a warmth pool in my stomach as he maintained his touch.

"This is the great room," he said, his touch still unfastening me.

"I gathered that."

Pushing me forward, we walked down a hall. "There's a powder room behind that door. And this door leads to an exercise room. The library is at the end of the hall. And the music room is connected to it."

"Music room?" I asked, feeling my heart rate quicken.

"Yes. A music room."

We walked down the long hall, stopping every so often for Luke to push open a door, leading into one of the various rooms he mentioned. We stood in front of the large French doors at the end of the hall. Between books and music, I couldn't wait for him to open the door.

"This is one of my favorite rooms in the house, besides the master." The way his voice slowed on the word master made my insides rattle. I felt his smile as he opened the doors. He knew what he'd done to me.

It was beautiful. There were floor-to-ceiling bookshelves, wrapping the entire room, but I didn't see another door, and he'd mentioned a music room connected to this one. I spotted a ladder that was on tracks in the far corner but no door.

"Does that just wheel around the room?" I asked.

"It does." He nodded.

I took a step inside and could smell the books. The room didn't need any decoration besides the bookshelves that were filled with colorful spines. It rivaled any public library I'd ever stepped foot into.

"This is beautiful," I muttered.

"Glad you love it."

"Where's the music room?" I asked.

"It's a secret room."

"Are you serious? And you wanted to laugh at my whole interrogation theory on the marble room?" I asked.

"The marble room. I like that. Has a nice ring." He smiled.

"So where is the entrance to the secret room, or are you going to make me guess?"

"You won't be able to find it." His eyes twinkled with amusement.

"How can you be so sure?" I asked.

"It's the design. It's not meant to be found."

"Is that a challenge?" I asked.

"I guess it could be," he acknowledged.

"Well, I bet you that I can find the entrance to the music room," I replied, crossing my arms.

"And what are you willing to bet, Hannah?" His eyes darkened in such a way that I almost fell over. I glanced nervously around the room.

"I don't have much to offer," I replied, blushing.

"I doubt that to be true." Luke was completely amused but changed the subject. "How about if I lose, I'll cook you a four-course meal?"

I nodded. "And if I lose?" My heart was racing.

"A kiss," he responded simply.

"That I think I can handle. But there's not much incentive for me to win," I replied, laughing.

"I'm a fabulous cook." He smirked, watching as I began to make my way to the nearest wall of built-in shelving.

I began running my hands along the shelves, feeling for anything that was out of place.

"You would need to be." I continued moving my fingers along the wood as my eyes noted the amazing collection of titles. I could spend the rest of my life in here and be completely content. It was so odd being in Luke's presence. In one moment, my past was coming back to haunt me and in the next, I was able to dream of another way of existing in realms I'd never imagined.

"Am I getting warmer?" I asked.

"And you think I'd tell you?" he joked.

I continued walking along the wall, spying any books that looked out of place or any shelving that looked off. I'd finally moved onto the far wall and still nothing, when Luke's cell rang and he picked up on speaker.

"You here, Mia?" Luke asked.

"Pulling up the drive. Just wanted to make sure you were decent," Mia informed him.

I busted into laughter.

"And you're on speaker. Thanks for that," Luke replied, smiling and shaking his head. His gaze dropped away from mine, and for once, I caught a little embarrassment flitter through him.

"Whoops. Shit," Mia chimed. "Anyway, we'll be there in a few."

Luke disconnected the cell and turned to look at me. "Sorry about that."

"What's to be sorry about?" Our eyes locked on one another and I felt a tingle run through me.

Luke ran his fingers through his hair and looked around the room. "I think I might have won this bet."

"How so?" I asked.

"Do you have an answer for where the entrance is?" His brow quirked.

"There wasn't a time limit," I reminded him.

He pressed his lips together. "I assumed that was a given."

"Never assume..." My eyes darted behind him to a bookshelf where I noticed a book tipped against another. All of the books in the room were upright. None were out of place. I bet that had fallen when the door moved. I was sure that was exactly where the entrance was. I quickly skimmed over the area and brought my gaze to his. I didn't want to win this bet.

"So Mia and Mitch are almost here. That's probably good," I said.

"And why's that?" Luke asked.

"Like you said, I lost the bet. So when are you going to cash in on your winnings?" I teased, my pulse quickening.

"We've got a lot to discuss, and I'm hoping that tonight's events persuaded you to tell us what's going on. That was too close a call, and I don't want to lose control of the situation. But in order to design a defensive strategy, I need answers," Luke replied.

"I'll try."

His gaze deepened. "So to answer your question, I'll cash in when there's no chance of being interrupted." Luke's seductive grin added another layer of complexity to my feelings. The look in his eyes revealed a powerful man who didn't have a problem asserting what he wanted in life, and in this moment, I was what he wanted to claim. And even though I was more nervous than I could ever imagine, it felt really good.

He pressed his hand against my back and softly moved me forward just as the alarm beeped, alerting us that Mia and Mitch had entered the premises.

"Let's get settled," Luke murmured as we walked into the hall. "There'll be plenty of time for the other."

My heart nearly popped out of my chest as a mischievous smile spread along Luke's lips. I'd never taken that next step before, and recently that seemed to be all I could think about when I was around Luke. I couldn't let my feeling for him overshadow what I needed to do, and I worried that every day I stayed, I endangered us all.

CHAPTER TWENTY-EIGHT

Luke

I could no longer worry about rushing Hannah. I needed answers. We'd nearly been run off the road because I'd let my personal feelings for Hannah get in the way of taking precautions. If the man had tapped our bumper a moment sooner, I probably wouldn't have been able to correct our vehicle, which was why he landed over the cliff and we didn't.

"Sir," Mitch greeted me in the foyer. "Mia's in the kitchen."

I nodded and without thinking slipped my hand in Hannah's as we walked through the hallway. She didn't say a word once we left the library, but her eyes said it all. She felt responsible for this and had made up her mind. She was going to go if I didn't stop her first. I needed to distract her. And against my better judgment, the plans for tomorrow had to go on. I needed to get her mind on something else, remind her of what a life can be.

"Mia," I called out.

Mia came running from the kitchen and gave me a big hug just as Hannah slid her hand out of mine. Hannah's walls were going back up piece by piece.

"Needed a beer," Mia smiled. "Finding out my brother and roommate almost got run off the road scrambled my composure."

"We're fine. Can't say the same for the other guy," I said.

I glanced around the room and dismissed Mitch. We needed to talk, alone. Mitch walked out of the room toward the control room to follow up with police about the identity of the man who'd nearly driven us off the road.

Mia walked over to the couch in the family room and fell onto it, her body succumbing to the tension in the room. I grabbed a beer from the counter and popped it open as I watched Hannah take a seat next to Mia. They both looked exhausted.

"Hannah, regrettably, I've let my personal feelings for you endanger not only you but, also, my sister."

Hannah blushed and looked out the window, which only drove me more insane for her. Her power over me made me feel guilty and that wasn't an emotion I was used to.

"Don't go there," Mia said, her eyes narrowing on me. "If you hadn't shown an interest in

Hannah, she would've been captured."

"Or worse," Hannah's words shook me to my core. "Don't blame yourself. If anyone is to be blamed, it's me. I shouldn't have allowed myself to imagine a different life."

Mia frowned and shook her head. "That's ridiculous to lose hope and sure as hell isn't how my brother and I operate. No one here is to be blamed. Bad things happen to good people. Isn't that how the saying goes? My brother and I learned that a long time ago. We're all in this together. No one's going to run." My sister's gaze caught Hannah's. "And no one is going to waste time playing the blame game."

Everything I wanted to say, Mia just hung out there, and I hoped Hannah would absorb it better coming from Mia. I stared at Hannah waiting to capture her gaze but she wouldn't look at me.

"What is it you know, Hannah?" I questioned. "What has you running? What has them chasing?"

She didn't answer and continued to look away. Anger was beginning to boil through me, but it wasn't directed at her. It was at the situation. At her not being able to trust. It was a feeling I knew well, but I wasn't going to give up on Hannah. I wanted to gain her trust.

"Look. I know there's more to it than what I've been able to piece together. There are a lot of cults in the world and lots of small communities have sprung up across the country over the decades. Why don't you tell me what sets yours apart?" I asked. "Is it religion? Is it drugs?"

Hannah's eyes flashed to mine, and she pressed her lips together. She looked distant. I was losing her before I had a chance to claim her, claim her heart as my own.

"There's evil in this world so dark that it can't be seen." Hannah interrupted me, her lips moved slowly. "I grew up thinking the opposite. That people wanted to do good, be good. That was what the community preached. If we all lived together peacefully and without conflict, blessings would come our way. In hindsight—ignorance—not innocence was a virtue. We were taught selflessness. But in truth it was selfishness that drove our existence in the community. How can one truly be selfless, if all we do is concentrate on ourselves? They had us so focused on self-development that if something happened to a neighbor we'd blame it on their lack of self-improvement. It's brainwashing for the betterment of humankind." Hannah's smile was cynical, her eyes darkening. "It worked on my own family. I wanted to see something in my mom that set her apart. I believed that since she was my mom, I could get her to see the light. That was four years ago. I never did break through."

"I'm sorry," Mia said, shifting on the couch. Her eyes connected with mine. She was going to lead Hannah to tell us. "Start with what makes you comfortable."

"It's complicated, and I'm worried the more I tell you the more danger I'll put you in."

My stomach tensed. We just went back ten steps. Was she going to run? I had Mitch on alert, but that didn't mean anything. Mia sensed my worry and stood up quickly.

"Have you shown her the guest rooms yet?" Mia asked.

"No. We hadn't gotten that far."

Mitch came rushing into the family room.

"Mr. Fletcher, we've got an identification on the individual who tried to run you off the road."

"Who?" I asked.

Mitch took a deep breath and handed over a piece of paper. "Terrance Bridges."

"Bridges?" I repeated, glancing at Hannah.

She shook her head. "The name doesn't sound familiar."

Mitch walked the photo over to her.

"I don't recognize him," Hannah replied. "But I'm beginning to realize that doesn't matter."

"This is a business for them, played out on the streets. But it's our turn to change the rules. Instead of being the hunted, we need to become the hunter," I said, my eyes connecting with Hannah's. A trace of excitement shot through her expression. "But first, you absolutely have to tell us what we're dealing with. I don't want to lose a man to these cowards because we're not prepared."

Hannah nodded slowly. "I think I'd like to change first. Maybe, get settled in the guest room."

"Certainly," I replied, glancing at Mia. "Will you show her upstairs?"

"Totally," Mia said, grinning.

Mia and Hannah walked out of the room and I turned my attention to Mitch who'd walked back into the room.

"They're sending a message loud and clear that this is no longer only about Hannah. I want to ensure that they don't regret including us in their plans. We're going to give them a run for their money. They've made it personal."

"Absolutely, sir," Mitch responded.

I grabbed a beer and glanced at the clock. It was getting later and later and I still had no answers from Hannah. We couldn't plan until we knew what was worth chasing her across the country.

"If you'll excuse me, I need to clear up some things with Hannah."

Mitch nodded and retreated to the study down the hall.

I climbed the stairs trying to talk myself out of tomorrow. I had all the plans set up to take her somewhere magical and out of this world. But with everything happening, it didn't feel like the time. But on the other side of it, I was so worried that if I just happened to look in the other direction, Hannah would run. And I wanted her to stop running. I wanted to show her what it could be like.

Damn it. Now I was actually analyzing things as if there was a future with this girl. She needed my help, end of story. The weight of guilt and regret threatened to crush me. I should've seen this coming. This was what I did. I'd protected dignitaries and saved lives. What was different about this case?

I heard Mia and Hannah's voices coming from the third bedroom on the left. Mia had brought over some clothes for Hannah in case they needed to stay longer than a night. I took a deep breath and commanded myself to get control. But as soon as Hannah's eyes connected with mine, I knew that was impossible. I was only fooling myself if I thought I'd be able to walk away from this girl after we made her problems become a thing of the past.

"Every minute I waste is a minute the others don't have to give," Hannah whispered.

"Others?" I asked, taking a seat across the room.

Hannah nodded and Mia's expression was frozen in a state of shock. Hannah must've told her something.

"Imagine sins so evil that drug running is chosen as a cover-up to soften the blow. The drug world is less toxic than what the NLC is actually into," Hannah replied, her eyes holding mine. "They'd rather throw off the authorities by sacrificing a relative or a community member every so often to ensure that their real activities are never uncovered." She paused. "It worked on you."

I nodded. "It did. We traced the drug connection pretty quickly."

"And that's where most people would stop, including the authorities, I'd imagine," Hannah stated.

"So they're throwing the authorities a bone," Mia whispered, nodding.

"And it's an enticing bone. The smuggling ring they've built up is impressive, at least on paper," I admitted.

"Yes, and if the FBI is busy investigating that network, they're unlikely to find out what's really going on," Hannah replied. "Not that I have much faith that they're investigating much of anything."

"And it's far worse," Mia replied, her gaze connecting with mine.

"What they're actually into happens three times a year. The next event will happen in less than a month. I think that's why they're throwing so much attention my way. They don't want the next shipment to be in jeopardy. They're worried that I've gone to the authorities or will. But they don't want to stop the shipment in case it turns out I haven't gone to the authorities—too much money to be lost," Hannah's voice broke off.

I nodded, prompting Hannah to continue.

"I have to survive if for nothing more than to end it. I have the proof, but I haven't been able to trust anyone with it. I tried, but it went nowhere. I'm sure that's what killed my sister and best friend, but I got away," her voice trailed off.

"And what is it, Hannah?" I asked. "What is the NLC doing?"

CHAPTER TWENTY-NINE

Hannah

I looked at Luke, and Mia grabbed my hand. I knew by divulging this information I was putting them both in direct danger. They were already targets, but this solidified it, and I hadn't intended to do that. Not initially. But if something were to happen to me, I couldn't let this atrocity continue. It was a hidden epidemic just running through the undercurrent of society. I'd kept it hidden long enough as I attempted to gather the information, the proof. There was nothing more crushing than when I tried to present all of my findings to the people who were supposed to protect, only to be dismissed.

I went to the local police, and that's when I realized the NLC had dug in far more than I knew. That moment was the first moment I could actually taste fear. My next step had been the local branch of the FBI. They met with me, listened to me, and never returned my call. That was why I trusted no one. But it was time to change that, and I was looking at the two people who I'd finally allow myself to place trust in. I only prayed it wouldn't backfire. I'd never forgive myself if something happened to either of them.

I took a deep breath in, my eyes locking on Luke's as I readied myself to tell them about the people who'd haunted my every nightmare and thought and the energy it took to push it all away just to survive.

"Human trafficking." The words left my lips and an immediate chill touched my skin.

"And you have proof?" Luke's eyes didn't leave mine.

I nodded.

"Where?"

"I placed all the documents in a storage locker on my way into California."

Luke ran his fingers over his hair while exhaling loudly. "So they want to know who you've told. That's why they want you alive," he replied.

"Yes. Before they kill me, they want to know what I know and who I've told. I'm sure of it." Saying the words aloud solidified it. I was ready to fight. "They don't want to cancel their next shipment unless they have to. Too much money on the line."

"Shipment," Mia whispered.

"Shipment," I repeated. "That's how it's

referred to in every document. It's beyond sickening. Humans as cargo. Both men and women a commodity."

"And you went to—" Luke stopped himself.

I nodded. "I went to the local police."

"So that's how they know you know enough to be a problem. They had an informant on the inside who reported back," Luke said, glancing at Mia.

"It's not like out here. Back home is just a small, local police force. My guess is that the person I spoke to is the one who's involved with the NLC. That's usually how my luck goes."

"Did you go anywhere else?" Mia asked.

"I found a local branch of the FBI, reported everything and never heard back."

Luke's jaw muscle tensed. "We'll need to get the FBI involved. I have several contacts at the bureau that I trust, but I agree that timing is of the essence."

"If the NLC gets suspicious at all, they'll stop the upcoming delivery, and the whole process will be disrupted, and all of the information I gathered will be useless. The dates, names, addresses would all be a thing of the imagination," I said, feeling the panic set in.

"They'd find new sources, kill the old ones," Luke agreed. "I see your hesitancy. We won't do anything to jeopardize what you've gathered."

"I don't know how you've done it," Mia whispered.

"In order to function, I've had to compartmentalize everything, including my existence. I didn't dare allow myself to think of the lives that were in danger, the lives that had already been extinguished in years past. I knew if I let myself think about everything in too much detail, I'd become paralyzed in fear and sorrow. One of the items I came across about six months ago was a photo album..." I stopped.

"A photo album?" Mia questioned, her eyes filled with sorrow.

"Pictures of the captives with country of origin, date of birth, etc." A lump in my throat made it impossible to continue with details.

"Do you have a copy?" Luke asked, his voice softening.

I nodded. "It's all in a storage locker. That's one of the things that I worried about the most. That something would happen to me, and everything in the storage locker would just get lost. No one would know it existed and everything would continue to go on."

"What you're doing is very brave," Luke said, walking over to where I was sitting.

"No. It's not. It's just the right thing to do," I said, his eyes locking on mine. "These people need to be stopped."

"They do," Luke agreed, as Mia stood up.

"I'm going to go grab a drink," Mia said. "Need anything?"

"Two beers," Luke replied, putting my hand in his as he took a seat next to me.

"The ugliness in the world made me question what I thought about being human, and the more I grappled with that question, the less I could function. When I first discovered everything, I withdrew and fell into a deep depression. I literally couldn't function," I revealed to him.

"I can understand that," Luke said softly.

"But then I realized inaction wasn't helping anyone, and I pulled myself out of the despair by devising a plan. Interacting with my fiancé, who I'd continually avoided, became a priority. I wanted to look like I belonged in my community again. I hoped it would allow me the freedom to follow up on what I'd learned."

"I'm curious how you first ran across this?"

"A year ago, I was hiking around the woods, contemplating my life. My upcoming marriage to a man I didn't love had been arranged and announced, and I just wanted out. The forest provided me with the solitude I needed to think, so I often roamed around for hours, discovering little creeks and caves. I'd actually talked myself into leaving the community. I'm sure that sounds silly, but it was a big step. I'd be leaving everyone and everything that I knew behind."

"It doesn't sound silly," Luke replied.

"As selfish as this sounds, I sometimes wish I'd never discovered what I did in those woods. I imagine what it would've been like if I just turned around, packed my bags, and never returned. But then all of the images of the people flood my mind. And I realize I'm better than that."

"What did you find in the forest?" he asked.

"A large barn. At the time, I didn't think much of it. I went inside and it was completely empty, but it was on our property, and I'd never heard it mentioned, which was odd. And it wasn't for our animals. We had barns close to the compound for our horses and cows. You probably saw them when you were there. Anyway, I didn't give it any thought until I was out traipsing around a few months later with my best friend, Tracy."

"Only this time it wasn't empty," Luke whispered, finishing my sentence.

I nodded. Tears began to moisten my lower lids as the reality of everything hit. I was no longer hiding the sins of others. For the first time in a very long time, I felt like I might be able to stop the destruction of the NLC. Knowing that I wasn't carrying this burden alone any more created a sense of genuine hope, which was something I hadn't felt for a very long time.

"I'm so exhausted," I whispered. "Tonight just about threw me over the edge. I can't believe what happened. I'm trying to push it out of my mind, but I can't." I pressed my hands on my chest. "I swear my heart's still beating twice as fast as it should. It could've been us."

"We'll take these bastards down," Luke whispered, bringing me into his arms. "But we need to make sure you're safe too. I want you and Mia to go into hiding—"

I broke from his embrace. "Absolutely not. I didn't come this far to hide until it's all over."

Luke's expression remained firm. "You aren't any use to anyone if you're dead. Being a martyr isn't..."

"I don't intend to be a martyr," I interrupted

him. "But I do intend on being there when these people get caught."

Luke let out a sigh. His expression didn't change, but I felt the energy between us switch. The closeness from earlier returned. "I think everything you've acquired needs to stay where it is until we're certain that the proper course of action is laid out and will be taken."

Luke was very matter-of-fact as he picked up his cell and began to search for something.

"I still plan on working at Buttons. If they're following me as closely as it looks, they would certainly notice my sudden lack of interest in employment."

"There is no reason for you to continue. I'll cover..."

"There is every reason in the world for me to continue," I interrupted. "First, I do need the money, and I will not be taken care of. Second, I don't want anything out of the ordinary to signal that I'm getting antsy or might have talked. And third, I need an outlet. I have survived this long because I'm good at distracting myself. If I just sit and stew, my life will be unbearable. I need to continue to compartmentalize everything. All details need to be in their place. My nightmares are bad enough. I don't need the images to surface during the day."

A few moments of silence passed between us, and I thought about Luke's comments. It wasn't the first time he'd mentioned it, putting me in hiding. I admit there was a part of me that was very intrigued by going into hiding, but I felt it was the cowardly thing to do. That wasn't my intention when telling Mia and Luke everything. I wanted to look into the eyes of the NLC as they were led away in handcuffs. And maybe that was more dream than reality, but it was the fuel I needed to continue.

I glanced at Luke and saw a drop of conflict behind his expression. It made me worry that what I was feeling between us was his uncertainty growing. I hoped not, but I'd understand. There was nothing but complication for the both of us, and it was only getting worse with each new development. Not to mention there were far more important things to be concerned with than a fleeting attraction.

"I respect your opinion," Luke's voice shattered the silence. "My firm didn't grow because I did everything singlehandedly. It grew because I have an excellent team and a large network composed of people who I can trust, both inside and outside the firm. You gave me the courtesy of trusting me, and I'll return the gesture. If you think you need to return to your job for appearance's sake, I understand. I wouldn't do anything to put you or my sister in further harm's way." Luke balled his fists and glanced at me. "But I'm sure at some point you counted on being able to involve the authorities?"

"Yes," I responded.

"Then you'll understand my need to contact a man within the bureau who I feel can be trusted?" Luke asked. I had fallen into a professional slot, and I'd be lying if I didn't say a part of me was relieved.

I nodded. "But, please, keep me informed every step of the way."

"Absolutely." His green eyes flashed to mine and I felt a rush, but as instantly as it was felt, it vanished. He was about to say something, and thought better of it.

The tension between us was almost unbearable. I needed to break it up the only way I knew how.

"So I guess our date tomorrow won't be happening?"

Luke laughed and leaned back in the chair. "I'm not going to let an attempted murder stop our fun. Besides, you want to keep up appearances, and I think that's the only way to do it. It wasn't easy finding a place that fit your requirements. We're definitely going through with it."

I couldn't help but smile at the heat behind Luke's expression.

"I'll do what I have to do for appearance sake," I smiled. "Besides something tells me that we won't be alone."

"You can count on that." Luke smiled and stood up, stretching.

My eyes accidentally trailed to where his shirt lifted and my heart sped up at the sight of his bronzed skin. Good God.

His eyes connected with mine, and he grinned while I flushed with heat.

"You're protected here. I have a few more men

coming over who'll be on watch. Try to get a good night's sleep. We're going to have a busy day tomorrow. It just might be what we both need." He was only a foot away, and I could feel the spark between us intensify, but rather than kiss me, he smiled. He gently touched my cheek with his thumb before walking out of the room, leaving me completely in need of something I'd never had before.

But before I could get wrapped up in the thoughts of desire that were threatening to make my night full of dreams rather than nightmares, I heard Mitch in the hallway, filling Luke in on some developments on another case. He was headed out tonight on an emergency call and my insides twisted into knots at the thought of him leaving.

CHAPTER THIRTY

Luke

I knew I needed to push Hannah away. It was the safest thing to do, but the thought nearly destroyed me. She'd been through enough, and I didn't need her thinking I was toying with her. That wasn't my intention, and I would never do that to her or any woman, for that matter. Mitch's appearance was a welcome one since I was about to turn back around and say something to her that I would surely regret, but I hated to leave her. I knew she needed me. I felt it. Saw it in her eyes, or maybe, it was what I wanted to see.

"What've you got for me?" I asked Mitch in the hallway.

Hannah stayed in her room, and I looked over my shoulder and watched her crawl under the covers. Feelings that shouldn't take priority did.

"The congressman had a break in while his family was asleep upstairs," Mitch began, bringing me back to the reality that I needed to stay in. "Police have already canvassed the area, and came up empty-handed. But he wanted us to survey everything. He's kicking himself for not hiring our firm. He didn't want to believe the threats could be real."

"I don't blame him. Our services aren't cheap." I smiled. "What makes him think it's the same people?"

"They tagged his living room wall with the same symbol as in the letter," Mitch replied.

"Gotcha. Well, we'll go take a look around and figure out how many men to station at the residence. Let's send a team over to observe the premises."

"Will do, sir," Mitch replied as I headed to the kitchen where Mia was taking a sip of her beer.

"Oh, shoot!" She slapped her hand against her forehead. "I forgot to bring you the beers. Wait. What's wrong? Why do you have that look on your face? Is it Hannah?"

I shook my head and walked over to my sister. "No. I just need to go out tonight. Duty calls."

"Shoot. I thought we'd have some well-deserved brother sister time."

"Yeah, right," I laughed.

"Can you believe everything the poor girl's been hiding from?" Mia asked, her voice quiet.

"No. I really can't imagine it. My mind has run through so many scenarios, but I never once thought of human trafficking."

"Kind of makes sense though."

I nodded. "Yeah. I can see a connection. If they've already got networks and smuggling operations built up for the drugs, why not just change up the product."

"Brutal," Mia whispered, taking another swig.

"Yeah. It really is."

"But something tells me with you on the case, their time's almost up," Mia said smiling.

"Such faith you have," I teased.

"You know it's true."

"I just hope there's a day that Hannah will be able to experience what life is supposed to be about. Having to constantly look behind you and feel like the weight of the world is balancing on your shoulders is more than most can handle for a long stretch," I said.

"Something we're all too familiar with, wouldn't you say?" Mia asked.

"True. But at least I've been able to protect myself and my family. Or what's left of it."

"You know," Mia paused. "Don't discount Hannah. She's known about this for a while now and has managed to stay out of their grasp. She made it all the way across the country without them finding her. She's going to come out okay."

"I'd say just making it out alive was a good start," I confirmed.

"Exactly. So don't underestimate what that girl can handle."

I nodded. "I wouldn't dream of it. But I do dream of making her life better."

"And that is why I think you're such an

amazing guy." Mia beamed and I rolled my eyes.

"Yeah. Yeah. I'm gonna go get changed. Do you mind letting Hannah know about tonight?"

"Sure. I'll go tell her that you're putting yourself in harm's way in the middle of the night. That usually always goes over well with girlfriends."

"It's just tossing some security detail on the congressman. Nothing dangerous," I said, flashing a warning glance to my sister. "And she's not a girlfriend."

"Whatever you say, bro," Mia snickered, as I left the room.

CHAPTER THIRTY-ONE

Hannah

"Hey, girl," Mia said, pretending to knock. "We've had a slight change of plans."

"Plans?" I asked. "I didn't think I had any other than to go to sleep. What do you mean?"

"Some congressman needs to be babysat or something."

"Somehow I doubt that's all." I eyed her suspiciously.

"My brother's the best in the business," Mia assured me, but it felt like she was saying it more for her own benefit.

I didn't doubt it, but that didn't calm my fears any.

"Does this happen often? Middle of the night excursions," I asked Mia. "I heard Mitch and Luke in the hall."

Mia let out a sigh. "More than most people

would enjoy. But honestly this one tonight is no big deal. He's just doing a quick once over or something."

"Was there a bad guy involved?" I half-joked.

"Yeah. There was," she acknowledged.

"And they're still out there, aren't they?"

She sighed, "Yup."

"Well, that's not safe in my book," I muttered.

"It's what he does. But anyway, he's getting ready and just wanted me to fill you in."

"Thanks."

"Have a good night. If you need anything, come find me." She smiled and left my bedroom.

The thought of Luke going somewhere in the middle of the night was unnerving and unease crept up my spine. There was so much more I wanted to learn about Luke. The thought of getting to unwrap him and discover what created him strummed through me. The way he looked at me, his smile, humor, and touch were all things I wanted more of. I needed to see Luke. I couldn't let him leave without thanking him for everything he'd done so far. He'd saved my life.

I threw off the duvet becoming more and more determined to tell him thank you. As I walked down the hall, rehashing what I wanted to tell Luke, I realized it sounded like I was worried he wasn't coming back. Reworking my words came to an abrupt halt when I heard Luke speaking into a cell. He was in the master bedroom at the far end of the hall, but I heard enough that garnered my attention.

I walked slowly along the wall, listening to

him explain everything and more. The NLC's drug connection and everything else Luke had dug up on his own was hurriedly coming out of his mouth, followed by what I explained earlier. The door was open and I walked into the room, not expecting to see him half naked. Luke's back was turned toward me as he changed into dark clothing. Luke wasn't wearing a shirt and my eyes fell along his beautifully chiseled back. The dips and curves of his muscles were even more carved than I had imagined. As he turned, his green eyes caught mine and a flicker of amusement appeared before he continued his conversation.

"Yes," Luke replied. "And I understand that. We'd like to meet with you in two days."

His eyes looked to mine for confirmation, and I nodded.

"Okay. Take care." Luke disconnected the call and turned to look at me.

I looked away quickly, blushing. I'd been caught. But rather than look at him, my eyes drifted along his chest, committing every beautiful curve of his body to memory. I imagined my fingertips running across his flesh, feeling every dip of definition. The tattoo I'd only seen glimpses of was now in full view. The black outline of a scorpion, tail up and ready to sting, caught my eye. I wanted to know the story behind it.

"Interesting how chemistry works, isn't it?" Luke asked, his voice lowered.

My eyes darted to his. "How so?"

"Even in the darkest hours we're still human. We still crave touch...love."

I took a step forward and debated what to say, but as I stood quietly taking in this God of a man, wondering what my next move should be, he closed the gap. His hands gripped my shoulders and his gaze fell on mine. He was only the distance of his arms from me, but it felt like miles. I wanted to be in his arms. I wanted to be held by him. I wanted this entire mess to vanish. The frisson of electricity that ran between us was impossible to ignore. It cut through everything else that attempted to overtake our lives. It made the fight seem worth winning. I knew he felt it, the slight buzz of current running through us with every step closer we took toward one another. So why was he ignoring it, pretending it no longer existed?

"Tonight's no big deal," he muttered.

"As long as everything goes according to plan," I replied.

His grip tightened and his gaze intensified. "Everything will go according to plan."

I tried to take a step forward, but his arms stiffened, keeping the distance between us.

"I don't understand." I searched his expression for answers and found none.

"I've jeopardized too much that's important to me because I was impulsive. I didn't follow protocol."

"That's why I wanted to leave. I had no intention of putting your sister in harm's way. I thought if I could just get enough—"

"I was referring to you," Luke interrupted, his voice low, almost hoarse. "I missed signs. I didn't enforce rules to help protect you, hide you. That needs to change. I never involve myself with clients. Impulse doesn't work in my world."

"I was never a client. I never asked to be protected." My pulse raced as the words left my mouth. "You're not running from this because you're worried about protecting me. You know very well, you can protect me with your eyes closed. It's what you do, remember? You're running because you've never done a relationship. Well, neither have I, and I'm willing to try. I'm willing to get hurt, have my heart broken, if it means that I get a chance to give my heart to you in the first place. I've never fallen in love, but I'm willing to bet that I'm about to, if you'll let me have that chance."

There was silence and I wondered if I assumed too much, misread our signals.

"You're right," he murmured at long last.

My heart started pumping faster at his admission. His hand moved along my jaw and framed my face, as he brought me closer. I never expected my words to hold such power over him, but they did.

His other hand ran along my hair, stopping at my shoulder. "You're beautiful...so beautiful. Your heart is filled with love in a world full of ugliness, and I don't want to take that away. I don't want to damage you. I don't want to become part of the ugliness."

"Why do you think you would be?"

"Because I don't do this..." his words trailed off as his mouth curved slightly, only inches from mine.

I traced my hand along his bare skin, feeling the hardness of his abdomen underneath my fingertips. The coolness of his skin as my fingers trailed up his torso made my breath quicken. The thought of being this close to Luke without ever getting to truly have him made my heart want to shatter into a million little pieces.

"I wish I could change your mind," I murmured, touching my lips to his.

His mouth parted as his hands moved to my waist, bringing my body next to his. With each deepening kiss, I imagined new possibilities as I melted in the feel of his soft, warm lips pressed against mine. His firm hands skated along my back, sending a frantic wanting through me, as if every kiss and touch provided a new thrill to be discovered. But the moment had to come to an end. Reality had to be dealt with.

"Did you try a Jedi mind trick or something?" Luke murmured, smiling, as our bodies slowly parted and my fingers crawled up his chest.

"I just may have. What's it to you?" I teased. "It worked, didn't it?"

"It did." Luke's smile absolutely melted my heart. "This is a lot to handle. You know, my lifestyle isn't for everyone."

I laughed. "I can imagine not, but I'd like to try."

He grinned as a spark flicked through his green eyes.

"You believe the NLC will be brought to justice, correct?" I asked.

His brow arched and he nodded.

"Then someday soon, my life will be *my* life again. When that moment comes, I'll have a lot of things to think about and a future to plan. But until then, I can only put one foot in front of the other. And I think that's all I can ask of you. I'm not asking for anything more than you can give in any one second. So go kick some ass," I told him. "And we'll see what tomorrow brings."

"You're so intriguing," Luke whispered, his mouth crashed down to mine once more. His lips warm, as our kisses intensified before he quickly broke away. The strength behind his eyes made my body quiver as I imagined what it would be like to unleash that desire between us. I wanted to experience that moment with him so badly it almost hurt.

"I've got to get going," he replied.

I nodded. "I understand. I actually just came in here to say thank you for everything. I'm not sure where it all went wrong."

"That was quite a thank you." He grinned. "And a wake-up call."

I smiled as his gaze lingered along my body.

"I get too wrapped up in myself sometimes, a lot of the time, actually. It's nice to be reminded that there's more to life than just my rules."

"Love doesn't follow rules," I replied, not realizing what slipped out. But I didn't try to correct it.

Luke touched my cheek gently before slipping

his black Henley over his head and let out a sigh.

"No, it doesn't, does it?"

I nodded and followed him out of the room.

Luke clipped a pistol to his pants, along with a knife. Even though it wasn't supposed to be a dangerous outing, it was hard to watch Luke prepare for something like this. But this was part of him, and if I wanted to be included in his life I needed to accept all of him. Mia caught my glance and smiled before taking a step forward to give her brother a hug.

Luke grabbed a jacket and slipped it on.

"Alex will meet you at the congressman's," Mitch replied.

"Thanks," Luke answered, his gaze avoiding mine.

Mia and Mitch left the entry and I just stood in place.

"I'll see ya in the morning," I said.

"Yes, you will," Luke murmured, his fingertips tracing along my arm.

I looked into his green eyes and felt my body responding to him immediately.

"Be safe."

"Always," he assured me before touching his lips to mine.

CHAPTER THIRTY-TWO

Luke

The congressman's house was trashed and his family scared, but from the looks of it, everything would be fine with just a few men on site until the person was in custody. It wouldn't take too long for the man to be caught. His face had been captured on camera. He was an amateur and really nothing I wanted to be bothered with today. Today was about Hannah. I wanted her to have one day to just have fun. She charged me with finding a spot that would take her cares away and I had done just that. I'd barely had four hours of sleep, but I felt completely reenergized at the thought of getting to spend the day with her.

"So are we still sticking to my original rules?" Hannah giggled.

Hearing the beautiful ring to her voice made

my body respond to her instantly. There was something so innocent about her, but she wasn't naïve. She was just good, a good person.

"I am. I honored your request and happen to know about a little place built on dreams that allows everyone to be a kid and imagine a different kind of existence." I glanced in the rearview as I turned off the exit into Anaheim. I had several employees who'd be watching us so I wouldn't feel so exposed. They were two cars back.

"I can't even imagine that such a place exists. What makes you so certain that it will have this effect on me?"

I laughed and drove along the busy West Ball Road that was lined with gingerbread hotels and candy themed motels. "Anywhere that can turn a rodent into a beloved hero obviously has magical powers to wipe away all sense of reality."

"A rodent?" Hannah asked, turning in her seat.

"Yeah. A rodent who is worshipped by millions," I chuckled.

"This is really not calming my fears. I'm not sure you got what I meant."

"Oh, I think I did." I turned into the drive and passed through the large gates, stopping at the booth. I rolled down my window and handed the attendant my debit card.

"Anywhere in the blue area that's marked Mickey and Friends," the man replied, handing me a ticket. "Enjoy your day."

I looked at Hannah who was glowing.

"Welcome to Disneyland," I told her.

"I can't believe I didn't guess this! I've never been."

"No kidding," I teased, as I pulled the car next to Daisy duck grinning at us all. I found an empty stall on floor two and turned off the engine. I could feel Hannah's excitement filling up the car, and I loved every second of it.

"I've heard about Disneyland. Actually, more so Disneyworld, but I always knew that wasn't in the cards," she said.

"Well, Disneyland is the best place to put all of your problems aside and just enjoy life. Plus, their frozen lemonade is pretty good. And the churros."

"Sounds like my kind of breakfast," she said, opening the door and hopping out before I had a chance to say anything more.

Hannah was dressed in a pair of jean shorts and a camisole. She had a sweatshirt tied around her waist, and I prayed it didn't get cold enough for her to want to put it on.

Hey, I was only human.

We walked through the parking garage to the elevator. A family of five stepped on with us and so did my three agents. I had assigned two males and a female so it didn't look like a bunch of creepy men hanging around an amusement park.

Hannah's hand found mine, and my world literally stopped. I didn't think a woman would ever be able to hold this kind of power over me, but I had found my match. Now it was up to me to keep her.

The elevator opened at ground level, and my

agents and the other family walked off the elevator. All of the tickets had been pre-purchased so we wouldn't have to wait in line. Every so often Hannah would stop to look at a bronze Minnie statue or glance at a Pinocchio poster. Having her this close to me was a wonderful thing, and I didn't want it to end.

I watched as my team blended in while Hannah took in the scenery as we made it to a large stone entrance. She spotted something across the way and glanced up at me, smiling.

"I think this Sebastian character has it right." Hannah grinned.

She let go of my hand and walked through the stone tunnel. I wasn't sure what caught her eye. We hadn't even made it into the park yet, and it was already having the intended effect on her. If only for a day, her cares would be taken away.

"What's that?" I asked, walking up behind her as she stared at a poster with Ariel, Prince Eric, and a large lobster grinning with one of life's mottos underneath. I felt a current run between us as I placed my hands on her shoulders and kissed the top of her head.

"That the human world's a mess," she replied. I didn't need to see her face to know that she was smiling. "Sebastian's kind of cute and he's got brains. I wonder if he's available?"

I started laughing. "You've never seen *The Little Mermaid*, have you?"

She shook her head. "Why?"

"Because Sebastian is the lobster, not the prince."

Hannah started laughing hysterically and flung her hair back. "Boy, I really did miss out."

Before we entered the park, I slowly turned around and brought her into my arms. Her beautiful eyes looked into mine reflecting the same desire I felt. I placed a soft kiss on her lips and took a step back, squeezing her hands.

"The rodent awaits."

"Well, when you say it that way," she gushed and pulled me through the gates.

Hannah was my taste of Heaven and I never wanted it to end.

CHAPTER THIRTY-THREE

Hannah

Wow! This place was absolutely breathtaking. There was something in the air that just made me happy. I snuck a peek at Luke and noticed him taking in my reaction. I was sure I looked like a complete nerd, but that would come out soon enough anyway. Let him run now.

The air smelled like sugar, and the buildings put me in another time and place. I stood still for a few moments, holding Luke's hand before moving forward. The sign scrolled in fancy lettering read Main Street, and I saw old-fashioned storefronts lining the entire path. There were ceramic pots overflowing with flowers and striped awnings dotting the sidewalk. Women dressed in Victorian clothing, carrying parasols, walked down the street and handed out carnations.

"There's a bakery over there," Luke said, pointing about four doors down.

"How do you know?" I asked. It was hard for me to imagine Luke just hanging out at Disneyland on his off-hours.

"It hasn't changed for years. I used to bring my sister here all the time to take her mind off things."

"I swear I can smell the goodness from here," I said, walking with Luke toward the bakery. But on the way I found myself stopping every few feet wanting to look at the storefronts packed with Donald, Minnie, and Pluto. I'd never had a lot growing up, and certainly never had stuffed animals like these. Some were as tall as I was. It was like this place zeroed in on the kid in me and made me want to exist how it used to be in another era.

"Any one in particular catch your eye?" Luke whispered into my ear.

I glanced up at him and a shiver ran through me at the thought of how close we were.

"You'd be willing to spoil me with rodent merchandise?" I teased.

"Anything you want, I'd be more than willing to spoil you with."

"Anything?" I asked.

He nodded and his eyes darkened a shade. "Maybe I should've planned on this being a weekend event."

"What on earth would make you say that?" My brow arched as he whisked me into the store.

There were cute Minnie Mouse pajamas

directly in front of me, and more stuffed animals piled high next to me. As I continued browsing, I began seeing all kinds of things I could imagine buying. I didn't even have a house, but all of a sudden I desperately felt the need to own Minnie Mouse salad tongs, potholders, and salt and pepper shakers. This place was good. Luke was right.

I stood in the far corner of the store still smelling the sugary aroma and watched Luke wander around the store. He was dressed in a slouchy pair of faded jeans and a navy t-shirt. He had a pair of Oakley sunglasses slid back on his head, and he looked absolutely incredible. He must have felt me watching because he glanced over at me and smiled. I held up a Minnie Mouse backpack and wiggled my brows as he came over.

"How sexy would this be?" I teased.

"Sexier than you can imagine," his voice low.

I giggled and tossed the backpack down as his hand wrapped around mine.

"On to the bakery and coffee shop," Luke said.

"Sounds like a plan."

We wandered back onto the street and I watched as the "real-life" Minnie walked along the sidewalk, giving away balloons and waving to everyone in her path. This place certainly knew how to shift reality in a lovely way.

"I wonder how they get those jobs?" I muttered.

Luke's brow arched. "You wanna be Minnie?"

I shrugged. "Seems like it could be fun. Make

people happy every day? That would be a dream come true." I saw a group of princesses, in satin gowns, walk down the middle of the road giving us all the beauty pageant wave. "Ooh. I could be Cinderella."

Luke smiled as we walked into the bakery. The scents of butter, sugar and coffee combined to create an even more delectable fragrance than outside. I looked into the glass cases and thought I'd just about died and went to heaven. And the best part was that they were all shaped as the star rodents or their friends. Rice Krispy treats were shaped as the lovable mouse with the ears dipped in chocolate, the cinnamon twists were wound into magic wands, and the croissants somehow resembled Pluto. This looked like a way better place to work than Buttons. I was becoming surer of that with every passing second.

"What would you like?" Luke asked, as we stood in line. He placed his hands on my shoulders and gently massaged them like we'd done this millions of times before, and I loved it—loved being with him—and imagining another reality outside of the one I'd been dealing with.

"A mocha and a cinnamon twist." I smiled and added, "And a Mickey Rice Krispy treat."

The cashier motioned to us to move forward so she could take our order. I slipped my hand into Luke's back pocket and watched as the barista prepared our drinks.

As the cashier handed Luke back his card, she

asked, "Are you guys on your honeymoon?"

I chuckled and Luke beamed and replied, "No. Not yet."

It felt like all of the air had been sucked out of the room as I glanced at Luke who was gauging my reaction. I knew he was only teasing, but hearing those words solidified an idea of a future, which I desperately needed to hear.

"Well, you two definitely have something special." She smiled and waved the next set of customers forward as we stepped aside.

"You are in so much trouble," I said, grabbing the bag with my two pastries inside.

"Sure I am," he laughed, grabbing his iced coffee.

"Are you always so confident?" I asked.

"No." He took a bite of his Pluto croissant as we walked outside and I started laughing.

"There's something about a tough guy biting Pluto's nose off."

"Tough guy, huh?"

"Definitely."

"So are you ready for some rides?" he asked.

"Like what kind?"

"Anything you can imagine."

"Do you have any favorites?" I asked, before I took a sip of my mocha.

"Several." He smiled. "*Pirates of the Caribbean* and *Indiana Jones* are my top two. But those are followed closely by *The Haunted Mansion, Space Mountain,* and *Splash Mountain.*"

"Well, let's hit Indiana. That was the first movie I ever sneaked," I revealed.

"You didn't have television?"

"No. They thought it took away from self-reflection or at least that's what we were told. They just wanted to keep us in the dark. Anyway, Indiana was my hero."

"So which Indie did you watch?"

"There's more than one?" I asked.

Luke smiled. "Dear God, I'm going to have to corrupt you."

"I think there was a temple in the title."

"*Temple of Doom*. Nice. That was the second one. When things settle down, we'll do an *Indiana Jones* marathon, only sticking to the eighties versions of course."

"Of course," I laughed.

His words made my tummy flutter. Imagining a time when a movie night didn't seem frivolous felt almost in reach, like a real possibility. And getting to share it with him was beyond words.

"There's *Raiders of the Lost Ark* and *The Last Crusade*," he continued, as we walked along the path where the makeshift town turned into something of a jungle. We'd left the old-fashioned delights of fragrant bakeries and ruffled parasols for jungles and Tiki torches. Disneyland was an incredible place.

"As long as there's popcorn involved in our marathon, I'm totally game."

"It's a deal. So did the pastries fill you up?" he asked, as I tossed the bag away.

"For now. But I keep seeing people with corndogs walking around, and I don't know how long I'll last without one." I rubbed my hands together, and he squeezed me closer as we walked by little shops with safari-themed novelties.

"Your wish is my command," he laughed.

"That's what I like to hear. Oooh, wait! Check this out." I grabbed a hat that looked just like the one from *Indiana Jones* and plunked it on his head. "Now that's what I'm talking about. That's completely sexy."

"Is that so?" His brow arched as he scanned the goods. "Then turnabout's fair play."

Luke grabbed coconut shells and tossed them over to me.

"What's this supposed to be?" I asked, holding them up.

"A bikini," he laughed. "Hold them up. You'll see the strings."

I couldn't help but laugh as I did as he instructed. I tied the string behind my neck and fastened it behind my back, and I quickly adjusted the shells over my tank.

"Almost there," he replied, scanning the shelves. "This."

He threw a grass skirt in my direction and I caught it.

I stepped through it and pulled it up, adjusting the hula skirt over my shorts before I shimmied my hips.

"Too much?" I asked.

Luke's smile made the entire store light up as I twirled around. "Not at all," he said, pulling me toward him. He untied the strings at my neck and worked the clasp open as my body heated up from his touch.

"Will you wear the hat today?" I asked.

"Only if you'll wear this later," he murmured.

"I might be able to work that out," I laughed. "Is it bad that we're dorks?"

I scooted the skirt over my legs and handed it to him, along with the shells that he was already holding tightly.

"Not as long as we're both in it together." He smiled as we walked up to the cash register. "Good thing this hat has a strap. Some of these rides are pretty intense."

"How intense?"

"Enough so that the hat could be blown away."

"Sounds exciting," I smiled, but I was completely terrified.

He paid for the merchandise and we walked back outside.

"That's where we're headed." Luke pointed ahead to the left where large trees towered and rope bridges dangled. "Doesn't look like much of a line. Guess it pays to go during the week."

As he pulled me down into the maze of ropes that guided guests, my heart quickened at the thought. I was scared of rollercoasters. I'd only been on one and that was enough for me. Back in high school, my friends and I managed to sneak into a carnival two towns away. Even remembering that frightened me.

"Is it scary?" I asked, squeezing his hand as we ran between the ropes.

"There's only one crazy moment," Luke assured me.

"How crazy?"

We ran through the tunnels, stopping every so often to look at the treasure, skulls, and artifacts that guided us to the entrance of the ride. When we made it to the end, I saw a woman who was about eighty years old piling into the vehicle with her grandkids.

"Still worried?" he whispered.

"I'll handle it," I informed him, as we climbed into the vehicle and the attendants slammed down the safety bar. I buckled in and the bumpy ride took off, and I felt immediately transported to another time. As we barreled deeper into the caverns, I was in complete awe over the sets. It was visually stunning and such a blast.

"Way different than the carnival," I laughed and Luke wrapped his arm around me just as a large boulder came rolling toward us. As I was about to scream, the ground beneath broke away and our vehicle slid down a steep hill and the scream I saved echoed from my belly.

"That was awesome," I whispered, catching my breath, as we continued to creep along through the ruins, finally coming to a stop where we had first started. I released my seat belt and the bar unlocked.

Luke helped me out of the vehicle, but I honestly didn't want to leave.

"How was it?" he asked.

"Amazing. I totally want to go again," I snickered, feeling like a kid. "But your hat totally makes it."

Luke certainly did an amazing job of finding a

place that took me away from everything I'd been running from. I only hoped that someday I'd come here not to escape my life but to add to it.

He pulled me down a tunnel that had been roped off, and I watched as fellow riders started running toward the exit in the other direction. Where we stood was dark and far enough back that it was doubtful that anyone would see us or even think to look. He slid both hands along my hips and looked down into my eyes as my stomach fluttered at the closeness. I felt the warmth from his body as he pressed against mine, and I prayed to be kissed as I closed my eyes, waiting for his lips to come to mine.

CHAPTER THIRTY-FOUR

Luke

This was the first time I felt Hannah relax. Feeling the tension leave her body as I held her through the ride was something I wasn't sure I'd ever see. I never guessed Indiana would've accomplished this so quickly, but I was grateful to him. The excitement that rolled off her was contagious, and I didn't want this day to end. But I knew it would. And then tomorrow would come.

Hannah's excitement was something that continually pulled me to her. Her curiosity about new things and her ability to not take things for granted were astounding attributes. I'd been surrounded with people always into the bigger and better, but not Hannah. She just enjoyed being. And that was something I didn't ever want taken away from her.

She laid her head against my chest as the vehicle took the final turn on the ride and I could smell her heavenly scent. It was almost more than I could handle when she slid her hand along my chest. My agents were stationed at the entry and exit of this ride so that did buy us a few minutes of privacy. I wanted the damn ride to be over so I could feel my lips pressed against hers.

Once it came to a stop, I hopped out of the ride and helped her out. I spotted a tunnel that looked like it went nowhere and pulled her into the dark cavern with me. I felt like I was fourteen all over again and I had no idea how she did that to me. There was something about Hannah that literally made me weak for her. I heard her breathing change as my hands slid down to her hips, and I pulled her into me. Feeling her softness against me was almost soul crushing. I wanted so much more. I prided myself on being practical, organized, and in control, but that always changed the moment I was around Hannah. All I wanted to do was taste her, feel her against me.

Her hands ran along my chest and she looked into my eyes, which was my undoing. I watched her lashes fall as she closed her eyes, and my lips crashed to hers. There was no softness. I craved her too much to be gentle. My tongue ran along the seam of her lips, and she welcomed me in, parting slowly as I felt the warmth of her mouth connect with mine.

I took a step forward, lifting her as I moved, and she wrapped her legs around my waist. We belonged together. Everything was instinctual. There were no awkward moments. Her hands ran along my neck as her kisses deepened, and I fantasized about her nude body next to mine. Imagining our bodies as one created a tidal wave of desire. Feeling her fingertips scatter across my skin aroused me beyond no return. There was no coming back from Hannah. I was falling in love with this woman.

She let out a soft moan, and I couldn't help but smile knowing that I was unraveling her, and this was only a kiss. I slowed the urgency and broke my lips from hers. She unwrapped her legs from my waist and started giggling.

Damn! I loved hearing her laugh.

"Is that included in the price of admission for all girls?" she teased.

"Only you," I assured her.

She moved her hand into mine as we walked back into the main hallway toward the exit. Her cheeks were flushed and her steps full of energy.

"Where to next, Indiana?"

I laughed and spotted my guy at the end of the tunnel as we exited.

"I was thinking something a little more romantic. Say pirates?" The sun was blazing and the heat intensifying as we trekked down the path, dodging kids with cotton candy and swords.

"Sounds amazing," she whispered, pressing her head against my arm as we strolled down the walkway. "This place is absolutely magical."

"I thought it might be just what we both

needed." Before tomorrow, I thought to myself.

We continued filling the rest of the day with ride after ride, only stopping to try some new rodent shaped snack or to sip on frozen lemonade. It wasn't until the sun set that I realized how quickly the day had slipped away, bringing the uncertainties of tomorrow closer.

The temperature had dropped slightly and she'd slipped on her sweatshirt. We'd decided that we were all done hopping on rides so it was safe to buy some of the items she'd had her eyes on. As of now, I was carrying around a huge Minnie Mouse and a Dopey from *Snow White*.

"Did you want to stay for the fireworks?" I asked, hoping her answer would be yes. Maybe I shouldn't have given her the option.

"Who wouldn't?" She winked, taking Minnie from my arms. We'd circled the entire park and hadn't even made it into California Adventure. "Too bad the Haunted House was closed."

"That just means we'll have to come back," I murmured, sliding my arm around her waist.

"I would like that very much," she said, sighing.

"What's up?" I asked, feeling her body tense.

"Tomorrow. Just kind of sneaking up on me."

"Sam's a good guy. He'll help get done what needs to get done." I nodded, squeezing her a little tighter.

She looked into my eyes and forced a smile. "I'm counting on it."

"I'm not going to let anything happen to you," I whispered.

"It's not me I'm worried about." She glanced away, and I felt the entire day's events get overshadowed, and I knew this had to end. I was going to do everything in my power to make Hannah's life okay again. I wanted to make her worries disappear and her struggles vanish, but there was only one way to do that, and it would take her cooperation.

Music began playing over the speakers, and I towed her over to a vacant spot that would be a great vantage point for the sky's displays. We sat on the curb and looked above as the music blared through the park, and the first silver firework crashed into the sky, sprinkling pieces of glitter in every direction. Red splashes dotted the night sky, followed by blue and green. I felt her body relax again and drew her chin toward me.

Her lips parted as I pressed my mouth to hers, feeling our worlds slowly begin to merge. This woman was worth fighting for with every ounce of strength I had, no matter what we'd face. Her breath quickened as my hand ran through her hair and I felt like my world shifted. We had power over one another, and I just prayed for a day when that was all we needed to live a happy life together.

CHAPTER THIRTY-FIVE

Hannah

It seemed like the innocence of yesterday was years ago as I sat in Luke's car, staring at the building I was about to go in. Luke had the entire parking lot surrounded by his men. There'd be no one coming in or out of this lot without a serious problem to deal with. At least that's what I'd been told and I had no reason to doubt it.

It should have made me feel better, but it didn't. Luke promised to be with me every step of the way and that meant the world, but I didn't like that I started to count on that, on him. It scared me.

"You ready, babe?" Luke asked, bringing me back to reality.

I nodded and climbed out of the car. The agent we were meeting was already inside the building. We'd driven a couple hours inland to a vacant warehouse that Luke owned. For what I wasn't sure.

"You've got this. And if there's anything you don't want to answer, or that makes you uncomfortable, don't feel obligated. You're the one in control."

"I don't feel very in control," I whispered, as we walked toward the entrance.

Luke opened the door and led me to an office right off the entry. The interior was as industrial as the exterior with exposed metal walls and concrete floors. A man, who I assumed was Sam, sat on a leather couch. As soon as he spotted Luke, he stood up and walked over.

"This is Agent Fredricks," Luke said to me, shaking the man's hand.

"Nice to see you again, Fletcher," Agent Fredricks replied.

"Pleasure's mine. This is Hannah," Luke replied, introducing us.

"Hannah, you can call me Sam."

"Thanks," I replied.

Sam looked to be around forty with a few flecks of silver spotting his otherwise dark hair. He was an attractive man, muscular, but he didn't project the strength that Luke carried. Sam's brown eyes watched me carefully as Luke ushered us to a small conference table near the back wall.

"Luke has briefed me on some of the background information. I was able to get some leads on what he's told me as well," Sam pulled out a folder and began rifling through papers. "I looked up that Donald Jamison character who was recently arrested. I found no ties to the NLC, but don't get me wrong, I have every reason to believe he's involved."

I nodded as relief began seeping into my pores. I was finally talking to the right person.

"We believe that your accusations are valid, but we must proceed with the utmost caution," Sam began. "We need to take things slow, let them play out a little longer."

"Attempts have been made on Hannah's life. How slow are you talking?" Luke asked. His hands fisted into a tight ball.

"Long enough to make sure whatever case we build against them is unbreakable. Everything needs to be solid. This isn't the private sector, Luke. We have to do things by the book."

Luke placed his hand on my knee. "I understand that. The information I sent over, was it helpful?" Luke's brow arched. I could tell he had Sam where he wanted him, reminding him not so subtly of the help he's afforded him.

"Yes. It was. We were able to trace the offshore accounts that funneled to one custodial account," Sam said, turning his attention to me. "This is where things get a little dicey and patience is of the utmost importance."

Luke remained silent.

"The NLC isn't named on the custodial account. We're tracing the sources of deposits and should know who all is involved, who owns the main account."

"And you got the information from my

sources. Isn't that correct?" Luke asked. "You didn't bother waiting for search warrants now did you?"

Sam let out a sigh and smiled. "No, Luke. We didn't. And I thank you for forwarding the information."

"What I'm about to tell you doesn't leave this room," Sam replied.

"Of course," Luke said.

"They're well funded whoever they are, and with the information that Miss Walker has provided we can guess how," Sam replied.

"But you're worried about the bigger fish in the sea," Luke sighed. "It's not the NLC that your agency is as concerned with but who they're working for. Correct?"

"We don't fly on conspiracy theories," Sam replied coldly. "We need to sort out all of the possibilities before we make a move in any direction. If we go after the NLC too soon, guaranteed the others will vanish into thin air."

"No. I got it." Luke shook his head. "But knowing there's another shipment coming in, does that speed up the process?"

"Only partially," Sam acknowledged. "By the looks of it, the shipments happen a few times a year. The truth of it is that if we don't have a solid enough case, we won't go in before this next one. We'll wait it out."

My stomach twisted at the thought of this never-ending hell that had become my life. And the thought of another shipment going through successfully made my head begin to pound.

"There are lives at stake. Far more than just mine. Those people have no voice and one more shipment might not seem like a lot to you, but those are hundreds of lives that are forever changed, possibly ended," my tone bristled.

"The agency understands that," Sam replied.

"Don't give me that agency shit, Sam." Luke pounded the table.

"Listen, there's far more going on here than I'm at liberty to speak about. We have intel that the shipment is about to move up a week early. That's why I'm telling you we might not make it in time. I'm just trying to be as open about things as I can so you can continue to watch out for Miss Walker."

"Where'd the info come from?" Luke asked.

"I'm not authorized to tell you that," Sam replied.

"Then how do I know it can be trusted?"

"I guess you don't."

"Do you trust your people?" Luke asked.

"As much as I've trusted you over the years." Sam smiled.

"I guess that's saying something."

"The first house you stayed at when you got to town?" Sam started.

"What about it?" I asked.

"How did you find it?" Sam asked.

"Both my best friend and I were planning to make a run for it. But they killed her first. She was the one who set it up. Why do you ask?"

"The NLC found you very quickly out here. I was curious if maybe someone at the house was involved somehow with getting you found." Sam closed the folder and pushed it to the center of the table.

"Nothing would surprise me."

"Was there anyone else who knew of your whereabouts after you left that house?" Sam asked.

"No."

"That seems odd."

"Wait. One girl knew that I had accepted a job at Buttons. But she wouldn't have said anything to anyone. There's no way, and she didn't know where I lived."

Sam's expression fell and he glanced at Luke. "Was her name Rikki Stevenson?"

I took in a deep breath. "We didn't do last names. I'm sure you can guess why. But yes. Her first name was Rikki." My heart rate began to soar as I waited for Sam to continue. The look on his face told me everything, but I wanted him to say it.

"She was found dead."

"How?" A lump formed in the back of my throat.

"A bullet to the head. She was found in a park, but her body had been placed there. I have reason to believe that's how they found you again."

"I can't believe it," I whispered. "She did nothing wrong. Her only fault was coming into contact with me."

"We interviewed Nancy and couldn't come up with anything solid. But I wouldn't doubt that she's also involved. But again, we have nothing to go on there. Not yet anyway."

I stared at the table as I tried to absorb that Rikki was gone, just like my best friend and my sister. Everyone my life touched was doomed.

"We have documents that will link everything to—" Luke began, squeezing my hand under the table.

"You have them with you?" Sam interrupted.

"No," I replied.

"Then what good are they?" Sam asked.

"As good as your promise to speed things along, I suppose." Luke leaned back in his chair. "I've dealt with the agency long enough to know that I've always gotta provide some incentive. If you can focus on the men that are after Hannah and take at least two into custody within seven days, then we'll hand over the documents."

"How can we be sure the documents are worth that?" Sam asked.

"Have I ever screwed you before?" Luke questioned.

"I'll need to run this through our division. I don't know how this is going to be interpreted," Sam muttered.

"Interpretation is always subjective. Cover your tracks and all will be fine with the black suits," Luke laughed. "But there are copies of everything. Past shipments, deposit amounts, names and ages of the kidnapped, names of all the NLC who were involved, along with government officials and law enforcement, it's all there to not only build the case on everything going forward but everything going backward as well."

"You've got a deal," Sam said. "But Hannah we need you to continue to live your life as open and normal as possible. Go to your job, keep up appearances..." Sam's voice trailed off.

"I will." I nodded.

Luke stood up, which signaled to Sam the meeting was over. Rather than experience relief, I just felt like the end might never be in sight.

"It was nice meeting you, Hannah. If there are any other developments you can call me directly." He handed me his card and shook Luke's hand once more before heading out of the room.

"Well, that went well," Luke replied.

"How do you figure?" I asked.

Luke pointed at the folder on the table that Sam left behind.

"I thought you said he was your friend? That didn't seem very pleasant."

"I don't think I ever called him that. But open the folder. It was his gift to us," Luke said, sitting back down.

I grabbed the folder and opened it up.

"I can't believe Rikki was murdered," I whispered, as my eyes fell to the first page.

"These people will stop at nothing," Luke agreed. "But this will come to an end. Soon."

"I wonder who the NLC works for," I muttered as I began scanning the pages.

"I think Sam just gave us the answer." Luke brought the pages closer to us and read aloud, "997F Cartel."

"Who is that?" I asked, reading over the legal jargon.

Luke flipped the page. "997F has been around since the 1970's. Started as a drug running operation and expanded into over nineteen countries through the last several decades. They also began their luck with human trafficking beginning in the 90's."

"Boy, this is way bigger than I ever imagined," I sighed.

My blood turned icy. They'd been doing this since then? How had the NLC been getting away with these things for so long?

"I say we get out of here," Luke said, his eyes searching mine.

"Sounds good to me. I need some time to digest things."

"We'll continue looking everything over tonight when you get back from Buttons," Luke replied. "I'm not happy with the idea of you there."

"It's safer working there than at a grocery store or somewhere where just anyone can get in," I reminded him, trying to calm my own fears at the same time.

"You can bet it's going to get a hell of a lot safer too."

"I can only imagine," I laughed, but truthfully, I was relieved. "So do you believe that Sam will keep us informed and try to speed things along?"

We walked to the car, and I held the folder tightly. Everyone had become suspect to me now, including my own family.

"He'll do what he can, but he won't do anything that'll jeopardize his career," Luke said.

"Can you fault him?" I asked, climbing in the car.

"I guess I can't," Luke acknowledged, before shutting the door and walking around to the other side. "But it never stopped me. Maybe that's why I'm not still there."

I turned in my seat and stared at him, realizing how little I knew about the man I was falling in love with.

CHAPTER THIRTY-SIX

Luke

I dropped off Hannah and drove back to my house. I sighed as I turned on the stereo. Knowing she worked there was bad enough. I didn't need to watch her engage with customers to prove that I didn't like it, but one thing at a time. That's why I had two guys stationed in the parking lot, keeping an eye on things.

I spread the papers from Sam out on the dining room table as I tried to bridge any connections I could find. There was something that didn't sit well with me. I dangled the bait and he accepted. Asked him to bring in two guys in exchange for the papers that Hannah had to offer. He wouldn't accept that offer unless they were getting very close to a bust. Sam had a lot he didn't want to tell me and that was worrisome, especially as Hannah was still out and about. I rubbed my hands over my face and tried to shake off the exhaustion. I didn't know how Hannah did it. I was here barely functioning and she was at work carrying a tremendous load.

"Everything okay, sir?" Mitch asked.

I'd forgotten he was in the far corner.

"Yeah. Just a long day."

"Long day?" Mitch smiled. "Try a few long weeks."

I laughed. "True. You know, something's just really bothering me with how they always manage to find Hannah."

Mitch stood up and walked to the table, taking a seat across from me. "You said they tapped into her cell records and pinged her location."

I scratched the whiskers along my chin. I didn't even remember when I'd last shaved. "They did. They obviously have people with the same access to technology as we have."

"Or connections within an organization that does."

Mitch nodded. "The NLC seems to enjoy psychological warfare. Maybe they wanted to continue to weaken her mind before capture so they can get what they want easier."

"There's no weakening her mind," I laughed. "She's tougher than most men, but it's a definite possibility."

"Mia was talking about going back to her house."

"Not a chance in hell. Mia's..." I muttered.

"Mia what?" Mia asked, taking a seat next to me.

"Going home until it's over," I sighed, preparing for a fight.

"Everything's always up for negotiation," she countered. "So where's Hannah?"

"Sam thought it best to keep up the same routine so she's at Buttons. I tend to agree, even though I hate that place. Hannah wanted to continue."

"Can you blame her? I'd want to keep occupied as well."

Mitch excused himself and wandered toward the kitchen.

"I guess I don't blame her. I just wish she'd let me help her," I said, taking a sip of water.

"You're helping her. But she doesn't want to be taken care of. You've got to respect that. She's not ready to give up control."

"I'd never want her to give up control. I'd just like to make her life easier."

"I see something developing between you two. I think anyone who has eyes sees it, but I don't want you to forget that this girl hasn't had a chance to really live. She might not be ready for what you want to give."

I sighed. "You think I haven't thought about that?"

"I'm just saying..."

"Believe me. I'm quite aware of where she's situated in life, and I don't want to do anything that will have her regretting her choices. No matter what they are. I don't want to make promises that I can't keep."

"Don't let her make promises that she can't

keep either," Mia said softly.

I nodded.

"On the other side of it, if you let her get away and lose your soul mate, I don't want to be blamed," Mia chuckled with an evil grin.

"You're pure evil," I joked. "Thanks for that."

"I'm just glad it's not me," Mia said, glancing in the mirror over the buffet. "But if it were, I'd forget everything I just said and would go for her."

"Thanks for the advice. And might I add, if either of us ever took relationship advice from one another, the world would have to be ending."

"Maybe it is," Mia teased. "So what's got you in here all tense besides the usual?"

I let out a deep breath and closed the folder in front of me. "I feel like there's a missing piece here that I'm overlooking, and I'm worried it's an important one."

"Like what?"

"I'm in the business of tracking and protecting. I've seen what lengths criminals will go to in order to get what they want. But I feel like they're putting extra effort into Hannah's whereabouts. Only not."

"How so? She's got a lot to offer," Mia replied.

"She does." I nodded. "But I feel like some of the information they're getting is being handed to them on a platter. I think information is coming to them far too easily."

"How would that be possible?" Mia's expression hardened.

"I don't know, but I think once I figure it out,

the rest will fall into place." I glanced at my phone and saw the time. I needed to leave now to get Hannah. "I'm sure it'll come to me."

"It always does." Mia stood up. "I'm gonna check out and head to bed. Tell Hannah sweet dreams."

"Will do," I said, grabbing the keys off the table.

The thought of getting to see Hannah soon made my worries slip away. I didn't have a choice about Hannah Walker. She'd gotten into me and there was no turning back. I felt like there was so much more about her than she revealed. Wanting her had become as constant as my heart beat. I couldn't wait to explore who she really was and who she wanted to become. I only hoped I would be a part of it.

CHAPTER THIRTY-SEVEN

Hannah

The night had gone well, but I was exhausted. The only thing that kept me perky was the thought of getting to see Luke soon. I had one more table left before I could close out for the night. They were on their umpteenth bottle serving, and I'd already arranged for a cab ride home for them. It was a table of four and the bill was already at three thousand dollars. I hoped to see at least a twenty percent tip for all of us to share. That was pretty standard and a pretty great chunk of change to stash away. Fifteen was the minimum and often the members chose to show off by paying more.

"You've had your hands full," Liv whispered, as I passed by the bar and grabbed two Maraschino cherries to snack on.

"Why was it that I wanted to work here?" I

teased.

"Uh. The money. Duh," Liv answered.

"Oh yeah. Do you mind covering for a few? I want to go freshen up in the back."

"Not at all, doll. Take your time." She winked.

"Thanks."

I walked through the restaurant to the back hall that led to the offices and our dressing room. I heard a heated discussion coming from Emily's office and slowed down to listen. Obviously I hadn't learned my lesson about sticking my nose where it didn't belong.

As I got closer, I recognized the male's voice as Sean's. I pretended to adjust my silk boxers and camisole in case someone came out of the office.

"You can't just expect me to ignore deposits this large," Emily said angrily. "The first time I was willing to look the other way. But this is the third one, Sean."

"What does it matter if it's going in the account to help the business," Sean replied. "It shouldn't matter. Say it came from my personal savings."

"I'm not going to say it if it's not true. If we ever get audited, they would love to know why a part owner was busy dumping money into a business that was plugging along just fine."

"Exactly. We're plugging along."

"What are you expecting out of this place, Sean? You pay the servers miraculously well."

"I don't pay them miraculously well. The tippers pay them miraculously well."

"Whatever the case. You're not in the red," she

continued.

"I'm not in the red, but let's rehash. As you pointed out the servers do amazingly well. How well? Many of them make more than I do," I heard anger at the revelation.

"You just proved my point. Why would you, the owner, dump such a large sum of money into a place that might not offer the return? That is a question the auditors would ask. They'd also want to know where the money came from."

"You're basing everything on something that might not even happen," Sean replied. His breathing sounded exasperated and I heard footsteps, but they were leading away from the door.

"I'm trying to look out for the business and what's best for you," Emily said.

"If you're worried about what's best for me then look the other way, and I promise there will be no more large deposits," Sean's voice softened.

"You promise?" Emily's voice got far too breathy.

I took that as my cue and continued walking to the dressing room. I really hoped Mia was done with Sean, fling or not. It grossed me out. Granted, since I'd never gone down that path, maybe I was making too much of a big deal out of it. But I doubted it. The thought of sharing Luke was out of the question. Not that I actually had him to share but still. It wouldn't happen. I opened the door and walked over to my little area. Grabbing a fresh bottle of water, I sipped it as I wondered if Luke knew anything about Sean's feelings about the place. Something told me no. It seemed like Sean was far too prideful to talk about where he was financially compared to where he wanted to be, especially if comparing to anything Fletcher related. I took another sip and got my bearings as I thought about the possibilities. Was it true we made more than Sean?

Liv stuck her head in the dressing room. "Table's on the move." She grinned.

"Thanks." I tossed the water on the chair and wondered if Liv knew about Sean and Emily. Maybe it was common knowledge, but I wanted this job enough to stay quiet regardless.

I followed Liv into the main area where the four men were wallowing in their sorrows over having to leave and go back into work the next day. In this instance, I actually felt sorry for them too. There wasn't one of them that took it easy tonight. They'd be feeling it in the morning for sure.

"Thanks aahhso much, my beauty," one of the men slurred. He slinked his arm around my waist and gave me a slight squeeze. He smelled so strongly of alcohol I had to turn away and just as I did, Luke walked in.

Perfect! Just my luck.

I never allowed men to get this close and the one time…

As quickly as he slipped his arm around me he let go, and his group hobbled out of the restaurant to the waiting cab.

Luke caught my gaze across the restaurant, and I felt a wave of heat roll through me as his eyes darkened. His stride quickened, and he didn't look away as he walked across the room. My pulse accelerated as I watched his unchanged expression. There was something beyond appealing about his reaction. The idea that I could make him respond to me in this way was enticing, like I was his to be claimed. His green eyes held an intensity that I'd seen before, but this time, I felt like he wanted to do something about it, and I wanted him to.

I flashed him a smile and a smirk appeared on his lips as he shook his head.

"Let me guess. That's never happened before," his voice low as he reached me and slipped his hands around my waist.

"It seriously hasn't. Not like that," I grinned, as he pressed his forehead to mine, looking into my eyes.

His fingers circled the base of my spine, sending a bolt of desire through me and I felt my heart flutter.

"Let me close up the tab, and I'll be ready to leave," I whispered.

"The sooner the better." He released me, and I immediately wanted back in his arms, but instead I walked over to the terminal. I felt his eyes on me, which only made a wave of heat travel through my body. I closed out the bill and waved at Luke before heading to the dressing room to grab my bag.

"You and Luke pretty serious?" Liv asked, as

she followed behind.

"I'd say so. If that's possible with him."

"Lucky you," she laughed, as we walked into the dressing room.

I grabbed my bag and strapped it over my shoulder. I didn't feel like changing out my outfit. We were headed straight to his house so it didn't matter. I said a quick goodbye to the girls and walked out. Luke was leaning against the wall, waiting. He looked absolutely delicious. He grinned and I shook my head and smiled. The feelings this man evoked were sensational, and I had to do something about it before I exploded. Slipping my hand into his, I pulled him along through the building.

"In a hurry for something?" he teased.

"Possibly."

We walked to the car, and I slid into my seat, hoping that my exhaustion wouldn't take over the other ideas that were beginning to form. Luke climbed into the driver's seat and flashed me a smile. Exhaustion definitely wouldn't win tonight.

"You look beautiful," Luke replied, slowly backing out of the stall.

"Thanks. You're not looking so bad yourself," I teased. "So I still haven't seen the music room."

"You haven't found the entrance."

I started laughing, and found it almost impossible not to reveal that I knew where the entrance was the entire time. I just wanted to lose the bet.

"We'll see," I said, resting my hand on his

knee.

"I guess we will."

We continued the drive in almost silence, but it wasn't awkward. It was peaceful, content. Neither of us felt an overwhelming need to fill the air with small talk and I liked it. Whenever I'd been around my fiancé, I felt completely uncomfortable and like I needed to fill every second with babble about something inconsequential so that we never spoke about anything too personal. I didn't want him to get to know me, and I had no desire to know him. With Luke, everything had changed. I wanted to know every single detail about him. Where he grew up. What schools he went to. What his favorite subjects were. Everything.

Luke turned up the drive and opened the gate. Driving down the driveway and into the garage, I felt safe. We drove down the ramp and parked on the bottom floor of the garage.

"I bet you're exhausted," Luke said, his lip curled up slightly.

"Yeah. Exhausted for sure," I said, hiding my grin as I unbuckled and climbed out of the Tesla.

"Before I forget, Mia wanted me to tell you sweet dreams. She's in bed." He came around to the side of the car and led me to the elevator.

"That was sweet of her. I have something to show you in the library," I offered.

"Lead the way," he laughed, his touch gentle as we climbed on the lift. "But I doubt you're as good as you think you are."

"Those are fighting words," I joked, as the

elevator opened on the main floor.

There was something changing between us and with every step closer to the library, I almost felt like I was going to spontaneously combust. We walked down the hall and I stopped him in front of the door.

"I want you to brace yourself," I whispered. "This will blow your mind."

"I hope so."

I opened the door and beelined to the shelf with the tipped over book. I ran my hands along the shelf and pushed gently as the wall moved, revealing the music room.

"Always hide the evidence," I laughed. A click echoed through the library and I glanced over my shoulder to see Luke locking the library door. My heart rate quickened with an anticipation of the unknown. I turned my attention to the room revealed in front of me, the beauty catching me off guard.

A Concert Grand Piano sat in the center of the room, shiny and black. Gold script lettered the maker. It was a Bösendorfer, something I'd only read about in magazines. I couldn't even imagine the price, but my guess was well over six-figures. My sister would've bowed down to the piece. I glanced at a harp that anchored the far corner and a Cello stood next to it.

A collection of guitars hung on the wall to my left, ranging from classical to electric. To the right was the collection I wanted to devour. There were glass cabinets with violin cases on the shelves. Two of the cases were open, the red velvet interior showcasing the prize. I took a few steps inside, daring myself to look at his collection. I heard the click as the door closed behind me, creating a muffled echo. One oddity about the room was the lack of windows, but I did spot a door next to the guitars.

I walked over to the violins, spotting little cards describing each. My heart hammered once I realized I was looking at a Guarnerius. The tips of my fingers began to tingle with the idea of holding this beautiful instrument.

"Instead of a secret garden, I have a secret room," he whispered, bringing me into his arms.

"It's magical," I said, feeling his body against mine.

I turned around and stood on my toes, my mouth brushing against his.

"Do you play?" I asked, breaking away from him and walking toward the piano. We had an upright at home. Getting to admire this instrument up close was a dream. My sister played the piano. I played the violin. We'd often perform duets with each other. Another memory I'd chosen to pack away.

"The piano. I dabble with the others," he replied, his voice smooth. "But I love to collect instruments. It turned into a passion. I wish I could do the instruments justice, really. I just loved the beauty of them and the beauty of what they can become in the hands of a chosen few. I'd love for you to play for me."

"How about when this is all over, I'll play something for you?" I whispered, my hand tracing along his arm before I took a step away. "Has anyone played violin for you?"

He shook his head. "I would be honored."

I felt him behind me, his hands slowly moved along my sides. The tenderness of his touch created a thrill.

"Why aren't there any windows?" I asked.

"I figured that if I had to have a safe room, I might as well be locked away with something that I'd enjoy," he replied.

"This is a safe room? Wow." I looked at the door across the room. "Where does that door lead?"

"My bedroom."

A shiver ran through my body and I giggled quietly.

"Every day I'm near you makes it harder to stay away," he murmured, his grip stopping at my hips.

The excitement and desire rippling through me turned to nervousness. Not because of Luke, but because I was worried I wouldn't be enough for him. That my inexperience would spoil his pleasure or make him regret his decision to be with me. I had no expectations. He had plenty. I slowly turned in his arms and looked up at him.

"Then why stay away?" I asked, brushing aside my worries.

His gaze connected with mine, as my hands traveled along his arms. He held me while the rush between us grew, and my mind began dreaming of all the things that could come tonight.

"I don't want to pressure you. Make you do anything you'll regret," he murmured, his lips dangerously close to mine.

"I'd never regret giving myself to you," I whispered, my heart racing with the admission. "I'd regret that I didn't."

Luke's gaze filled with desire as he pressed his body against mine. I felt his firmness press into my stomach, but it wasn't enough. The excitement of the unknown took over completely as my hands ran along his back, bringing him in even closer as I leaned against the wall.

"Upstairs," he whispered, his lips touching my throat before taking me to the door I'd spotted only moments earlier. "It leads to my bedroom." He stopped himself. "Only if you're sure."

"I've never been more certain in my life."

His lips broke into a smile as he carried me upstairs. The staircase led into a large bedroom where he placed me down, my hand in his. I didn't know what I expected, but this room fit Luke perfectly. A King bed covered with ivory and beige linens was centered in the room, and a fire was already blazing in the corner fireplace. French doors looked out into darkness.

Luke grabbed a remote, closing the curtains and flicking off the lights, and I felt a flutter of excitement as I thought about this next step, with only the shadows from the fire providing a faint glow.

He took a step closer to me and tossed the remote on an upholstered chair before enfolding me into his arms. I felt his hands glide along my spine, sending an amazing trill of sensations through my world. I wanted him. I wanted more.

"You remind me that there really is a heaven," he whispered.

My breathing quickened while I stared into his eyes as he cradled me in his arms. There was something so pure about this moment, the way he held me, touched me. My hands trembled as I attempted to unfasten each button on his shirt.

"Take it slow," Luke whispered, pushing a piece of hair from my face. "Your first time will only happen once."

So he knew.

My heart raced with the way he looked at me, like his entire existence hinged on this one moment. And maybe it did. Mine certainly felt like it might.

He touched his lips to mine, and the insatiable need I had growing inside of me challenged me to remain calm even though I felt anything but. His mouth parted and his kisses deepened as I ran my fingers through his hair, pulling him into me. His mouth traveled along my jaw down to my throat. I worked my hands down his chest and lower to his stomach, settling at his waist. His jeans already sat low, but I ran my fingers along the edge, dipping along his v-muscles, letting my hands wander as the excitement remained unstoppable. This type of anticipation was almost unbearable. Almost.

His lips skated along my skin, sending prickles of delight through my body, but with every breath, I wanted more. His hands slowly worked down my back, stopping just short of where I wanted them to settle. I squirmed, only to hear a little growl as his lip turned up slightly.

"Is that so?" he asked, his voice low.

I nodded as he ignored my request. Instead, he cupped my chin and hovered his lips deathly close to mine, building a desire inside of me that only grew with every passing second. How could this man do this to me?

His green eyes filled with longing as my hands dipped lower. I unbuttoned his jeans and smiled, but he shook his head and laughed as he picked me up and carried me to the bed. Setting me down gently, he took a step back and slowly unbuttoned his shirt. Watching this god of a man undress only made my longing worse. As I watched him take his shirt off, my eyes cascaded along his broad shoulders, corded with definition. They made most sculptures look inadequate. My breathing changed as my eyes followed down his pecs to his abdomen. My fingers ached with need to touch him as he climbed on the bed, his jeans still on.

Luke gripped my hips and slid me down the bed toward him as heat flooded through my body. He slowly raised my camisole, exposing my skin to the cool air as his fingers grazed the surface. He sent shivers through my body with each touch. Sometimes trading touch for kisses, I felt like I was going to melt in his arms. He pulled my camisole the last little bit over my head and tossed it to the floor. I felt completely exposed but completely wanted as his eyes ravished my body.

His lips glided along my bare belly, upwelling my desire and sending heat clear through to my bones. With every tender kiss and caress of his tongue against my flesh, my mind spun out of control. The tingle of the unknown pulsed through my body as he worked his mouth lower and lower. With every kiss, a fire continued to build that burned intensely.

Every emotion rose to the surface when his lips left my flesh. I didn't want him to stop. Instead, he teased, reading my body. I felt him move away and this time he didn't come back. I opened my eyes and saw Luke balancing on his elbows as his body hovered over mine.

"Why'd you stop?" I whispered.

"Are you sure this is what you want?" he asked, touching his lips ever so gently against my belly. A wave of shivers ran through me.

"When you put it that way, yes," I teased, but my breath caught as he slid his body against mine. His jeans still on, his fingers slid along my sides to my back, finding the bra clasp to unhook. I felt his hands move along my spine to my shoulders as his fingers worked along the lace. He slid my straps down and his breathing quickened as my bra fell to the floor. The power I felt in this one moment was glorious. His fingers stroked along my breasts as my body begged for more.

"You're so beautiful, Hannah," he whispered, as his fingers moved along my arms. "I'm such a lucky man."

Instead of feeling completely exposed, I felt admired, loved, and I wanted more.

"Thank you," I murmured, his eyes locking on mine. My fingers fell to the waist of his jeans as I attempted to pull at them unsuccessfully.

"Is that so?" His smile was captivating as he propped himself up on his knees, his legs straddling my waist. I imagined having him inside of me and my body responded. I slowly moved my hips, but he began working my shorts down my legs.

Sitting on the bed, his fingers slid along my thighs. My body trembled with the closeness of his hands to where the longing burned within me. His hands came so close, only edging my panties before retreating. He stood up as my heart raced with a craving that grew with every second he wasn't touching me.

"Please," I whispered, unsure of what I wanted more, his touch or to see him undress.

He smiled, his eyes hooded as he moved onto the bed, hovering over me. My hands quickly worked to push his jeans and boxers down. He helped the rest of the way as I began kissing his chest as his fingers brushed aside my panties. I wanted him so badly it hurt. Every stroke of his fingers made my entire body tingle as his lips teased my breasts.

"Kiss me," I moaned, tracing my hands along his sides. His mouth met mine, hungry and craving so much more than only kisses could give. Luke's body pressed against mine, and I felt his firmness press into me, making the need almost insufferable.

"I want more," I moaned softly.

Our kisses transformed, becoming more demanding with every passing second. His fingers tangled through my hair as he pulled my head away from his. His gaze burned with intensity as he moved his lips to my throat, his tongue tracing along my flesh. But it wasn't enough. I wanted more. I needed more. I wrapped my legs around his waist, feeling him press into me. His breathing changed as he ran his mouth along my collarbone. A quiver ran through my body as my craving for him became insatiable. A moan escaped from my lips as I attempted to squirm underneath.

"Not yet, my love. Patience is key. I'm not going to rush a single thing," his voice deep, his breath tickling my over-sensitized skin.

"Please," I begged.

He shook his head as I tried to slide my panties down. He grabbed my wrists and kissed each one before pinning them above my head. I'd never felt this much desire. It was turning into an obsession. I tried wiggling out of his clasp, but he only smiled, shaking his head slowly. He was always gorgeous, but seeing him above me like this was beyond my wildest dreams. His chiseled features working to bring me pleasure as I moved under his body, begging for so much more.

"Let me love you, how you should be loved," he whispered next to my ear. His words made me tremble with yearning as he placed a soft kiss underneath my lobe.

"This is excruciating," I whispered as he let go of my wrists.

"That will only make the end even more pleasurable," he promised. "Learn to trust."

Unable to speak, I nodded as he moved his mouth down my belly lower and lower.

His fingers moved the lace aside and my body quivered in delight. Pleasure bolted through me, and I knew now what he meant as my hips writhed to a rhythm he created.

"Now," I murmured.

"I need you to say it. I need to hear it from your lips." His eyes stayed on mine as he moved across me, his flesh pressing into mine as he tossed my panties away. I squirmed underneath him as excitement pulsed through me.

"Make love to me," I whispered.

A smile broke onto his lips as he gently parted my legs. My pulse raced at the thought of what was to come next. Luke propped himself on his elbows, his mouth only inches from mine. I tangled my fingers through his hair as he slowly entered. The weight of his body disbursed as I felt our bodies connect and the passion between us unleash. Our kisses intensified as our worlds interlocked. For once in my life, I felt wild and possessed and I never wanted it to end.

With every movement of his hips, I felt another pulse of goodness shake through me as the silhouettes of our body became one against the shadows of the night. I felt his body shudder just as mine released, my body arching in pure ecstasy.

"I think I'm falling in love with you," I murmured.

Luke moved to his side and cradled me in his arms. "I guess I'm one step ahead, Hannah Walker. I'm completely in love with you."

CHAPTER THIRTY-EIGHT

Luke

The morning light trickled in through the shades, and I turned over slowly, still feeling Hannah's arms and legs wrapped around me. I glanced at the clock and saw that it was ten o'clock in the morning. I couldn't remember the last time I'd slept like this. Feeling the warmth of her skin against mine made me never want to leave the bed. It also made me want her again.

I tried to be gentle with her last night but there were moments I wasn't sure that was actually possible. Hannah stirred slightly, and she ran her hand down my waist, dipping lower and lower. I felt her body shudder as she started laughing.

"Next time maybe you'll wear the Indiana hat?" Hannah giggled, and I scooped her into my arms as she buried her head under the covers.

"Next time, huh?"

She began kissing my chest and it made me want to devour her right here and now.

"I wanted to give you a proper good morning," her voice rang as she appeared from under the covers.

Her hair was completely disheveled and it looked cute as hell. She was wearing nothing but a sheet and I loved it. For the first time in my life, I could imagine spending my life with someone as long as that someone was Hannah.

A knock on the door interrupted my intentions, and I groaned as I threw off the covers and grabbed a robe.

"Sir, I'm sorry to bother you but this was delivered to Mia's house by courier. One of our guys watching the house just picked it up." Mitch handed me an envelope and I thanked him before shutting the door.

"What's up?" Hannah asked.

"Not sure. But it's addressed to you," I sighed.

Hannah froze, her eyes staring at the envelope like she'd just seen a ghost.

"What's wrong?"

"That's my mother's handwriting." She shook her head and scooted back in bed. "How can that be? I don't understand."

I slid my finger under the flap and tore it open to reveal a letter inside. Hannah was sitting in bed shaking her head. I handed her the letter and sat next to her on the bed.

"I don't want to read it," she replied.

"I know, but I think you should."

"You read it first." Hannah stood up with the sheet wrapped around her slender body. She left the letter on the bed and walked to the bathroom.

I heard her turn on the shower and knew to give her some time. I glanced at the letter and read it through quickly, taking as many mental notes as possible. Her mother left the NLC, wanted to meet with her, apologize. I needed to get a hold of Sam. I left the letter on the bed and hurried toward the study. Hannah would read it when she was ready, and something told me she'd be ready after her shower. She was like me, always curious.

"Everything alright, sir?" Mitch asked.

"If the letter can be trusted, Hannah's mom is in the state. Wants to meet her. It's undoubtedly a setup, but I wanna give Sam the details immediately."

"Absolutely," Mitch said, following me down the hall. "I apologize for interrupting."

I laughed. "You did the right thing. I'd like to think someday there won't be these kinds of interruptions, but until then..."

Mia was in the kitchen sipping a cup of coffee. She looked at me and smiled until she saw my expression.

"What's wrong?"

"Hannah got a letter delivered to your house," I replied. "From her mother."

"Dear Lord." Mia shook her head and sighed. "You think it's legit?"

"Hannah recognized the handwriting

immediately," I hollered over my shoulder.

I took a seat at my desk as Mia brought in some coffee.

"Think Hannah would like some?" she asked.

I nodded. "I'm sure she'd love some."

I picked up the phone and dialed Sam's number.

"Sam, it's Fletcher. Yet another piece to the puzzle."

CHAPTER THIRTY-NINE

Hannah

I looked at the piece of paper with my mom, Bethany's, handwriting sprawled on it. Of course, the NLC could've coerced my mom into writing it, but I still held hope for my mom. I didn't want to believe that she'd be so willing to turn her back on her children. If the letter could be trusted, she'd left the NLC and was in California. I wanted it to be true so badly it hurt, but my mind couldn't justify the sudden change of heart. She'd spent over three decades of her life involved with the NLC, which was also what pointed to why this was probably a trap. The only way she could've found me was through the NLC. That, again, would point to this being a setup. The thought that she had Mia's address was frightening. If my mom knew where Mia lived, the NLC knew where she lived. I just wondered who she got the information from, how she got the information. The answer worried me, but not finding out worried me more

I let out a sigh and trudged up the stairs. Gripping the letter tightly, I held it close to my heart. It was my only connection to my mom, no matter how tenuous. I walked through the family room and opened the French doors to let the sea air in. I sat on the couch and watched as the sheer curtains blew gently in the breeze.

Luke was in the office with Mitch. He'd already placed a call to Sam, and then I heard them discussing some other cases, and I let them be. I didn't want to be anymore of a distraction than I'd already proven to be.

The place where my mom wanted to meet was close to where she was staying. It was in the middle of a busy open market with a café surrounding the center square. If she wanted to cause harm, wouldn't she pick a more isolated location? Maybe she didn't know how I'd respond. I looked at the letter carefully and tried to ignore my gut reaction, which was to burn it and pretend it never existed. I got up and walked over to my bag and fished out Sam's card. I knew he'd tell me what needed to be done that wouldn't jeopardize the case. I couldn't count on Luke for that right now. He was too focused on keeping me safe to worry about how this could help or hurt in the larger picture.

I folded the letter, slid it back into the envelope, and shoved it in a magazine. I grabbed the phone and card and walked out onto the deck, dialing Sam's number.

"Sam Fredricks speaking."

"Sam, this is Hannah."

"Yes, Hannah. What can I help you with?" His tone sharpened.

"I'm calling about the letter."

Sam was silent so I continued. There was something about silence that always drove me to say more than I intended. I needed to work on that bad habit.

"It states that she's left the NLC and wants to meet me."

"I'm assuming Luke didn't tell you that we wanted you to take her up on the offer," he replied.

"No. He didn't mention that yet," I sighed.

"I see. Are you contemplating actually meeting her? You know there's a high probability that it's not your mom, correct?"

"I know. But I don't want to jeopardize anything with the case. I'm worried if I don't show up they'll know that I feel like I don't need to be scared of them."

"And you knew Luke wouldn't want you to meet whoever would be waiting for you, regardless."

Sam let out a deep breath and I was met with more silence. "We already have a team on it and in place."

"Is that so..." my voice trailed off.

"Luke knew that even though he wasn't in favor of this meeting, you would be."

"So you're telling me in two hours I won't be

alone when I go to meet her?"

"That's exactly what I'm telling you."

The more I verbalized what had been written, the more foolish I felt. This had to be a trap. The NLC knew where Mia lived and they told my mom so why was I driven to see her?

"Your hunch is right. This needs to be played carefully. I'll be in touch on how to proceed." He hung up, and I leaned against the railing watching the waves move in and out. There were several tiny dots on the beach. The longer I watched, the worse I felt. People who cared about me were in the house, and yet I was aching to cling to a family that wanted nothing to do with my sister or me. I was too impulsive, and now I was left with the mess of feelings that often settled around me. I wished I had spoken to Luke sooner.

"Hey, baby," Luke said, walking up behind me. His hands slid around my waist and a surge of emotion pulsed through me. "You doing okay out here?"

I nodded as I felt his lips press against the back of my neck.

"You smell so good," his voice lowered, as the guilt flooded through me. "I'd like to take you out to dinner tonight. Somewhere quiet, romantic."

"Before my shift?" I asked, pushing away the tears.

"Mmhm," he murmured.

"I'd like that." A tear escaped as I thought about meeting my mom or meeting the trap that awaited.

Luke gently turned my body to align with his. His fingers softly landing on my chin as he lifted my face. "You're crying?"

"I'm sorry. There's just been a lot. I know the FBI's closing in on them, but I'm just worried it won't all fall into place. I don't want to continue living like this."

Luke smiled, pulling me into his chest. "I know, sweetie. It'll be over soon. All of it."

The longer he held me, the more I wanted to believe he was right. "I called Sam. I'm going to meet my mom."

"I know. I figured you would," he sighed, his hands running along my hair. "I would too."

"So you don't think I'm crazy or foolish?" I asked.

"I think you're human." He cradled me in his arms as I let my self-doubt slip away.

"Do you think it's really her?"

"I do. I think she'll be there, but I don't know her motives."

I let out a sigh. "It's awful that a daughter can't trust her own mother, isn't it?"

"It happens more than you probably realize."

I nodded, feeling comforted by the strength of his embrace. "What was your mom like?" I asked.

"She was a beautiful woman. Strong, bullheaded," he sighed, as he held me tighter. "Her spirit was kind, her soul enchanting. Mia takes after her."

"Was she around all the time?"

"She travelled a lot with her job, but she was there mentally all the time. We were really close and distance never stopped her from being there. She was very direct and no nonsense, but at the same time loving and soft, at least when it came to her kids."

"She sounds lovely."

"She was."

"My mom was around all the time, physically, but she was never there mentally. I understand what you mean about your mom being present. I never had that with my mom. There were times where she was sitting right next to me, but halfway through a conversation, I realized she wasn't even listening. Sometimes she'd actually get up and walk away mid-sentence. It taught me not to bother. Mentally, I also stopped calling her mom. I called her by her name, Bethany."

"Well, maybe that will change," he said.

"Maybe."

"Sam's sending a team," Luke said, as he took a step back.

"He said they're already in place. Will I be able to spot them?"

Luke shook his head. "Not if they're doing their job."

"I'd like to go early."

"That's not a bad idea. There's a coffee shop on the second floor where we could sit. It would give you a good viewpoint. Hopefully, you'll spot her beforehand."

I nodded. "I think that's the way to go."

Luke squeezed my shoulder and glanced at his phone. "Well, we should probably get going if that's what the plan is. I'll call Sam and give him a heads up. I'll have a couple guys with us. And I want to put a vest on you."

"A vest?"

"Yeah. You can wear it under that sweatshirt."

"Hope they don't aim for the head, right?" I sighed, pushing down the apprehension.

Luke's expression hardened as the words escaped my lips.

Mia popped her head through the French doors. "Everything okay?"

"Been better," I replied.

"I hear that." She smiled. "Is there anything I can help with?"

Luke's phone rang. "It's Sam." He clicked the phone on, greeting the man on the other end.

"Okay."

A pause.

"I don't agree."

Another pause followed by a sigh from Luke.

"I'll speak with her about it." Luke disconnected the call.

"He wants you to wear a wire."

"A wire?"

Luke nodded. "I don't think it's necessary, but it's your choice."

"That's assuming it's even my mom showing up."

"True."

"I'll do it. I guess. Do I need to meet with them?"

Luke shook his head. "I've got some. There's one that looks like a pendant that you can wear. I'll grab it along with the vest."

"A vest?" Mia interrupted.

I nodded and her expression fell as I followed her into the house.

CHAPTER FORTY

Luke

I didn't like this one bit, but I had very little choice in the matter. I knew Hannah would want to see her mother, if it was her mother. I also knew the NLC was well aware of that and wouldn't hesitate to use that to their advantage. We pulled into the parking lot and I glanced at Hannah. For a woman who was about to face the unknown, you'd never guess it. She was calm without a hint of nervousness. She glanced at me and squeezed my knee.

"I'm going to be fine." She smiled and touched my cheek, reminding me I still hadn't shaved.

"I know. I'm just in awe."

"In awe?" Hannah asked.

"Your composure is something that can't be learned," he whispered. "I recognize it."

"From where?"

"My mom had it. So did my dad. They understood that worrying did nothing but dilute the ability to solve problems."

"I'll let you in on a secret. I'm not calm. I'm numb." She smiled and sighed.

"Same difference."

Hannah nodded and reached for the door handle. "Let's get going. I just want this over with."

We both got out of the car and closed our doors. I scanned the parking lot, not seeing any of my men or the Bureau's, which was a good thing. Neither would be doing their job if they could be spotted from the parking lot. The building was a replica of a town square with worn timbers and ropes along the railings to give a sea-worthy appearance. We walked over to the outdoor staircase and climbed slowly. Hannah looked around every so often, but she generally kept her stare straight ahead.

The coffee shop's doors were wide open and, as I remembered, would give us an ideal vantage point. We took our seats along the windows, our line of sight centered on the meeting place in the square below.

Hannah glanced at the bakery case. "I'd like a black tea and a blueberry muffin."

I nodded and walked over to place the order at the cashier's, keeping an eye out in the mirror's reflection.

Grabbing the plate and drinks, I took a seat across from Hannah.

"Thanks." She took a piece of the edge of the

muffin and popped it in her mouth, but her gaze didn't leave the square below. "This thing is suffocating."

"We'll get it off you as soon as we can." Wearing the vest wasn't a favorite of mine either.

Hannah nodded and took another bite. I noticed her body tense and followed her gaze. We were fifteen minutes away from the meeting time, but I watched as a woman dressed in very plain clothes wandered to a concrete bench in the middle of the square. She wore a soft floppy hat that made it impossible to see her face. She had a large bag with her, which she set down next to her.

"She's here," Hannah whispered. "I didn't believe it was really her contacting me. I thought it was a trap."

"It still could be one," I said, my voice low.

"No. I know. You're right. I just didn't even think she'd be here."

I watched the woman look around the square. Her hand searched for something in the bag. Hannah was mesmerized, her gaze not leaving her mother's location.

"Are you going to be okay?" I asked.

"I am."

Her mother had a book in her hands that she had fished out of the bag. She cracked it open and laid it on her lap, but she didn't read it. Instead, she watched the location around her very carefully, very nervously. She looked like a woman who expected to be alone, but who was worried she wasn't.

Hannah took a sip of the tea and moved closer to the window as if those few inches would provide the answers she needed. I scanned the top level and saw a man in shorts, searching a magazine rack, with a rolled-up newspaper under his arms. He was with the Bureau.

I glanced at the phone. We had seven minutes until meeting time. Taking a sip of my coffee, I kept my gaze on Hannah's mother and then it happened.

A crack echoed into the air followed by another and Hannah's mother fell forward, her book falling from her fingers.

Hannah jumped up, her mouth dropping open as she attempted to scream. I lunged for her, wrapping my one arm around her chest and the other covering her mouth as I took her down to the tile floor. Her body flailed under my weight as she attempted to get away. She wanted to run to her mother. I watched the man who'd been browsing the magazines make his way down the stairs as others descended on the scene to help. As instructed, my men stayed back. Their instructions only included keeping Hannah safe.

"You can't go down there, babe. You can't go out in the open."

"I need to help her. She's my mom. I need to help her," she whimpered. "I didn't know this would happen. I thought it would be me. Not her."

"Help's on the way, baby." I slowly moved off of her when I felt her body collapse in exhaustion, and I knew she wouldn't run. The workers in the bakery were all huddled in the corner as they watched the scene unfold outside. Sirens could already be heard pulling into the parking lot as I helped Hannah to her feet, her hands trembling.

She looked outside only to see a group huddled around the spot her mother had been.

"Can we go in the backroom?" I asked the cashier who'd helped me earlier.

She nodded as I received a call from Sam.

"We've got the gunner and accomplice in custody," he replied. "Hannah safe?"

"Affirmative," I replied. "I'm in the backroom of the coffee shop, floor two."

"Good. I'll be there in one minute." Sam disconnected the call as Hannah slid down to the floor, holding her head in her hands.

"Sam'll be here in a minute."

"What for?" she muttered.

"To brief us on the situation," I replied, kneeling next to her. All I wanted to do was hold her, take the pain away. But I couldn't afford it. I needed to be on alert and having her in my arms was like kryptonite.

I heard Sam's voice in the front and the workers pointing him our way.

"How's the girl?" Sam asked, his voice gruff.

"The girl is fine. My name is Hannah," Hannah replied, wiping the tears from her face as she stood up. "How is my mother?"

"My agents found a pulse. They're transporting her to Valley Gen," Sam replied. "We got the gunner and his buddy. They're already talking."

Hannah's gaze was icy as she looked at Sam. "You knew they weren't after me this time. You knew my mom wanted to see me."

"We did."

"She was setup alright but not by the NLC." Hanna's eyes flashed with a fury I'd never seen.

"We knew Bethany had purchased a plane ticket out here."

"You knew that and didn't tell me?" Hannah's voice trembled with fury.

"We don't divulge information that isn't deemed necessary," Sam replied. "But the NLC did set her up. We didn't. We hoped to bring whoever we could into custody."

"Did you know she was a sitting duck too?" Hannah tried to keep her voice a click away from a yell.

"No, we didn't plan on that. We thought—"

"Like hell you didn't," Hannah muttered.

"We are very close—"

"Close to what?" Hannah seethed.

"From all appearances they don't know you were here. We need you to go about your day. Go to your job. We're close. We're really close on this," Sam replied.

"Like I asked. Close to what?" Hannah asked.

This wasn't the moment, but seeing this side of Hannah was something to behold. The fire in her eyes and the heat of her tongue as she put a seasoned FBI agent on warning was brilliant.

"Close to making your life a lot easier," Sam replied.

Hannah glanced at me, but I didn't provide any answers. This was her decision and I knew she'd do what was in her heart regardless of my input.

"I want to see my mother," she whispered.

"We can't let that happen. Not at this moment."

"You said she's at Valley Gen? I'm her daughter. I can see her."

"No. You really can't. We'll have her under protected watch. No one gets in or out without my consent."

Hannah bit her lip and took a deep breath in. "I will go to work tonight. And I will see my mother."

And with that, she walked out of the back room with me closely behind.

CHAPTER FORTY-ONE

Hannah

Yanking on the door to Buttons, I was surprised by how much resentment I'd built up over the last few hours. I wanted to believe that the FBI was trying to help bring justice, but with every day that they were involved, I felt less and less like I could trust their intentions. In their world, it looked like everyone was a pawn to be tossed aside as needed, and that had me worried. The FBI knew someone in the NLC had let her find the information as to my whereabouts to see if she'd run, and she did.

Luke was able to find out that my mother was in stable but critical condition. My plans were to get in there tonight after my shift. I hoped that the late night crowd at the hospital would somehow listen to my pleas.

Kevin's head popped up from behind the

counter and he waved. "Hey, Hannah. You on for tonight's party?"

"Guess so." I smiled and walked over to where he was standing. "Do you know anything about it?"

"I don't." He shook his head and wiped a few of the glasses from the wash racks. "But it sounds pretty epic. Sean's been babbling about getting everything perfect."

"Isn't that kind of unlike him?" I asked. Sean was usually pretty hands-off with the girls and nightly management. I assumed special events would fall into that category with him too, but I guess not.

Kevin shrugged. "I never know what makes that guy tick."

I laughed and walked to the dressing room where I heard a few chuckles from the girls. At least I wasn't alone, and I was intrigued to see who all was on tonight. Pushing the door open, Liv stood in the center of the dressing room wearing a long, teal cocktail dress. She looked stunning. My eyes darted to the other women who were all dressed in similar attire.

"No pajamas tonight?" I asked. "You look amazing!"

"Oooh. I'm so glad you're here." Liv smiled and gestured for me to follow her over to the far corner.

"Your dress is over here," she gushed. "The member picked out a dress for each of us to wear."

"Who's the customer?" I asked, tamping down

the uneasy feeling that surfaced.

"A new member. I actually don't know who he is. I think it's for his wife's birthday."

"Huh."

Liv looked very excited about the whole thing, and I certainly didn't want to squash her mood or let on that something was wrong with me.

Liv grabbed the zipper and pulled down on the garment bag. The bag opened, unveiling a beautiful ivory dress with tiny beadwork along the waist.

"It's gorgeous," I said, touching the fabric.

"Wow. I'm totally jealous. You're going to look like a goddess."

I rolled my eyes at the absurdity of Liv's statement. She was gorgeous and if anyone looked like a goddess, I'd pick her out in a heartbeat.

"So when's the event start?" I asked, unhooking the dress from out of the bag.

"In about thirty minutes. But I guess the guy doesn't want us all out at once. We'll each get introduced or something as the night moves on."

"Okay. How big is the group?"

"You're certainly full of questions," she chuckled. "It's a small group, like twenty-five or so, which is why we can afford to come out at different times. It's going to be in the private room even though the club's closed down for it. He wanted it to feel intimate. There'll be plenty of servers to cater to everyone before the finale."

"And what's the finale?"

"I think that's what Sean wanted to talk to you

about. But you should get dressed first," she said. "I'll help with the hair."

I shuffled over to my area, feeling more apprehensive by the moment, and slipped out of my clothes. I wished I had told Luke about the conversation I'd overheard with Emily, but so much had happened that I didn't manage to fit it in. I grabbed a tan bra and thong and changed out of the cotton polka dots I'd been wearing. My modesty had become a thing of the past.

"We'll do a loose updo. How's that sound?" Liv asked.

"Great." I changed the configuration of the bra straps to work for the outfit and slipped the ivory dress over my head. "Can you zip me up?"

"Gorgeous," Liv replied, tugging on the zipper slightly.

I looked down at the material and watched how it shimmered with every movement. "This dress must've cost a fortune."

"A small one, yes," Liv said.

"Do we get to keep the dress?" I asked Liv, trying to make it sound like I cared to be here, but truthfully I couldn't think of anything but my mom and the men who tried to kill her.

"Again with the questions. You'll have to ask Sean. I didn't bother to ask. Did you hear what we're getting tonight?" she asked.

"No."

"Well, if you knew, you probably wouldn't ask a single question. We're receiving four times what our average is for a single evening. The guy already paid in full for the event, gratuity included. It worked out to like a 40 percent tip, plus something or other."

"Doesn't that make you nervous?" I asked.

"Not really."

I sighed and looked in the mirror as Liv placed the last of the pins in my blond hair. I tried to look like I was alive, but I wasn't. I felt numb, dead inside, and I wasn't sure if that feeling would ever go away. I no longer believed that this nightmare would be over anytime soon. Instead, I felt like I was in a never-ending game where both sides would stop at nothing to achieve an end result that was in nobody's best interest.

"You okay?" Liv asked. "I thought you'd be as excited as I was about the money."

"I am. Sorry. I just... My mom's sick. I'm a little distracted."

"Oh, hun. I'm sorry to hear that. I'm sure she'll be just fine. Is she still in Ohio?"

I nodded.

"Well, with tonight's earnings you can go visit her." She smiled and tossed the brush on the counter.

"True."

The door opened and Sean appeared, beaming, holding a box. "Are you ready for tonight's event?" he asked.

"Totally," Liv shouted. "Should be fun."

"That's the plan," Sean laughed. "So if you're wondering why you're all in cocktail dresses, I'll give you the rundown. Lawrence is throwing a birthday party for his wife, Cindy. She's big into pageants. Grew up doing them and now teaches girls who want to follow in her footsteps. She was actually Miss Napa in 2003."

A couple of the girls groaned while a few others gushed at the sweetness of the husband. I didn't care one way or another. I just wanted the shift to hurry on by.

"So we'll be introducing you guys in pairs. Each of you'll be wearing a sash that lists a place that's special between the two lovebirds. Once you're on the floor, your shift begins. Hannah will be the only waitress who'll go out alone at the end. And she'll be carrying this." Sean opened the box, which had a glitzy tiara inside, and I did everything I could to not roll my eyes. "Lawrence wants you to pin this on his wife. He also wants this Tiffany's box to be on the pillow so when the tiara is removed the turquoise box is visible. He'll give it to her. Listen, team. This is our chance to get known for these one-off events. Let's make this memorable."

The more Sean spoke the less worried I became. My nerves started to calm and I realized we're just all here, like always, trying to make a buck.

"Here's to a great night," Sean said, walking over to me. He handed me the tiara, pillow, and Tiffany box. I smiled.

The other girls were putting on the last touches and adjusting the sashes that Sean delivered.

"How's Mia? She hasn't returned my calls."

"Does that really matter? I thought you two

were casual," I replied, coolly.

"We are. But she usually returns my texts. No biggie."

I laughed. "Well, she's doing fine. Busy on another series of paintings."

"She's something else," Sean muttered.

"Yes. She's truly something."

I didn't feel comfortable with how Sean was referring to Mia, but I didn't want to cause trouble. I'd been through so much already today, I felt like I was barely hanging on. Maybe I was just overreacting. After all, Mia made it clear she wasn't into anything serious. I watched Sean leave, escorting the first pair of women out onto the floor, and I felt a slight pounding behind my eyes. Just what I needed, a headache to accompany me and the jewels to the pageant queen.

My mind drifted to my mom. The idea of her in a hospital room all by herself saddened me beyond belief. We didn't have a close relationship, but she was still my mother. To say I was conflicted was an understatement. One minute I thought she wanted to do me in, and the next I was worried for her life. It made me wonder about my father and brother. Where did they land in the scheme of things? The longer I sat with my thoughts the more anxious I became. This was exactly why I kept busy and why I never let myself think.

The room cleared out and all the girls were on the floor. I only had a few minutes to burn as I waited for my turn to make an entrance. I reached for the dressing room's phone and dialed Luke's number. I might as well tell him about what I overheard yesterday. Luke's voicemail came on. A message would have to do. When his greeting ended, I began, "Hey, it's me. I wanted to tell you something I've been meaning to mention. I heard Sean and Emily talking last night. It didn't sound like things were going as well as Sean had hoped with Buttons. He's not destitute or anything, but something was bothering him, and Emily was upset about some sort of odd deposits. Anyway, since you're his partner, I figured I'd mention it. Gotta go. Love you."

I hung up the phone just as Sean appeared in the doorway. "You're up."

"Thanks." I grabbed the velvet pillow that had the tiara and Tiffany box on top and walked out the door.

"I'll meet you out there in a second. Just go into the room. You'll see where the wife is sitting."

I nodded and walked down the hall. The restaurant was empty but that was to be expected. The private room was across the way and the French doors were wide open. Music echoed through the air, and I heard the girls' laughter. I hoped some of their cheer would rub off on me. At this point, I was out of steam. I walked carefully to the entrance, not wanting to have the crown or jewelry box topple over, and saw the husband worshiping the woman in front of him. It had to be Cindy. She had platinum blond hair and I now understood why I was requested to bring out the gifts. Lawrence caught my eye and grinned, beaming, as he motioned for me to walk into the room. All the waitresses were lined along the side where the buffet table was located. Their sashes securely fastened, depicting different places the happy couple had visited. I walked steadily into the room and his wife's gaze landed on me. Her hands clapped in front of her as she gasped, eating up every second of the spectacle her husband had created.

"Happy Birthday, lovey," Lawrence told his wife.

I walked over to her and smiled as Liv came over to hold the pillow while I pinned the crown on the wife's head.

"This is beautiful," the wife whispered, as I fastened the crown to her hair. After I finished, Liv spun around, revealing the Tiffany box to the wife. Her eyes sparkled with excitement as Liv lowered the pillow for her to grab the tiny box. She opened the small turquoise box, which revealed diamond earrings and everyone began clapping.

"Happy Birthday." I smiled and took a few steps back, allowing the happy couple time to celebrate.

"So sweet," Liv gushed as I placed the pillow on one of the tables.

"It is," I confirmed. "Not my thing but definitely sweet."

Sean wandered over and gave Liv a quick hug.

"Nice work, Hannah," Sean said, glancing at

me.

"Thanks," I said, as the music turned up and the lights lowered slightly. I watched champagne get handed out and saw the happy couple begin to dance. It definitely looked like the wife was in heaven.

"You okay?" Liv asked, standing next to me.

"I'm just worried about my mom. I want to get a hold of the doctors," I confessed. "I'm not mentally here."

"I'm gonna go see if Sean'll let you off early," Liv offered.

I hadn't wanted to let him down.

"Really?"

She nodded.

"I'm sorry," I said, glancing around the party.

"Don't apologize. It's no problem. I'm sure he'll say yes. There's plenty of us around. We can handle it."

I nodded and walked out of the private room to get some fresh air. I didn't want any of the guests to see me so I slipped along the far wall and leaned against the bar, trying to force away the nausea from everything the day had presented to me. The bass of the music almost rattled the glasses stacked on the bar and I realized I just needed to get some peace and quiet. I'd give Luke a call and maybe I'd just get a ride with whoever he had in the parking lot.

"Hey, girl," Liv said, spotting me. "Sean said no problem."

"That's awesome. Please tell him I really appreciate it."

"Will do," Liv said, giving me a quick squeeze. "He was hoping you could toss this pillow in the storeroom before you leave." She handed me the velvet square and I nodded. I watched Liv return to the private room and sighed as the music continued to pound through the room. It was only going to get worse as the night wore on.

The storage room was right next to the dressing room. I'd never actually looked inside before. I glanced behind me and walked slowly down the hall, feeling some of the tension begin to slip away. I opened the door and flipped on the light. The room was pretty well organized, and I didn't want to just toss the velvet prop on the floor, so I scanned some of the shelves to find a good home.

I stood on my toes and found a place for the pillow. As I slid it onto the shelf, the lights turned off and my heart stilled.

"Someone there?" I asked into the darkness.

Silence was the answer. My heart began racing as I slipped on the floor and tumbled down. The dress made it impossible to move quickly. I had to get out of here. I heard footsteps and forced down my fear. I had to get back on my feet. Reaching the door, I wrenched hard on the handle, but the door wouldn't budge. I tried again and again, but I was trapped and no one knew to look for me because I wasn't lost. The bass from the music pounded through the air as I let out a scream that I knew no one would hear. I slowly slid down the door to the floor as the footsteps came closer. I looked into the shadows

and waited for what was to come.
     They had found me.

CHAPTER FORTY-TWO

Luke

"Look, I know you can't jeopardize the case. But something's going on here that needs attention and time's not on our side," I sighed into the phone, waiting for Sam's response.

"Listen, all I can tell you is that what Hannah fell into is way deeper than she realizes. She can trust no one. Absolutely no one. I've tried to get the director to put more resources on her, protect her, but they feel it's too risky."

"How so?" I asked, my temper rising. "What aren't you telling me?"

"A big bust is scheduled. We're looking at over a hundred arrests if all goes well. But all must go well. If anyone gets wind that the agency's been in contact with Miss Walker everything will be halted. Years of work will be for nothing. Lives will have been lost for no reason."

Lives will have been lost. Hannah could fall into that number and the agency wasn't worried about that at all.

I tapped my finger on the desk and glanced at the clock. Five more hours and I could pick her up.

"You knew Hannah's mother would be there and didn't tell me."

"I can't always tell you everything, especially if your heart's in the wrong place."

"What's that supposed to mean?" I asked.

"You're involved with Hannah, personally. We both know how that can jeopardize cases."

I let out a sigh.

"We both know she's in danger," I said, aggravated.

"Yes. We both do. And only one of us can do something about it," Sam replied. "Give us twelve more hours, Luke. And you'll see why I'm asking for patience."

"I'll do my best," I said, feeling my cell buzz from a new voicemail.

"Don't take your eyes off her, Luke. I know I told you she needed to keep up appearances, but I wouldn't trust anyone. Do you understand what I'm telling you?"

"Shit. I understand you should've told me this two hours ago." My heart hammered through my chest as I disconnected the call. Why didn't I think of this earlier? There was one person who had access to Mia, Hannah, and me. He would've been able to track her whereabouts with a simple question to Mia or glance at her work schedule. He had access to her cell through the work records. He knew where she lived. The intel was right in front of his nose. I'd been outthinking these people, giving them more credit than they deserved, thinking technology was on their side. They had an inside guy.

Button's main trunk line appeared as a missed call on my cell with the voicemail symbol blinking. I clicked it on and listened to Hannah's message. Another piece to the puzzle. I grabbed my pistol and dropped it in my holster as I called out for Mitch and Mia.

"What's going on?" Mia asked, running from the back of the house.

"It was Sean. This whole time. It was Sean."

Mia's hands rose to her mouth. "Oh my god. I never would've guessed."

"That's how they always found her. That's how she got the job at Buttons. That's why Sean had a sudden change of heart toward blondes. They must have gotten to him once she arrived in town. Money must've been enticing."

Mitch arrived in the room with two other men.

"My guess is that Sean was offered a large chunk of change to offer her a job once they tracked her down at that halfway house," I continued. "I knew I didn't trust that Nancy character. My guess is that Nancy somehow knew where Rikki was going to take Hannah that one day and Sean had Liv find her there to offer her the job."

"Damn it." Mia shook her head. "Makes

complete sense. You think she's in trouble right now? Even at Buttons with all the other girls around?"

"I'd bet my life on it. She's in trouble right now because she's at Buttons."

"Is the bureau on the way?" Mitch asked.

I shook my head. "We're on our own, at least for now. They're within hours of making the bust. They don't want to jeopardize the case."

Mia shook her head as anger covered her expression. "Like usual. Everyone's just a number."

My cell rang. It was Sean. A fire flowed through my veins as I thought about this man, this supposed friend.

I answered the phone on speaker. "What's up, buddy?"

"Slow night," Sean responded. "Hey. I've been trying to get a hold of Mia. You know where she's at?"

"Dude, I don't keep tabs on my sister. Last I knew she was working on some piece for a client. She got tired of you already?"

"Appears so," Sean answered. I detected a slight bit of hostility.

"I was thinking of surprising Hannah tonight," I sighed.

The silence over the phone sent a chill through the room.

"There's a private function here tonight," Sean said, after a beat too long.

"I guess I'll just have to wait until I pick her up then."

"You got it bad?" Sean asked.

"Sure do."

"Sorry to hear that, man. I hoped you'd be a bachelor for life. Join the ranks and all."

I laughed into the phone as Mitch caught my gaze and left the room.

"Well, sometimes the heavens need a good laugh," I said. "You up for drinks tomorrow?"

"Sure am."

"Great. I'll talk to you then." I disconnected the phone and tried not to punch something. The mere thought of losing Hannah was crippling, but I wasn't going to lose her. I was going to find her.

"The guys are on standby," Mitch said, coming back into the room.

"Get the team together. We're going in now."

CHAPTER FORTY-THREE

Hannah

My head pounded and I felt groggy. I tried to sit up, but quickly realized I was tied to a chair. The rope around my ankles stung as I attempted to move my legs. There was a musty smell, but I was surrounded by silence. I listened hard, depended on all my senses, but was met with only the ragged sound of my breaths.

I didn't want to open my eyes. I didn't want to know what I was facing. I knew enough to understand it wasn't good. As the fuzziness wore off slowly, I felt the fabric hugging dress still wrapped tightly around my body. I wasn't sure if it was the dress or the restraints that made it difficult to breath. But I kept my breaths regular, soft, to not arouse suspicion that I'd awoken. My mind wandered to Luke. Would he know that something happened to me before it was too late? Would he be able to find me? Would he ever catch the people who were going to kill me?

I concentrated on the distance beyond my closed eyelids. The darkness that sat surrounding me created a false sense of isolation, but I knew whoever was here had to be close. The quietness all part of a deception built to break me, but I wouldn't break. I was stronger than that. After all, I left. They didn't.

I heard a shuffle in the distance and a pink glow penetrated my lids signaling life beyond. Unable to gauge the distance, I listened intently for footsteps or voices. I was greeted by neither.

But I smelled something. I smelled something familiar, too familiar. To keep the unease at bay, I thought about Luke and what we shared. I remembered being in his arms and experiencing what it meant to feel alive and wild. I felt the sensation of overwhelming strength as we became one. I channeled my anger and fear into something that would make me more.

In order to move on in my life, I had to face my fears. I had to face the people who put them there. Now was my chance. I needed to shatter the sins they'd hidden for so long, the sins that became mine. I had no plans to die, but did anyone? Even if a person could taste death at the tip of their tongues were they truly ready? It wasn't a question I wanted answered, but it was one I was willing to face. If it meant I could be liberated from the demons that had followed me I would welcome it as long as I could take them with me.

"No need to act like you're sleeping," a man's voice said. I didn't recognize it, but I heard several sets of footsteps surrounding me. "You're heart rate tells us you're awake so rise and shine."

I stayed still with my eyes closed. I didn't want to be told what to do. I didn't come across the country to be told what to do by the same monsters I'd left behind.

A sting flashed across my cheek. "I told you to open your eyes."

Keeping my eyes closed, I spit in front of me.

"We have your boyfriend. Your fiancé is looking forward to meeting him," the man said.

My pulse quickened.

"Looks like we got a response out of her on that one. Love this little machine." He bent over me from behind. I felt his hot breath crawl over my scalp and it took everything I had not to vomit. "Why don't you tell me what all you think you know about us?"

I didn't respond. I focused on my breathing. Another slap seared along my cheek. This time I felt the sting for far longer, but I remained silent.

"Who have you told?" The man asked again.

He was greeted by my silence.

"I've never been great at starting conversation," he continued. He tugged on the restraints wrapped around my wrists that were tied to the back of the chair. Instead of loosening them, he tightened them. My hands immediately began to numb.

"I think Mia's a beautiful woman," the man

replied. "It's too bad about her. You want to know how they died?"

I didn't say a word. It wasn't true. They were fine. They had to be.

"We felt it only fair to pay them back. One of our best men went over that cliff. This time our man didn't screw it up. Did you?" I heard footsteps come closer, and I smelled the familiar scent.

They were using me, wearing me down psychologically. But as I sat here waiting, I knew I was developing a strength no one would ever be able to take away from me, here or in the beyond. I took a deep breath and smiled, opening my eyes to greet the man I knew. Pinning my gaze on the evil person who stood in front of me created a fury that burned my soul but freed my spirit.

As I looked into the eyes of my father, understanding of this cruel hoax forced its way into my being. Not every man born was a good man. His brown eyes narrowed as he watched my reaction. He had given my mother the information. He sent her to be shot.

"I've been waiting for a rebirth," I said, smiling.

"Too bad it's happening so late," my father replied.

"It's happening right on time," I responded.

"Why don't you be a good little girl and tell us what you know and who you've told. We took care of the two most likely candidates, but why don't you confirm everything for us?" my father asked, folding his hands in front of him.

My rage was quiet, always had been. But it was still there, ready for me when the time was right.

"All I know is that I don't want to be involved with any of you. I'm beyond you."

The men started laughing.

"If you were beyond us, do you think you'd be here?" my father asked.

"If I weren't, do you think I'd be here?" I asked, wondering if my brother was also involved. "Where's Sloan?"

"At home where he belongs. He wasn't ever cut out for this," my father answered. "Now, please tell us everything you know or else Mark will step in some more—"

"Mark might as well just step up to the plate," I interrupted, taking in a deep breath as I looked around the room. There were no windows. Concrete surrounded everything, floor, walls, ceiling. An industrial light hung in the middle of the room. I was in the back corner, which made my vantage point clear. We must have been in a basement, but I didn't know Buttons had one. I'd never seen a door leading downstairs. If I didn't know it existed, would anyone else? What if something had happened to Luke? What if they weren't lying? My pulse jumped at the thought, and I quickly tried to calm myself.

"Looks like something riled her up," my father replied, glancing at the machine.

Mark took a step toward me and pinched my chin between his thumb and index finger.

"What did you see?" Mark asked. His eyes narrowed on me.

"Nothing," I replied, and he squeezed harder.

"Try this," a man from the hall walked into the basement and tossed something to Mark.

"Does mom know about you?" I looked at my father.

"What's there to know?" he asked.

Mark held the small rectangular object in his hand. "Are you sure you don't just want to give us the info?"

I let out a sigh. "I don't have any information to give."

"We'll find out soon enough," Mark replied, taking a step forward. I glanced at the black object in his hand as his finger wrapped around a grey trigger. He pointed it at me and pulled the trigger.

An intense sensation sizzled through my body as I writhed in my chair. I lost complete control as my body seized and the chair tipped over. My cheek hit the concrete, and I gasped for breath as two men surrounded me, lifting the chair back up. I tried to regain control, but I felt paralyzed, unable to even lift my head.

"Again," my father replied.

The man pointed it at me and squeezed the trigger once more. Unable to brace myself, I felt the pain sear into my flesh as the volts ran through my body, my head drooping. My mouth felt completely dry as if I'd been without water for days. I attempted to raise my head, but nothing happened. I just sat there, my body sagging in the chair.

I heard the footsteps lead out the door into the hall as they talked amongst themselves.

"She surely would have told us something," my father said.

"Not everyone responds to this the same," Mark replied. "We have a few more options."

"I'm just not sure it's worth wasting precious time."

"We have nothing but time," Mark replied.

I thought of Luke and his sister. Had the NLC managed to overtake them? The thought made me ill as I attempted to push myself up in the chair. I had to see this through. I thought of the amazing times I'd experienced since I met Luke. I started to let myself imagine a future. Maybe that was what these people were missing. An imagination.

I took a deep breath in and thought about what few options I had. They weren't going to let me go. I was either going to be of use to them or not and if I didn't dangle something out there to prove my worth, my end might come sooner than I'd like.

"Hello?" I muttered.

I heard the voices quiet out in the hall.

"Have you come to your senses?" Mark asked.

I laughed, but it turned into a cough. The pain seized my lungs. "I guess you could say that."

"So what are you gonna tell us?" Mark said, kneeling in front of me.

"My sister. She was murdered by someone named Eric. That's what I know."

My father's gaze hardened and he began pacing back and forth.

"Is there more I should know?" I asked.

"Your sister wasn't murdered. She left the community," my father replied.

"You wanted to hear what I knew? That's what I know. I heard Miles and Eric talking the night I left. That's why I left," I lied. "So tell me was what I knew worth all this? Tracking me down across the country?"

I heard four loud bangs and the lights went out. Footsteps echoed down the hall through the darkness as I attempted to wrestle with the restraints. I heard several men bark directions as scuffles began to take place. I kept listening for Luke, praying that they hadn't done anything to him. A gunshot rang into the air, followed by more shouts.

"Apprehended." I recognized Mitch's voice, but why didn't I hear Luke's?

Another man's voice boomed through the air. Still no Luke.

I heard heavy breathing behind and felt a knife begin to carve through the ropes, freeing my wrists and ankles. It was my father. I jumped out of the chair and attempted to run, but his hand snatched my wrist and pulled me back to him.

"Not so fast," he said. "I might need you."

I heard men shouting, followed by several loud crashes before the lights turned back on. My breathing was ragged as I tried to get out of my father's grasp, but he held tight and slammed me against the concrete wall just as I heard Luke's voice finally bounce through the air.

"Let Hannah go. You're surrounded and we have all of your men. There's no use fighting."

"One step closer and I'll blow her brains out," my father said, his arm tensed around my neck. I felt the coldness as the barrel pressed against my temple. Luke avoided my eyes and kept his pistol squarely aimed on my father.

CHAPTER FORTY-FOUR

Luke

"I'm more concerned with you than her." I saw Hannah flinch at my statement. Her eyes filled with sorrow, but I focused on her father. What he'd done to his daughter made me want to pull the trigger without hesitation.

"You didn't love my daughter? It was all for the greater good?" her father asked. "She'll be so disappointed to hear it. Don't worry, sweetie. He fooled us all. I actually thought he cared about you."

Hannah's jaw tensed as I kept the red dot on her father's forehead. I didn't want to do this. I didn't want to be forced to do this, but he was leaving me very few choices. My men had subdued the others. No one had escaped. As of now, it was a small affair, and I wanted to keep it that way.

"Put the gun down," I commanded.

'I don't think that would make things very fair," her father growled.

"Dad, please just put the gun down," Hannah whispered. "It's all over."

"No. It's just begun," Hannah's father said.

"I don't think so," I replied. "Drop the weapon and step away from the girl."

"She's just a girl now?"

Hearing him mock his daughter sent an anger through me that was hard to control. It took everything I had not to shoot to kill as I watched him tease the barrel along his daughter's skin. But I didn't want to be the one who pulled the trigger on her father. That couldn't be me. That would destroy us.

I heard my team come up the hallway.

"We've got a hostage in here. Stay where you are," I hollered.

"Sir," Mitch confirmed.

"The government can protect you," my voice steady. "There are protection programs for informants."

"No one can protect us from them," Hannah's father replied. His eyes darkened. "You'd be a fool to think otherwise. That's why I might as well take my girl down with me."

I saw another red dot center on the thigh of Hannah's father as he shifted her forward. He moved the pistol closer to her temple.

"Learn to trust," I replied, watching Hannah. Her eyes held an intensity that I understood. She was ready to die.

"I trust," she whispered, her breathing heavy. Her eyes connected with mine. She heard my message.

"That's what this world needs more of," I said, glancing to my right.

Hannah followed my gaze as her breathing intensified.

I looked into the eyes of a mad man and asked the question my men would recognize. Their orders ready to execute once the answer was given.

"Why?" I looked at her father for a reply.

"Because I can," her father said.

The sound of the rifle firing blasted from behind. Hannah dove to her left as her father fell to the floor. The gun tumbled from his hand, and my men had him surrounded within seconds.

I ran to Hannah who was crumpled on the floor. Bringing her into my arms, I felt the hot tears soak through my shirt as the emotions she'd held in for so long finally came crashing out.

"I'm here for you, baby. I always will be," I whispered, rocking her against my body. "You're safe. I've got you."

She sniffed and slowly looked up at me with tear stained cheeks.

"I learned to trust," she whispered, glancing over at her father who was silently weeping.

"I know you did," I murmured, stroking her hair.

Mitch walked over to where we were sitting as the other men tended to Hannah's father and removed him from the room. "Sam's on the way."

"Better late than never." Hannah half-smiled.

"I'm sorry about your dad," Mitch said, kneeling down in front of Hannah.

"I'm not." Hannah glanced toward the door. "Have you heard any more about my mom?"

"She's still in stable condition and they expect her to be out of ICU in the next day or so," Mitch replied.

I glanced at him bewildered by how he got this information.

"I figured she'd ask," Mitch smiled, standing back up. "I'll be upstairs."

"So Sean was in on this?" Hannah asked, scooting back slightly. I noticed abrasions and redness on her skin, which only meant one thing. I should have pulled the trigger on her father.

"Thanks to your message, I was able to piece together that the NLC had somehow gotten to him. Paid him off."

"Jesus," she replied, rubbing her head.

"You down here?" Sam called.

"Yep," I replied, getting to my feet. I helped Hannah up and we walked over to Sam who had someone else with him.

Hannah gasped. "Eric?"

"He's a double agent," Sam replied.

"I don't understand. He—" Hannah stopped.

"The agency's been working on this case for a long time, Hannah," Sam began. "Eric came to us years ago when he found out some of the same things you did. We've been building the case ever since. We couldn't tell you anything. We were too close to making our bust. When you visited our field office back east our hands were tied."

"But he killed my sister, my best friend..." Hannah's voice trailed off. "And he's on your side? What? He's considered a good guy?"

"Sometimes casualties occur. You of all people should know that," Sam replied, looking at me. His words hit me like a sword to the chest. Like usual, Sam was being his cryptic self, but I knew there was meaning in those words. He had known something about my parents. I'd been looking in the wrong place.

"I didn't kill anyone," Eric said, pressing his lips together. "I regret every single moment I spent with the NLC and the 997F Cartel, and I'm so sorry for everything. But I never pulled the trigger. When people were killed, I had to turn the other way. I couldn't jeopardize everything we'd been working for."

"What do you mean?" Hannah asked. I could tell she was holding back her anger as best she could.

"We made the arrests tonight. The package you sent us contained the last pieces we need to make the case airtight. We were able to move everything up earlier. We got to them before the next shipment. We have enough to lock the bastards away for life. The CIA was able to grab the cartel members that weren't on our soil. But it's done. They're all in custody. That's why I couldn't send help sooner."

I looked at Hannah, confused. She'd sent Sam all of the proof she'd had?

Her gaze met mine and she whispered, "Sorry. I had Mia pick everything up and deliver it to Sam, just in case."

She had absolutely nothing to be sorry for. I held her tight. "I'm so proud of you," I whispered.

"If it weren't for Hannah, we wouldn't have been able to stop them before the next shipment."

There was a look in Sam's eyes that told me there was more to the story, and I intended to find out. In the meantime, it was time to get Hannah home. We'd had enough.

CHAPTER FORTY-FIVE

Hannah

Everything came late to me, but that didn't make me less. It made me more. It made love more. It made me love more, and it made me appreciate the love I had more. The world seemed like a different place. Everything changed in that one instant, that one moment of becoming when I looked in my father's eyes. The air changed. It wasn't so heavy. Even the color of the room had changed. It looked brighter and today I felt brighter. I felt lighter. I knew the world could become a better place. We could do better. Nancy was wrong. There weren't always strings attached. Sometimes love was all it took. I glanced over at Luke, who was sitting on the patio. He was holding a beer just looking out at the beach. This was my moment of perfection.

It was beyond unsettling to find out that the

FBI had not only listened to me when I reported everything back east, but they'd begun monitoring me.

Last night, he held me tightly and let me cry. He let me mourn the life I thought I had and the one I thought I wanted, but that's all I needed. I just wanted to be heard and let that happen.

"You doing okay?" he asked, taking a sip of beer.

I nodded and caught a glimpse of something in his eyes. "You?"

"I think so."

"It's hard to believe that the FBI had been following me from the moment I'd left the NLC," I sighed.

"It's hard to believe how many times they put you in harm's way," Luke said.

"That too." I got up from my chair and sat on his lap, leaning my head against his chest. "I keep asking myself, now what?"

He nodded, pressing his lips to the top of my head. "It's a loaded question."

"It really is." I let out a deep breath and felt his arms wrap around me.

"I've been thinking about my parents a lot with all of this," Luke sighed. "I've seen the agency use people time and again, but somehow seeing how they worked around you made me reevaluate some things in life. I think I've been looking in the wrong places about my parents."

"Maybe it's time you concentrate on finding the answers you've wanted for so long."

Luke kissed me and nodded. "I think they've

been at my fingertips for quite some time. I just wasn't ready."

"You think you are now?" I asked.

"I do. With you by my side. I do. I think Sam was trying to tell me something in not so many words."

"Seems to be his specialty."

"That it does," Luke laughed. He pressed his forehead to mine and his gaze dropped to my lips. I felt the familiar warmth inside my chest and smiled, hoping he would kiss me.

"I love you, Luke Fletcher," I whispered. "And I'll be there however you need me. We have nothing but time. You chased my ghosts away and I want to chase yours."

His eyes flashed before he brought his lips to mine. Our connection grew with every passing moment and the heat of our exchange made me want him desperately.

Luke's cell buzzed and I let out a groan as I broke from his embrace.

"There's something I need to tell you."

"Oh, god. Haven't we been through enough?" I teased.

"No doubt. We have," he agreed.

"What's up?" I asked.

"Last night when we were in bed, I got some information from Sam."

"Yeah?"

"It's about your sister."

"What about her?" I asked. I remembered back to the night I heard Eric and Miles discussing her fate. Maybe her body had been found. Shivers ran through my spine at the thought and I looked out toward the sea.

Luke grabbed my hand and looked toward the French doors. I followed his gaze to find Mia holding my sister's hand. My body started trembling with confusion as tears came pouring.

My sister ran to me and held me in her arms as we both sobbed.

She was alive.

WANT TO READ MORE ABOUT LUKE, HANNAH, AND MIA?

CHECK OUT BURIED SINS, REDEMPTION, AND MIA!

*A*BOUT THE AUTHOR

Karice received an MFA in Creative Writing from the U of W. She has written more than thirty novels, and she has several exciting projects in the works (or at least she thinks they're exciting). Karice lives in the Pacific Northwest with her awesome husband and two cute English Bulldogs. She loves anything to do with snow, and she seeks out the stuff whenever she can, especially if there's a toasty fire to read by.

Check out her website for a list of available titles.